MONSTERS
OF VENUS

ALSO BY MARTIN BERMAN-GORVINE

Seven Against Mars
Save the Dragons!
Heroes of Earth

MONSTERS OF VENUS

MARTIN BERMAN-GORVINE

WILDSIDE PRESS

For Daniel

And with thanks to my friend Naomi Schwartz Jacobs for help with Aramaic, and to my wife Jackie, my real-life gal with moxie, for her endless love and support.

1

Those jerks from Venus were going to be good and sorry they'd kidnapped Sonya Goldberg-Webb. Sonya herself had told them so, several times an hour, for the past three weeks, ever since they'd grabbed her on the way home from school on Mars and stuffed her in this rocketship. That meant, by rough reckoning, and even allowing time off for sleeping and eating, she had told them so more than three thousand times. But far from getting tired of it, she was enjoying it more and more all the time.

She loved watching the face of the tall kidnapper, the one she called Fatso because he had a slight paunch, bunch up and freeze as if his jaw muscles were developing a cramp from being clamped down so hard and so often, while his nostrils flared out so wide they looked like garden hoses. She loved even more making the short kidnapper, the one she called Spazzo, jump about a mile by reminding him suddenly just how sorry he was going to be, right when he was least expecting it.

"Hey SPAZZO!"

"AIEEEEEEEEEE!" The short guy had dozed off in his bunk, and Sonya's shout made him crack his head on the metal frame for the one hundred and twenty-ninth time. She was keeping count.

"You know what they're gonna do to you when they catch you?"

"Just ignore her, Gildie," the tall kidnapper said. "Don't give her the satisfaction."

"Please, please let me gag her again, Ross," the short one said. "I promise this time I'll make it loose enough for her to breathe."

"They're gonna lower you slooooowly, oh so slooooooowly, into the boiling-hot magma of Olympus Mons," Sonya said with satisfaction.

The face of Sergeant Guild N. Stern—that was his full name, as she'd learned when she found his wallet during another of his naps, just before reducing its contents to shreds—turned almost as red as the soil on her parents' Martian farm. Which was *very* satisfying. He started snarling and spitting, like a rabid dog only not as cute.

"No they AIN'T! Cause they ain't gonna catch us! And if they did, your bleedin'-heart queen has abolished the death penalty!"

Sonya ignored this. "Do you know what sound lava makes when it swallows a person up? Well, I do, 'cause I done heard it when that rotten no-good skunk King Ares was shoved in! It goes gloo-OOP!" She made some extra-juicy slurping noises to demonstrate.

Spazzo Stern clapped his hands to his temples and shrieked like a tea-kettle on a too-high flame. A hand reached down and grabbed Sonya by the neck.

"Hey, you better let go of me, Fatso," Sonya gasped. "I'm sure Da Mayor didn't go to all the trouble of sending you two goons a hunnert million klicks just to strangle me!" She was lifted up, wriggling, until her face was on a level with Fatso's clenched jaw.

"I'm getting so I don't care what Hizzoner Beppo Bellissini wants," the taller goon rasped. His breath stank like vomit.

Shouldn't have put quite so much salt in his instant coffee this morning.

"By the Great Venusian Monsoon I swear, by the rings of Saturn I cast a mighty oath, as my name is Captain Ross N. Krantz of Bellissini's Bullyboy Bastards of Venus, if you don't sit down and shut up like a good little girl I'm gonna open the airlock door and HIG-IG-IG-IG-INK!" he howled as Sonya jabbed her fingers up both of his nostrils. He let her go and staggered around the cabin, clutching his face with both hands as blood dripped from the middle of it.

Sonya was scurrying around two steps ahead of Spazzo Stern, when the ship's loudspeaker suddenly came on and started bawling louder than both kidnappers put together.

"Hello, PEEPS!" it roared, and the two thugs both stopped where they were and piped down, except that Krantz was still making wet snuffling noises.

"Yes, Yeronner," they mumbled, using the traditional form of groveling to the head honcho of humans on Venus.

Sonya perked up. "Hey, are you Da Mayor?"

"That's me, missy," the loudspeaker said after a ten-second pause.

Sonya did some quick math. The delay meant they must still be a good million and a half kilometers ("klicks") from the planet that was Earth's morning star. Her Martian science teacher, Mrs. Wynetski, would have been amazed to learn that she'd actually been paying attention in class.

"So, you're the one responsible for kidnapping me," Sonya said thoughtfully, while her captors held their breath.

Ten seconds later the loudspeakers gave out with a gravelly chuckle. "That's right, missy. I've got you now and there's not a damn thing you can do about it. I'm gonna use my Corrector to make you nice and docile. You'll be my little blond lap-dog, and you'll do whatever tricks I tell you to."

Cold prickles cascaded down Sonya's back and arms. King Ares had had a "Corrector," and she'd heard lurid rumors about what he could do with it. *Nasty* stuff to girls and young women. Even Queen Anya, who back then was only a princess and a dangerous rival to the tyrant, had almost given in to the thing's hypnotic power. Or that's what Martian people said.

Sonya's bossy stepsister Katie, and Katie's know-it-all, carrot-top best friend Rachel, who were from Earth like her, had a way of looking at each other and smiling mysteriously whenever the subject came up, but they kept saying she was too young to know the full truth and she'd just have to wait until she was a little older.

They said that about a lot of things, like how they'd all gotten to Mars in the first place, when Rachel and Sonya had been trapped along with their families in a crumbling apartment in the Warsaw Ghetto where the Germans forced them to live, and Katie had been living with *her* parents in faraway Texas. It seemed to Sonya they had all somehow been magically transported into the world of Rachel's imagination—the red-head used to write crazy stories about rockets and monsters on distant planets, back in Warsaw—but Sonya couldn't be sure, and it might have helped to know what kind of threat she was facing.

Instead, all she could do was bluster, so she raised her voice and began to shriek so loudly her captors clapped their hands over their ears, threatening the Venusian dictator that her best friend Queen Anya was going to declare war on his whole stupid planet, which he was too stupid to realize was named after a girl, and when the fearsome Martian war-riors captured him they were going to throw him alive into the enormous red-hot cauldron of Olympus Mons.

Eventually she had to pause for breath. Fatso grabbed her from behind and tied her to a chair, making the knots so tight she gasped in pain. More chuckling came from the speakers, but Sonya's arms were bound too tightly for cold prickles this time.

"Is that all you've got, *little girl*? I'm going to take a good look at you when my men bring you in, and decide whether I want to keep you around until you're a little … *riper*. And if not, I'll use the Corrector to command *you* to walk into a lava crater … and you'll be happy to do it!"

* * * *

Queen Anya wasn't, in fact, considering throwing anybody into red-hot lava. Instead she was meeting with Sonya's adoptive parents, Mike and Mary Webb, and her best friends, Katie and Rachel, to deliver the grim news.

"I'm afraid she's no longer on Mars," the red-haired queen of the Red Planet said quietly.

Mike Webb's lower lip vibrated. "We've got to get her back. She's a good girl, after all."

"No she ain't, Boo," his wife Mary said. "Remember what happened when we tried to have her help out with the milking?" They shuddered at the memory of swollen udders and seriously pissed-off cows. "But she don't deserve to be kidnapped to another planet," Mary quickly added. "What can we do to rescue her?"

Anya sat and pondered the problem, her lower lip sticking out slightly on the left, which was her "bad side" since the struggle against King Ares and his Corrector had come within a whisker of killing her.

As if Anya really has a bad side, Rachel thought. *That little scar on her left temple just makes her more beautiful!*

Love, admiration, and a trace of envy flowed through the Earth immigrant as she regarded her greatest creation. For the young queen of Mars had been born, along with the rest of this improbable world, when Rachel dreamed them up on her typewriter two years ago, when she was hungry and cold and scared, living with her parents, Sonya and her little sister and their parents in that tiny apartment in the Warsaw Ghetto.

By Rachel's personal reckoning, it should now be the summer of 1944, not late in the year 2173—but then if reality had proceeded in this reasonable, everyday way, Rachel and Sonya would probably both be dead, murdered by the Nazis. Instead the force of her imagination, and the magic of the typewriter, had somehow transported them both to this fantastic world of the future. There she had met a fan of her stories—Katie, who really *was* from the future, albeit a much drearier version of the twenty-second century than the one they'd been living in for two years now.

Of course, this world had its dull moments too. Like last week, when Anya didn't want to attend her own birthday party and made Rachel go instead.

"I have a headache," she'd whined—no, sorry, this was Anya, she hadn't *whined*, she'd *purred*. "Please, my dear sister. It'll only be for a couple of hours."

"All I have to do is greet a lot of boring senators and businessmen—*capitalists*," Rachel spat, "plus eat so much fattening cake we won't be able to keep up this charade much longer. Your Majesty," she added in afterthought. Anya, of course, never seemed to put on weight no matter what she ate. That was what Rachel got for having dreamed up a fantastically perfected version of herself.

"Oh, thank you, Ray!" Anya had cried, embracing her so that she'd really have had to be stone-hearted to refuse her best friend's and near-twin's request.

The ceremony was every bit as awful as Rachel expected, and then some, and she had definitely put on at least a full kilo.

Well, maybe I shouldn't worry about that too much, because I can see which way this *little crisis is heading.*

Katie said it first. "We'll have to go look for Sonya." Her parents both shouted at once, but she waved them off. "So what if I still need a wheelchair to get around? That don't mean I can't help look for my own sister!"

"I'd better go with her," Rachel said. "The bad guys will see that wheelchair and make the mistake of 'messing with Texas,' and who's going to stop her from killing them if I'm not there?"

Katie stuck her tongue out at Rachel. "I can see pretending to be queen all the time has made you put on airs. What would all your 'Young Guard' buddies think if they saw you prancin' around in royal robes?"

Rachel's face heated up at the mention of her socialist Zionist youth group back on Earth. They were supposed to be training to go to Palestine and live on a kibbutz. The SS had other ideas.

Anya held up her hands. "Friends, this isn't helping Sonya. You can't just go running off looking for her, if you haven't got any idea where to look."

"I think I can help with that," a new voice said. Everyone turned and Rachel felt her heart skip a beat at the sight of Zap-Gun Jack Flash, larger than life and twice as full of surprises. He bowed and grinned. "Your Majesty," he said, and when she leapt to her feet he added a more informal greeting.

"Nice lip work," Katie said, after a few seconds. Her parents looked away.

"Oh, I don't know, Tommy has his moments too," Rachel said quietly.

"How is Junior Gdanski? I ain't seen him since finals last month."

"Busy with the kruckle bean harvest."

"If I never have to see any of them beans again, it'll be good for my heart. The more I eat them, the more I fart."

"Kait-LYN!" Mary Webb said.

"Hi girls. Mr. and Mrs. Webb," Jack said, coming up for air. "Well, as soon as I heard from Anya about Sonya's disappearance, I started making some discreet inquiries. It may interest you to know, Anya, there was an unauthorized launch from Quack at the same time Mary Webb, here, was reporting Sonya missing."

Quack was really QWAC, short for Queen Wanda Catapult-port, a name that recalled the ancient Martian method of spaceflight.

Anya bit her lip. "Think they bribed someone on the spaceport staff?"

Jack shook his head. "Not necessarily with money. There are still a lot of bad guys left over from Ares's time who would be willing to do anything to embarrass or hurt you. And I mean *anything*."

"You have such a comforting way of putting things, Jack dear," Anya sighed. "Better that than yes-men, though. Give me anything but yes-men. I'd rather know the truth, no matter how awful it is."

"So you won't mind my telling you that the kidnappers were apparently from Venus, and are probably working for Da Mayor, Beppo Bellissini," Jack said. "I took the trouble of plotting a course from QWAC to Aphro-Port, at the maximum speed for a scout-ship. That would put our friends on track to arrive in a few days. I asked Karolla to monitor the radio traffic, and sure enough, he's picked up some suspicious encrypted radio signals from a rocketship that's on such a course."

Rachel tried to visualize how Jack's friend Karolla, a Venusian native from a tribe called the N'Bialy, could operate a radio set with his seven-fingered hands. It would have to be a very big radio set. His body looked as though it might belong to a miniature Tyrannosaurus Rex, one almost three meters tall, except that it was covered with purple scales that felt like downy fur. Also he had the head of a sheepdog, and eyes bluer than any she'd ever seen except Tommy's. And even Tommy didn't have a chest THAT furry …

Concentrate, Rachel! Ask some astute questions! "Has he been able to get a look at the ship?"

"Umm, not really, Ray," Jack said, struggling to keep a straight face, "what with the permanent cloud cover over the whole entire planet and all."

Katie scowled at him. "Don't you smart-mouth my friend, gunslinger!" she warned, wheeling herself menacingly close.

Jack raised his hands and smiled. "I wouldn't dare do that, Katie. I was just going to say that I think I can probably handle this one on my own, maybe with a little help from Jim."

Jack's younger brother had gone back to Venus, which was their home planet, almost two Earth years ago. Anya had offered to make him an officer in her new, smaller Martian Army, but after having spent fifteen years kidnapped and drafted against his will into the old Martian Army, he had said thanks but no thanks.

Rachel remembered writing about him in the stories that had somehow created this mad universe. She'd meant it as an interesting backstory for Zap-Gun Jack and a possible set-up for a future adventure. She couldn't have dreamed that she was making herself responsible for ruining an actual human being's life. But Katie kept telling her she wasn't to blame, seeing as how this world and all the people in it wouldn't exist without her—Jim included.

But if I'm the god of this crazy world, how come I can't stop bad things happening in it? Or help the people I love most?

Sometimes at night, when she came home to the plain old Martian sandstone house she'd asked Anya to give her instead of a palace for "services to the Crown," Rachel would lie in bed staring at the ceiling, sleepless with grief over not having been able to rescue her parents from the Nazis and bring them to this fantastic Mars. All her skill with words and all the awesome powers she seemed to command when she sat down at her magic typewriter hadn't done the trick, and so she'd smashed it. When she got in those moods, even Tommy had a hard time making her feel better. Though his warm smile and warmer embrace did help …

Katie put her hand on Rachel's shoulder and started shaking her roughly. "Ray! C'mon and back me up!"

"Huh? What?"

"Mr. Musketeer here is trying to say I can't go save Sonya! My parents, too!"

"Sugarplum," Mike Webb began, but Katie cut him off.

"Don't you 'sugarplum' me, Pa! You're always saying not to sit around feeling sorry for myself, that I should just get out there and do things like everybody else does! Ain't rescuing my kid sister more important than helping out around the farm?"

"You'll do anything to avoid chores, won't you, Kaitlyn?" Mary Webb said.

"You don't even need me! Ain't Pa always saying the soil's so rich out here by Olympus Mons that all you have to do is look at it to make the crops grow?"

"Kaitlyn, that's not the point—"

"Enough," Anya said. She spoke quietly but everyone else stopped talking as soon as she opened her mouth.

It's good to be the queen, Rachel thought. *I can pretend to be her and even fool a lot of people, but she really does have something I haven't got. I made her that way!*

"Kaitlyn and Rachel, you are not to imperil yourselves going with Jack on this mission. We have need of your services here."

I HATE it when she uses the royal "we"!

"And neither are you to place yourself in peril unnecessarily, Mr. Flash!"

Jack put his left foot back and bowed a mocking bow, crossing his arms while holding his beloved zap-gun "Annabelle" over his chest. "Whatever you say, Your Majesty!"

"We'll have none of your cheek, Mr. Flash," Anya said, trying hard not to grin.

"Aww, but I shaved this morning, Anya honey!"

"C'mon," Katie growled to Rachel, "let's get out of here before them two start smoochin' again!" She propelled herself out the door with her powerful arms—even though she'd designed and built an electric wheelchair in two afternoons, she refused to actually use the thing herself, saying that building her muscles built character.

Rachel sighed as she jogged after her friend, who had more than a little of her flinty Texas parents in her. They made their way across a field where Mike Webb had set up some spindly tomato trellises, betting that the Martians' love for anything red would trump their suspicion of Earth fruits and vegetables. So far the bet hadn't panned out.

Katie kept wheeling herself along until she'd put a good fifty meters between them and the house, where Anya's palace guard added to the number of potential eavesdroppers.

"You're thinking the same as me, I'll wager," she said, stopping abruptly.

Rachel shut her eyes and rubbed the bridge of her narrow nose. Then she nodded reluctantly. "Katie, I'm afraid we might be up against another Johnny Marshall on Venus."

Katie nodded. "That's why we got to take that dirtball's old Remington out of hiding."

The manual typewriter that Johnny Marshall (alias the Martian King Ares III) had brought from Texas and used to try to take over the universe Rachel had created was locked away securely in her house. It was covered with a dustcloth and she intended it to stay that way forever. The thought of the power she would wield with her fingers on its keyboard didn't thrill her—it terrified her.

"There's got to be some other way we can stop Bellissini, Kaitlyn!" she said.

"Don't you Kaitlyn me no Kaitlyns, Ray. You know there's been rumors for years that Da Mayor of Venus has his very own 'Corrector.' A typewriter from our home universe … the kind that can rewrite this entire world!"

"I wish you wouldn't call it a 'Corrector,'" Rachel said, shuddering at the memory of Anya's near-death experience when Johnny/Ares tried to bend her to his will. "Anyhow, when you use a typewriter you need a corrector to fix your mistakes!"

"Don't quibble, Ray. That ain't the point and you know it. The point is Hizzoner Beppo Bellissini just proved them rumors true. Or else whyfore would he go and kidnap my bratty little sister? He must've heard the same rumors about us. Grabbing her is a good way to find out if we have our own Corrector, so he can protect his little monopoly."

"You're probably right," Rachel sighed.

"I *am* right. And that bein' so, we better bring Johnny Marshall's antique Remington manual typewriter with us when we ride to Sonya's rescue—in lieu of a Remington rifle."

"But if we keep tampering with reality, we'll end up as bad as he was!"

"I don't like the idea of messing with this world either, Ray. I like it just fine the way you and I made it."

Rachel stayed silent: she knew her friend was her co-creator, in the most literal sense. They'd found out through trial and error that until Katie read any changes Rachel made in the world, they remained nothing but words on a page.

Once, they'd switched Anya's hair color as a test, and nobody but them had noticed: to everyone else, Anya had *always* been a blond, until they switched it back and she had *always* been a redhead. It was downright creepy, which was why Rachel didn't want to use that power for anything that wasn't life or death.

But with Sonya in peril, this really was a case of life and death. Rachel bit her lip, staring down at the black volcanic soil nourishing Mike Webb's tomato crop. At last she nodded.

"I'm sorry, Ray, but this is the way it's got to be," Katie said. "There's an old Texas expression, you know: don't bring a knife to a gunfight. Or a quill pen to a typewriter war."

"You made that last part up."

"You made up a whole dang universe!"

2

"Yeronner," the flunky said.

Da Mayor, Giuseppe "Beppo" Bellissini, watched closely as the flunky flung himself face down on the carpet and crawled on his elbows and knees. That was a lot of tongue the guy was using on the crimson shag carpet. Maybe too much. Wasn't he overdoing it a little? Could he really trust a total spineless moron like this guy?

"Yes, Major Stoppard, you may get up on your knees now. What is it?"

"Bad news, I'm afraid, Supreme Boss."

Bellissini knew he should be glad Stoppard wasn't a total yes-man who was too afraid to give him the truth. But he wasn't in the mood. "Bad news, eh? Well, out with it, man!"

The major's face paled. "Yer-yeronner, I'm afraid that, well, well …"

"WELL?!"

"TherocketfromMarscrashedinthejungle. Sir!"

"I see," Da Mayor said, squinting at the major. Something was bothering him about the man. Something besides the fact that he was bearing bad news.

"Captain Ross N. Krantz and Sergeant Guild N. Stern are dead. Sir."

"I see," Da Mayor said again. He stood up slowly, relishing the six inches he had on the little man.

Stoppard gulped as his boss advanced on him. But he hadn't finished delivering his bad news. "And the prisoner, s-sir …"

"Yes?" They were standing face to face now, Stoppard tipping his head back to look up at Bellissini.

"Sh-she's not in the wreckage. Sir. It seems she escaped into the jungle."

"I see," Da Mayor said a third time. He saw Stoppard's clenched jaw relax a bit. *Must be glad I haven't already shot him.* But shooting was too good for this sniveling toady. Da Mayor reached out, grasped the flap of the major's uniform shirt pocket between thumb and forefinger, and started delicately rubbing the material. "What is this on your shirt pocket, major?"

"Sir?"

"I said, what is this on your shirt pocket?"

"N-nothing sir. I haven't earned any medals yet."

Hizzoner gave out with a mighty snort. "I am referring to the condition of the fabric, major."

"The—what, sir?"

"Its condition, man. The fact that it is torn."

"That, sir? That's just a little rip at the corner. I'm going to fix—"

"LITTLE RIPS BECOME BIG RIPS, MAJOR!!!" Bellissini shouted, and taking the pocket flap in both hands, ripped it from the shirt, leaving a gaping hole through which the major's tattered white undershirt showed. Da Mayor tsk-tsked and reduced the rest of the shirt and undershirt to shreds. Then he spun the man around, planted his foot on the flunky's rear end, and kicked him hard. Stoppard fell face down and began crawling out of the room. "Better come back with that lousy little Martian brat, major," Hizzoner said, sitting calmly back down. "Or don't come back at all."

The old methods are always best, Bellissini thought with satisfaction as Stoppard scurried away.

* * * *

It figured that those two idiots couldn't land their stupid rocketship without crashing it. Of course, it might have had *something* to do with the fact that Sonya had been hollering her head off, wriggling and kicking while Captain Fatso buckled her into a crash couch, and meanwhile Sergeant Spazzo was having trouble trying to pilot the ship by himself, especially when she bit his arm. Her teeth *still* ached from that. But there were lots more painful aches now clamoring for her attention as she staggered away from the wrecked ship, which had crashed in a smelly bog.

The truth was, Sonya was a city girl. Though she'd now spent nearly two Earth years on the Webbs' Martian farm, she'd never really taken to it. Mr. and Mrs. Webb weren't so bad, she'd figured out how to deal with them and avoid doing most chores and such homework as didn't fit into her busy pranking schedule.

If all else failed, there was always the orphan card for emergencies— all she had to do was look the angry parent in the eye, tear up and start blubbering about how much she missed her REAL parents to turn those flinty Texans into big piles of mush. That didn't cut much ice with Katie, but fortunately the wheeled terror was so busy with her own studies and advising Queen Anya that she didn't have all that much time to boss her around. With any luck, Katie would soon get her doctorate in engineering and go on to make the lives of generations of Martian students miserable.

Yep, Sonya knew she had it pretty good with her adoptive family, and they lived close enough to Krakowicz that she could walk to town. Hanging out brooding in the desert like Rachel liked to do wasn't Sonya's cup of tea, and exploring this scary, stinky jungle wasn't her idea of fun either. The muddy water came up to her waist, the gravity made her feel like she weighed a ton after spending all that time on Mars, there were thick gray reeds two meters tall blocking her view in all directions, and there wasn't even anybody around to talk to. A big orange caterpillar crawled onto her arm, and she flicked at it in annoyance, whereupon it opened its mouth and revealed big pointy teeth. Sonya shrieked and thrashed around trying to get it off her. She was so convinced the thing had bitten her that she actually saw blood for a moment before realizing there wasn't any.

Darn that Rachel anyway. Why'd she have to dream up such a crazy world?

Sonya hadn't forgotten that Rachel's dreams had actually saved her life—if she hadn't used her magic typewriter to send then-Princess Anya to the Warsaw Ghetto to rescue her, she, Sonya, would undoubtedly have starved to death hiding in the room where her parents and little sister had been dragged away before her eyes (an event she carefully walled off in its own little ghetto in her mind). But still, did she have to be rescued to a world full of monsters and flying rocketships and kidnappers armed with zap-guns—and *school* to boot?

If I were in charge you can bet I wouldn't have had any school in my world! And nor would I have giant wasps that go moo like cows when you try and smack them!

When Sonya finally quit her second round of shrieking and splashing around because her throat was sore and her arms were getting tired, she slowly realized that there were still splashing noises coming from somewhere nearby. She froze.

Could Fatso or Spazzo have survived the crash after all? She began digging around in the cool mud at her feet, which kept trying to suck her down.

There's got to be a rock down here somewhere.

She stifled a cry as her right hand hit something sharp. Sweeping her left hand slowly closer she was stopped by the edge of something hard. Something big.

It took almost a full minute of frantic digging and tugging against that powerful, slimy black mud before she could pull out the object, which looked like a broken piece of a dinner tray-sized clamshell. That would do nicely for a weapon. The splashing was getting closer, and there was a voice mixed in with it. Sonya raised the broken shell as high as she could with her right hand while cautiously pushing aside the reeds with her left hand.

Someone was thrashing around in the water at her feet. Someone big, but it was obvious the person posed no threat to her, being busy drowning and—singing? Sonya kept hold of the shell but let the hand holding it drop to her side as she watched and listened, fascinated.

"Covered with sweet flowers (*glub glub*)," sang the voice, in English. (Solar, they called it here.)

It didn't sound like Spazzo or Fatso. In fact it sounded more like a woman's voice. No, an older girl's. Someone Rachel and Katie's age, maybe.

"Which crying to the grave did go (*glub glub*)," the voice sang. "With true-love showers (*glub*)." A bare arm emerged from the water.

At first Sonya thought it was just covered with mud, as she herself was, but then she realized the drowning girl actually had dark skin. Now this was even more interesting. You didn't see any African people back in Warsaw, or in the crazy mixed-up funhouse version of Poland that nutty Rachel had put on Mars. Sonya decided she had to learn more.

"Watchya doin'?"

A head emerged from the water. A dark, shapely head covered with soaking wet, jet-black hair. It tried to say something but ended up choking and spluttering.

"I can't understand you. You're gonna have to spit some mud out first."

"I said, I'm hallucinating," the voice said. "Must be the oxygen deprivation—drowning (*glub*)."

Sonya grabbed a handful of hair and yanked the head out of the water. "You won't drown so much if you don't keep stickin' your head in the water. What's 'hallucinating' mean?"

"Seeing things," the drowning girl said. "I must be. Here I am trying to drown myself in the middle of this godforsaken swamp, and this annoying white girl is suddenly standing there asking me all kinds of dumb questions."

Sonya let go of the other girl's hair and folded her arms, being careful not to scrape her bare skin with the broken end of the shell. "Nuh-uh. I'm real. You're the one that ain't. You and the whole rest of this silly world that bossy know-it-all Rachel dreamed up."

"No, *you're* the one who isn't real. I'll just duck back under and this will all end (*glub glub*)—OW!"

"Whyfore you keep trying to drown yourself?" Sonya asked, clinging tightly to the girl's hair. She was *really* interested now.

"None of your business! I'm not discussing my private affairs with some hallucination—OW! Okay, okay, you're real." The girl groaned, and, with a mighty effort, heaved herself out of the water and onto a hummock of dry grass with a small tree growing out of it.

Sonya flinched. The stranger was taller than Mr. Webb, even. But she didn't seem hostile. She offered Sonya a hand, and after a moment the younger girl clambered up beside her.

"Name's Po Helia," the older girl said. "You may call me by my family name, Ms. Po. Only my friends get to call me Helia."

I hate snobs. But somebody has to lead me out of this swamp. "Sonya Goldberg-Webb," the younger girl said. They shook very muddy hands, and Sonya examined her new friend curiously. It was hard to tell under all that mud, but it looked like she'd been wearing nice clothes, a blouse and skirt like Katie and Rachel had to put on every time they went to the palace to see Anya. Seemed like a weird outfit to drown yourself in.

Sonya again asked why. She never let *anything* go, once she'd got her teeth in it, as the late Sergeant Stern had learned to his regret.

"And I told you, it's my private business! What do you care if my no-good boyfriend Mark Mahlett dumped me?"

Sonya scratched her head, working the swamp mud real deep into the scalp. "Sounds like he's a louse to me, but I still don't see why it made you want to kill yourself. I mean, wouldn't it be more logical to kill Mark?"

"Ladies do NOT kill their boyfriends."

"Nadia, the secretary of bad old King Ares on Mars, pushed him into the magma on top of Olympus Mons. I saw her do it myself. Now she goes around beating up any men that beat up their wives or girlfriends."

"Well, proper Venusian ladies don't act that way."

Much as she hated to admit it, a lot of Katie had rubbed off on Sonya. "Maybe your stinky planet would be better off if they did," she said.

Helia stuck her nose up in the air. "I will NOT debate the matter. Nor will I debate my ontological status with a brat like you."

"What's 'ontological' mean?"

"Whether I'm real or not."

"Oh." Sonya stood up and kicked Helia hard in the shins.

"OW! Is that how you thank people for improving your vocabulary?"

"No, that was for calling me names."

3

There is a very old, very simple idea about the Problem of Evil, and it goes like this: The bad guys don't really mean it.

Plato, one of the most famous of the ancient Greek philosophers, puts it this way: "For no man is voluntarily bad; but the bad become bad by reason of an ill disposition of the body and bad education, things which are hateful to every man and happen to him against his will." In other words, the bad guys are only bad because they don't feel well and had bad teachers—and they hate themselves that way!

Beppo Bellissini, Da Mayor of Venus, was personally insulted by this idea, having been a bad teacher for over twenty years before he discovered that a simple typewriter could give him grander scope for his own carefully chosen evil than he could ever have dreamed of. If Plato were in his power, he would make him drop and give him one hundred, then he would send him out into the jungle to harvest joowallah plants, and, if he came back alive, he'd force him to take part in the gladiatorial Death-Ball games. That might teach him a thing or two about evil.

Evil took a lot of creativity and a lot of hard work. For instance, Bellissini hadn't just happened to come across the Platonic dialogue *Timaeus* containing the idea that there is actually no such thing as a bad guy. No, to find it he'd had to confiscate dozens of books over the years from kids who came to his gym class late, or whose book covers had little rips in them (because little rips become big rips!)

Most of the books he got that way were just boring textbooks, which he'd toss in the trash without a second thought and with a sneering indifference to the sometimes tearful pleas of the kids who'd have to pay to replace them, or they were comic books, a few of which had made him a tidy profit after he let them sit around in his office collecting dust for a few years. But occasionally he'd find something really interesting that some nerd would try to hide in a corner and read instead of playing Death Ball (they called it Dodge Ball back on Earth, where it only occasionally resulted in death or a really satisfying injury) like a healthy red-blooded *manly* kid should.

In this way, Bellissini had acquired an education in fits and starts over the years, and he resented the über-nerd Plato's implication that he hadn't. Sometimes he thought he might use the typewriter to summon the philosopher and demonstrate to him just how wrong he was, but even these Venusian dopes were likely to notice something was a little bit strange if he did that. You had to know your limits, unlike that "Ares" character on Mars, another transplant from the real world whose overambitious plot to conquer the whole Solar System had brought about his downfall. *Hubris*, that's what those ancient Greeks had called the mistake of thinking too big. Bellissini had learned that from the same book that had the Plato stuff in it, which he'd taken away from a sniveling little nerd one cold November afternoon back on Earth.

"Please, Mr. Bellissini, I'm feeling nauseous, and I'm no good at football! Just let me sit here and read my books, I won't bother anybody!" the kid, whose name was Mark Mahlett, had begged him.

"Shuddup, you little girl. Geek philosophy, huh? That's you all over. And what's this? *Lost Classics of Science Fiction*? Well, it's lost to you now!"

And he added both books to his collection. Truth to tell, the philosophy book bored him, but he found the "lost classics" strangely gripping … especially an odd little tale called "Zap-Gun Jack Flash and the Dame-Eating Monsters of Venus." Wouldn't it be great to live in a world like that, Bellissini reflected, where men were real men and women knew how to be ravished!

The thought of bossing men around and having women under his power excited him more and more, to the point that he started neglecting his gym class and letting all kinds of intolerable things go on, like book covers with little rips in them and kids running around having fun instead of playing dodge ball. He was so busy daydreaming and scheming how to steal a spanking new IBM Selectric typewriter from the school secretary, a hot little number called Denise Fink (asking to borrow it simply didn't occur to him), that he didn't notice Mark Mahlett's complete disappearance, not just from fourth-period gym but from the school itself, along with Miss Fink—though that was all anybody else could talk about, and rumors swirled wildly.

Having liberated the temporarily unguarded typewriter from the office and half a ream of clean notebook paper from the binder of a seventh grader named Joelle—when she protested, he put a trash can over her shiny, straight brown hair, to the half-delighted, half-terrified squeals of the rest of the class, even though he'd thoughtfully emptied it first—he retreated to his little coach's office with its gaggingly thick stench of dirty socks, and proceeded to write what would one day be called "fan fiction," a vividly imagined addition to the world the anonymous author of "Zap-Gun Jack Flash and the Dame-Eating Monsters of Venus" had dreamed up. Hunting and pecking even slower than the Mahlett kid ran the fifty-yard-dash, Bellissini somehow produced a full page in just under two weeks, and then another, and another, until by winter break he had a completed story all ready to send off to *Thrilling Wonder Tales* magazine.

The response came just after New Year's Day. Standing by the row of metal boxes in his apartment building's lobby, Bellissini tore open the envelope with fingers that were trembling so badly he ripped the letter in two and had to hold up the torn edges to read the message it contained:

> Dear Mr. Bellissini, Thank you very much for submitting your story, 'It Takes a Strong Man to Rule the Woman's Planet.' Unfortunately, it does not suit our needs at the present time. Please do not take this as a reflection on your writing as opinions may differ, and another publication may well disagree with our judgment.
>
> Sincerely yours, Gloria M. Stein, Editorial Assistant.

As he stared at the letter, his face slowly turning scarlet, a scrap of paper fluttered out of the envelope and fell at his feet. He bent over to retrieve it, feeling as if his head would burst, and read the scrawled message on it.

> REJECT!!! This is the 1970's, science fiction has outgrown this kind of sexist, fascist garbage!

"Fascist?" Bellissini muttered to himself. "FASCIST?!" He shook with rage.

His downstairs neighbor, timid old Mrs. Feinstein, who had come out to retrieve her mail, scurried back into her apartment and slammed the door as he howled, "My name is BELLISSINI, not MUSSOLINI!"

And with that, he turned toward the lobby door, intending to jump in his power-blue Dodge Dart and race it from the Long Island suburb of Chatham's Ford where he lived and worked to downtown Manhattan and register his disagreement in person, with extreme prejudice. Instead he ran smack into the other ground-floor tenant, who had poked her head out of her own apartment to see what all the commotion was about.

Bellissini remembered just in time that he'd been trying to get Cherie Morgan to go out with him since she moved into the building. Her face looked like it was carved out of ivory, her glossy black hair was always carefully done up in the latest fashion, she dressed like a model, and if she said as much as "hello" to him he considered it a moral triumph. So he composed himself in the face of her arched, delicately tweezed right eyebrow and said, "Cherie, can you give me your opinion on something?"

"I'm kind of in a rush, Beppo." Her voice was like doves cooing at nightfall. "Can you make it fast?"

"This'll just take a minute!" he said, handing her the now half-crumpled pages of his story while hastily jamming the rejection letter and the insulting scrap of paper that went along with it in the right pocket of his burgundy track pants.

"Oh, all right," she muttered, her coral-painted lips twitching.

Surely she wasn't laughing at him? *No way can a girl this pretty be a lousy man-hating women's libber! Just look at those creamy white legs!*

Bellissini waited for her to finish, bouncing up and down on the balls of his heels. She was sure to see how great his story was and let him know about it! She might even fall into his arms! With every rustle of her turning the pages, his confidence grew.

"Well, Beppo," she said, at last, handing him back the manuscript, "I'm not much of a science fiction reader, but parts of it are, uh, stirring."

"I knew it!" Bellissini shouted, grabbing her by the hands. "That lousy editor was full of it! Now that you've read the story, you can come with me and show her how wrong she is, and after she agrees to publish it we'll go out to Delucci's for a candlelit dinner!"

"I'm on the way somewhere, Beppo. Like, I have date—"

She squealed in surprise as Bellissini started whirling her around in an impromptu dance, right there in the lobby. Faster and faster they spun, the metal mailboxes and the scratched glass of the front door turning into a blur around them. He'd never been so light on his feet, not since he was in high school!

Actually he was getting a little sick to his stomach, but he couldn't seem to stop … The ugly toothpaste-green walls seemed to be darkening in color and Bellissini wondered if all the blood was rushing to his head, he wanted to ask Cherie if she felt funny too but he couldn't seem to catch his breath, until all of a sudden he lost his grip on her hands and they went flying off into the walls at opposite corners of the room. He squeezed his eyes shut and waited for the world to stop spinning around him.

"Boss, we're waitin' for your orders," a voice growled. "Now's no time to be takin' a nap, capeesh?"

"Whazzat?" Bellissini grunted as the room swam back into focus.

A Neanderthal-looking individual with a single eyebrow extending the width of his forehead was leaning over him where he sat slumped on a burgundy deep-pile carpet, like the one he'd wanted for his apartment but the landlord wouldn't let him install. The Neanderthal helped Bellissini to his feet and into a red velour-upholstered easy chair—just the kind he had always wished for. Now he had one, and it was plunked down behind a polished wooden desk the size of a sailboat, a desk that would put the principal Dr. Muller's desk to shame.

Across the room Cherie was climbing shakily to her feet. Bellissini blinked when he saw she had on the kind of skirt he always wished she'd wear, the kind that showed off her legs and butt "and left but little to the imagination," as he'd written about all the women characters in his story, hunting and pecking each letter on the Selectric. Which had somehow come along with him, and now occupied the center of his magnificent new desk.

"Hot dog!" Bellissini exclaimed, sitting up straight so suddenly he barely avoided concussing the Neanderthal, who was named after a tough kid he always wanted to be friends with when he was in school but who used to sneer at him. "Vito 'Vise-Grip' Vinelli!'" he exclaimed.

"Yeah boss, dat's me," the Neanderthal said, giving him a wary look. "You sure you okay?"

"Never better!" Bellissini hopped to his feet, noting with pleasure that instead of a smelly old track suit he was now "dressed in the finest duds from Place Vendôme in Paris, France, Earth," as he'd written. The dark fabric whispered against his skin and he stepped in front of the full-length mirror in the corner to admire the way the crisp white cuffs of his shirt set it off.

He had written that Vito was a "machete-man" who'd paid his dues cutting joowallah plants in the thick jungle outside Aphrodite Port, Venus's capital and largest human settlement, for export to Earth, Mars, and the outer planets, where the thick raspberry-red juice was prized for its medicinal properties. In the fan-fiction story that had now come deliciously to life, Mr. Bellissini wasn't a lowly gym teacher who got his rocks off stomping schoolchildren half his size, he was "Boss-man" Bellissini, who had used his guile and a certain amount of discreet violence to work his way up from a bribe-taking customs officer to the leader of the powerful Joowallah-Juice Trust and alderman of Aphro-Port's South Side, just a short jump from the mayor's office.

"How long till the election?" he demanded as he straightened a tie so loud it should have deafened people way up on the North Side.

Vito raised his unibrow and said, "It's on Tuesday, boss. Duh foist Tuesday after duh foist Monday in Novembuh."

"I know that, idiot!" Bellissini said, smacking his loyal minion in the mouth without even turning around. "I asked how long UNTIL then."

"Oh, how long UNTIL then," Vito said, chuckling nervously. "Why it's, uh," he began counting on his fingers, his bleeding lips moving.

"Five days from now, baby," said a new voice.

Bellissini felt the grin slowly spreading against his face as the school secretary, Denise Fink, slinked (slunk?) into the room. Only here she was even younger and hotter than she was back in Chatham's Ford, dressed like Cherie's twin, and went by the name "Delores Fabuloso," which she had picked up as a showgirl in Aphro-Port's seedy Spaceman District.

Inside his mind, he licked his lips at the thought that the two hot brunettes were about to have a catfight over little old Beppo, but Cherie was standing rigidly with her arms at her sides, her dark eyes darting wildly from side to side.

Oh well. Have to slap her around a bit if she doesn't snap out of it. Meanwhile here's the luscious Delores ... Bellissini thought as he gave her a sloppy kiss.

"Or should I call you, Yeronner!" she said, tapping his nose with her forefinger when he came up for air.

"Yes you should, baby," Bellissini purred, kissing her again.

In real life he'd been forced back to bachelorhood after his wife, Teresa, got all mixed up another lousy gang of women's libbers. She always did have a mouth on her, but when they were just starting out he'd been willing to overlook that since she had such a nice butt.

Vito cleared his throat with a noise like a gravel truck running over a blender. "Your orders, boss?"

"Hmm? Oh, carry on, carry on," he said, waving his right hand.

"But you hadn't made your mind up about, uh, about whether we should do that thing."

"What thing?" But Bellissini was starting to realize he knew. He'd written about it in his story, after all. Stubborn Alderman Bill Penn was refusing to back his mayoral campaign, in spite of all bribes and threats. White-haired little phony thought he was better than that.

"Go out and round up some erasers, Vito ol' pal," he said, clapping the shorter man on the shoulder. It was like slapping a boulder.

"Erasers?" Vito said.

"Yeah, you know. Pen marks can be stubborn, but if you *rub them out* hard enough, they'll go."

"Oh!" Vito said, smiling a slow, terrifying little smile. "I gotcha, boss. Consider it done."

"Great! See ya later. See you at home, Delores," he said, tipping the former Miss Fink a wink. She winked back over her shoulder as she exited the room with Vito.

Bellissini shut the door gently behind them, then turned to face Cherie. *She'll still be in shock, so she'll do anything I tell her to.*

But there was such a hard little gleam in her eyes he took a step back.

"So, you think I'm another 'Delores Fabuloso' like in that stupid story of yours, huh, Beppo?"

Better show her who's in charge! Bellissini smiled the same smile he used when he was about to make some little scared-of-heights twerp climb the gym rope and stepped toward her. "What I think, toots, is that I'm a man who just magicked a whole planet into existence! So you'd better do what I say, or I'll vaporite you!"

"That's 'vaporize,' you dope," Cherie said, spitting the *p*'s. A glob of saliva landed on his fancy shoes. "And I'll bet you can't. I'll bet you don't even know how or why we both ended up here!"

He stepped close enough to smell her breath mints. "Willing to bet your life, toots?"

She shoved him away with both hands. "Yeah, I am, Beppo. I saw the look in your eyes when you stood up."

He stared at her for a long moment, then looked away, his shoulders sagging inside the expensive jacket. "Fine. Whaddya want?"

Cherie snickered. "Actually, I think I'll give you a hand, Beppo. You won't be able to run a whole planet by yourself. You can barely make it as a gym teacher."

He glared at her. "On what conditions?"

She ticked off the points on her violet-lacquered nails. "One, I ain't gonna dress like a tramp, 'cause I ain't gonna be your girlfriend. You're gross, and no suit's gonna change that."

"Why, you—"

He aimed a roundhouse punch at her but somehow found himself on his butt, in the corner he'd woken up in, with his chest aching as if a medicine ball had slammed into it.

Cherie leaned over him, still counting on her fingers. "Two, *I'm* the one who's gonna write this 'story' from now on. On your typewriter."

Bellissini decided now wasn't the moment to inform her that the machine wasn't really his.

"I'll take dictation from you, Beppo, and be your secretary, but I'll decide if what you're saying is so dumb it shouldn't be part of the story."

"Fuh-fine," he mumbled. "That it?"

"Three, I come and go when I please, and I set my own salary." She scratched her head. "Why'd you make 'solar' money the same as Polish money, anyhow?"

"I was feeling creative." Better that than admit he'd been writing fan fiction based on some dead Polock's story.

"Sure you were," Cherie snorted, gathering the Selectric under an arm that looked too skinny to hold it. Bellissini looked longingly at her butt before she straightened up and said, "See you tomorrow morning at nine, Beppo."

"But I thought I'd sleep in. I'm the boss, ain't I?"

"Nine o'clock sharp! Or maybe I'll run for mayor of Venus myself."

* * * *

The next five days were the busiest of Bellissini's life. Cherie was a regular slave-driver, and what was worse was, she was right: Fixing an election wasn't just about stuffing ballot boxes and throwing your muscle around, fun though that was.

No, you also had to make promises to the other aldermen and fat slobs like the commander of the spaceport, and you even had to figure out which ones to keep and which ones to break, along with the person you'd made the promise to, if you won the election. It had all seemed so simple when he was writing the story. Strong Man, meet weak, feminine planet yearning for a firm masculine hand.

But actually, all the politicians and businessmen he had to deal with were cigar-chomping tough guys who didn't seem any more eager to bend to his will than Cherie was. And then there were the crowds in Aphrodite Port. Cherie told him to promise the voters he would end corruption when he came into office. He didn't think that could possibly work, especially since he planned to take all the bribe money for himself, but sure enough they ate it up when he shouted that he was going to "throw out all the bums and crooks" and "restore Venus to her shining glory!" The chumps.

So it was with a sense of accomplishment that on election night he stumbled back home to the plastic-and-steel mansion he occupied with the beauteous Delores, a place he'd barely visited in the busy days since his unexpected arrival.

"Honey, we won!" he cried boozily. "You can call me 'Yeronner' for real n—" He stopped in mid-sentence when he saw her huddled over a form lying on the sofa. A male form.

"What's this?" he demanded, stomping over and shoving her aside. "Better get ready for your launch to Mars, pal, and you won't even need a rocket, you—you—what are YOU doing here?"

As Delores wept softly in the corner, the figure on the couch sat up and said, "Mr. Bellissini! What a surprise seeing you here!" His voice cracked on the last word, partly from nervousness and partly from the fact that he was a god. Damned. TEENAGER!

Bellissini forced himself to lower his voice to a growl. "Listen here, you sissy boy Mahlett, what's the big idea horning in on my little fantasy?"

"Your fantasy?! She was mine first!"

"Yours first?" Bellissini echoed, staggering backward as if he'd been punched in the gut.

Then he actually *was* punched in the gut—by Delores. *What is it with the women on this planet?* "You leave my son alone!" she screeched.

Bellissini's eyes bugged out. "Your son?" he rasped. He knew perfectly well that Mark Mahlett wasn't Miss Fink's son—she didn't have any children. He glared at the nerdball, his eyes narrowing. "You—little—pervert!"

"She wasn't like this until a few days ago!" the kid squeaked. "She was a school secretary here, too! Miss Fink was always so nice to me back at Chatham's Ford Junior High … I always used to wish she was my mom. All my real mom does is yell at me!"

"Sweetie, what are you talking about?" Delores asked, tears streaming down her face. "I *am* your real mom! I'm sorry I've been so busy the past few days. I just had to help Beppo win the election. Now that he has, we're all going to be one big happy family, isn't that right, Beppo?" She turned such beseeching dark eyes on Bellissini, nobody but a man with a void where his heart should have been could have resisted them.

Bellissini slapped Delores in the face so hard her lip started bleeding, although he was only a little annoyed.

"Never call me Beppo! I hate that name!" he said, clutching his hand to the void in his chest and massaging it while thinking fast. Of course he had only been "here" for a few days, so it could be the nerdball was actually telling the truth. It wouldn't do to put the boot in, not in front of this weepy feminine mess, so …

He smiled broadly and stepped forward, holding out his hand for Mahlett to shake. "Sorry, kid, I've just been under pressure from the campaign. Like your ma says, we'll all be best pals now! Put 'er there!"

Mahlett timidly stretched out his hand, and Bellissini put bone-crushing pressure on it while Delores beamed and clapped her hands.

Bellissini hissed at him softly, "Now, make yourself scarce while your Ma and me enjoy some quality time together, capeesh? Better give us a couple of, oh, weeks. No, better make it a couple months. Now skedaddle."

4

"To flee or not to flee," said Mark Mahlett, "that is the question."

No, that is not the question, reflected Jim Flash. *The question is how much more of this outrageous self-pity I can listen to before I up and strangle the kid?*

Mark certainly knew how to make a good thing turn sour in a hurry. After Da Mayor kicked him out of his mother's place he could have moved in with his girlfriend Po Helia, and what red-blooded boy wouldn't jump at that chance? But no, he wouldn't do it, and he didn't treat her very nicely either.

Jim gathered she'd been putting up with his pissing and moaning about his mom, and occasional sarcastic asides about how she'd be better off as a nun than staying with him, for ages by the time the younger Flash brother arrived on the scene from Mars. No sooner had he scraped the red dust of that filthy planet off his feet—best of luck to Anya running it, but really, he never wanted to see the place again—than he learned that his home planet Venus was just as badly off as Mars had been.

True, Da Mayor didn't seem to be planning any campaigns of conquest, unless he intended to take over the entire Solar System by means of sleaze. You couldn't sublet a miserable room in a slum on his planet without paying a bribe to the Housing Authority, you couldn't go to sleep without paying protection money to your friendly neighborhood thugs (unless you didn't mind bricks coming through the window), you couldn't even earn a living as a ditch-digger, as Jim tried to do when he first arrived, without paying kickbacks to your foreman and the Shovel Trust. And all of that money was funneled into the pockets of Bellissini and his henchmen, one way or another.

Jim walked off the job in disgust and drifted into the encampment of homeless, outlawed people who had been exiled from town and lived huddled against the outside of Aphro-Port's bucky-dome. *Outlawed was precisely the right word*, Jim thought as he walked past entire families reduced to living in tents that didn't always hold up when the monsoons came: they were outside all law, because Bellissini's crooked judges had declared them to be so.

It didn't used to be this bad when Jim was growing up, before Martian agents had kidnapped him for the planned Martian army of conquest. Back then, Venus was almost as crooked and sleazy as it was now, but the problem was too little law rather than too much. Nobody had ever heard of Bellissini and his Corrector. Now, this shantytown was home to the few disobedient Venusians deemed too pathetic to be worth a session with Hizzoner.

Among them was Mark Mahlett, a skinny, depressed-looking kid of about fifteen, who didn't seem to have a family. The reason why, as he told Jim within seconds of meeting him, was that Bellissini had "stolen" his mother and turned her against him.

"I don't know how he did it, but she doesn't even want to see me anymore," he said, looking as if he was about to cry. "She used to love me!"

"*I* still love you, baby."

Jim looked up and saw a magnificent black lady who had to be almost two meters tall but looked even taller under an exuberant Afro. Habits he had learned a lifetime ago and forgotten all about during his years as a forced conscript in the Martian Army took over and he jumped to his feet, pressed his heels together, and bowed from the waist.

She smiled sadly at him, and he realized that she was a lot younger than her poise and beauty made it seem. "An old-fashioned gentleman, I see," she said. "But there is no need, good sir. We Crewmen haven't been in charge here in Aphro-Port for a long time."

"Jim, my girlfriend Po Helia," Mark muttered. "Helia, Jim. Why don't you just betray me with him? It would make my day oh, so perfect."

"Mark, darling, how can you say such terrible things?" Helia said, her eyes welling up.

Jim wanted to slug the little twerp, and not just because the girl he was abusing was a gorgeous aristocrat—seeing anyone treated the way those brutal Martian drill sergeants had treated him made him want to go berserk. But he suspected this would not help the lovely Crewman (as the descendants of the original human pioneers from Earth were called), so he ground his teeth in disgust and decided to just pretend Mark wasn't even there.

He could try to make Helia feel better, though. "Some of us still feel honor is due the Crewmen," Jim said.

"Honor? Just because of the families we were born into? No, James, that wouldn't be right," she said with a heartbreaking smile. "The fact that my ancestors came here on the good ship *The Other Foot* doesn't make me anyone special."

"It should, though," Jim growled. "If your people had stayed in charge this world would be a better place. We wouldn't have land speculators cutting down the rain forests and driving the N'Bialy from their homes!"

Karolla's people were being driven further back every year, even from the "reservations" that they were supposed to be left alone in. Bellissini seemed to have it in for that tribe, for some reason. He could dimly recall when he was a kid that another Venusian tribe called the Malchussei used to suffer just as much at the hands of greedy human settlers, but now it seemed they had struck some sort of deal with Da Mayor, who left them alone while they kept going to war with the N'Bialy.

Divide and rule, that was obviously what Bellissini was up to, same as the old Martian Army used to do, and Jim wished he could explain that to the Malchussei. But how could he get them to listen to a nobody like him?

He shook his head sadly. "The whole planet was better off when the Crewmen were in charge," he said.

"It's kind of you to say so, Jim. But who knows?" Helia turned and began massaging Mark's shoulders. "Mark, honey, does that make you feel better?"

"I don't deserve to feel better, Helia," he said, but he closed his eyes and luxuriated under her strong fingers.

Jim shook his head, wondering what on Venus could possibly make a girl like that fall for a boy like *that*. The mystery only deepened with time, as days turned into weeks and it became clear that thanks to Helia, Mark was the luckiest guy in the outlaw encampment, but he didn't appreciate it any more than a pet snake appreciates the tame mice its loving owner feeds it—reptiles are simply incapable of gratitude.

Helia had catered five-course dinners delivered to him, and he'd sigh about how he missed his mother Delores's homemade roast scorpion-bunny. She had a miniature bucky-dome custom-built for him to shelter him from the elements, and so they could spend a little quality time together, and all he did was complain about how it wasn't as snug and warm as his bedroom in his mom's condo, "which Beppo Bellissini has probably made into an extra closet for his gym clothes or somethin'."

And Helia winced, but not because of the insult to her generosity. "Be careful what you say, baby, you'll get in trouble!"

"Yeah, I'll probably get my head cut off and mounted on a spike. Why do you hang out with a loser like me, anyway?"

Yeah, why? Jim wondered. But the strange thing was, in a perverse sort of way he was fond of Mark too. Partly it was sympathy—if you could get past his grating self-pity, which was a tall order to be sure, it was obvious that Mark really had suffered from being bullied all his life, just as Jim had in the Martian Army. But Mark claimed never to have had any friends at all back in Chatham's Ford (which seemed like a strange name for an Aphro-Port neighborhood; Jim couldn't recall ever being there).

One of the few things Jim genuinely missed about Mars was the friends he had made there, his fellow misfits and Wandanian pacifists. Mark, on the other hand, seemed intent on driving everyone away. It was perverse.

The best thing to do, Jim decided, was concentrate on survival. Yes, he could eat very nicely if he hung around with Mark and finished all those meals the kid never seemed to have an appetite for. But that was no way for a man to live.

Jim would rather do any kind of honest work, though that was in short supply along with everything else in this encampment of desperadoes. They were odd criminals, to be sure: there seemed to be a lot of families, solid working people and professional types who had managed to get by in the freewheeling days before the Bellissini mayoralty. A lot of them still had a bit of money left, and Jim wasn't too proud to do odd jobs; after all, he'd had to clean latrines in the Martian army barracks with nothing but a fake thistlecat-fur brush, so cleaning the mud out of an accountant's hand cranked washing machine and repairing its gunked-up parts didn't bother him in the least.

The accountant's grateful husband sent him on his way with a genuine 14-karat gold coin minted way back when Leroy II was mayor. (After his reign, the Treasury had switched to pyrite, which was abundant on Venus, since the aldermen had stolen all the remaining gold. Even under the easygoing, bribe-taking politicos who had come before Bellissini, it was forbidden to refer to pyrite by its common Terran name, "fool's gold.")

With real money in his pocket, Jim was feeling pretty good. He'd be able to buy himself the tools and materials for a decent shelter, maybe even a mini-bucky-ball like Mark's. He was whistling a little tune when he ran across Helia, who was trudging through the camp with her hands in the pockets of a pair of unflattering baggy trousers. She greeted him warmly, but her luminous black eyes were tired.

"Crewman Po, it ain't none of my business, but you shouldn't let that boy treat you so badly," he said.

Her eyes flashed and for a moment he cringed. But then she sighed and said, "You're right, of course, Jim. My father told me I'd better not bring Mark around again or he'll pistol-whip him! But I can't help it, I love him."

"Maybe it would help if you found some other interest. Back on Mars I used to stargaze when they had me stand guard at night, to help me forget this Martian girl called Agnieszka who dumped me for a lieutenant." The memory of that still stung.

Helia chuckled gently, the back of her hand half-concealing her mouth. "That wouldn't be too useful a hobby to have on this planet, I'm afraid. Not with the permanent cloud cover and all. What I really like is helping people get organized to do what they have to. So I'd probably be hanging around the outlaw camp even if not for Mark. But people here are so downcast, it's hard to do anything with them. I'm trying to arrange a litter cleanup and even that's proving nearly impossible."

Jim didn't know what to say. Part of him wanted to clap Helia on the shoulder and tell her to stick with it, but he'd have had to stretch up to do that, and his whole body trembled inside at the thought of getting all familiar with a Crewman. So he stammered something polite and continued on his way.

Jim decided to leave both Helia and Mark and their troubles behind. With the coin he'd earned he bought a prefabricated shelter—not as fancy as the one Helia had bought for Mark, but sturdy enough—and he even had enough left over to stock up on canned food and dried Venusian scorpion-bunny jerky, which he'd always had a weakness for. He set up his new home on the far side of the encampment and made up his mind to enjoy the peace and quiet, along with the freedom of being everyone's handyman.

A week or so later, the soft gray light of the Venusian day had hardly changed, but Jim lay on his cot realizing that strange feeling in his bones was something close to contentment, if not happiness. *Maybe I can spend my leftover cash asking a girl out on a date, if I can figure out a place more exciting than Adrian's Bar and Grill to take her.*

But a strange noise soon cut through his musings. It was an annoying blipping sound, like a drop of water falling into a still pool. Several moments passed before he figured out it was coming from the tiny sparkling emerald on his ring finger, but when he did, he stiffened as his peaceful easy feeling seemed to leak away into the jungle mud. Only one person could be trying to call him through the camouflaged miniature radio. And that was the person who had given it him.

"Hello, Jack," he sighed.

* * * *

A couple of million kilometers away in space, Jack leaned anxiously over his radio console, opening a channel he hadn't used in a long time.

"Jim, this is Jack. Come in, Jim."

There was a wait of over twelve minutes for a radio signal to reach Venus and a reply to wend its way back, and Jack spent the entire time fretting, wondering whether his brother had kept the radio-ring. What if he'd fallen on hard times and pawned it?

But then Jim's voice came through, reasonably clear despite the hiss of static. "Hello, Jack."

"Hello, little brother. Long time, no talk. Listen, I'll cut right to the chase. I need your help finding one of our young friends."

There was another long wait. Jack could only hope Jim would understand what he was talking about, and be willing to help.

The radio crackled. "Sure, big brother. I'm always happy to be of service, just like a good little soldier."

Just like he was on Mars, he means. What is this, an interplanetary guilt-trip? How could Jim manage to wrong-foot him so quickly and easily, when they hadn't even spoken in more than an Earth-year? *Maybe it's* because *we haven't spoken in more than an Earth-year.*

Jack gritted his teeth before pressing the green transmit button. "I'm sorry, Jim, I should have checked in with you sooner, but I was busy in the Outer System. How's it been, being back home again after all this time?"

Twelve more minutes went by. No, it was closer to thirteen. "Oh, you know. A little ditch-digging, a little back-to-nature living among the outlaws camped outside the dome of Aphro-Port. Nothing to interest a hero such as yourself."

By God, the little twerp IS guilt-tripping me!

Struggling to keep his temper, Jack said, "Sounds like you're having a tough time there, little brother. Why don't we meet at our usual place, say a week from Wednesday at noon, and I'll see what I can do for you?"

The "usual place" was Adrian's Bar and Grill, which Jack had designated their emergency meeting spot the last time he'd spoken to Jim, for three reasons: Adrian served the best imported Earth beer on Venus, he made the best roasted scorpion-bunny on Venus, and most important of all, Anya had paid off Jack's entire tab after Ares's agents had busted the place up while attempting to kidnap her.

"Sure thing, big brother, we'll meet then so that you can tell me what I can do for you. Over and out," Jim said.

Jack spent so long staring at the console, wondering how Jim had managed to get the last word in, that he almost forgot to call his other important contact on Venus. "Morningstar-1, this is Rogue. Come in, Morningstar-1."

Twelve minutes and forty-five second seconds later the speaker crackled. "Since all courtesy you lack, my old friend must be on his way back."

"Blow it out your ear, you furry menace," Jack said, grinning at the lame-o rhymes of his Venusian aboriginal pal Karolla. "Listen, I know you don't like the city, but could you make an exception and meet up with me and Jim next Wednesday at noon so we can help the friend in trouble I told you about?"

Jack's grin wobbled and collapsed at the reply. "To see you again would make me proud, but I fear in town I am not allowed."

"What? But the Treaty says your kind can enter any human settlement as honored guests!"

Jack knew what Karolla was going to say long before the pokey radio waves could make their way across the void and back, but it still made him furious and sad to hear it.

"Our rights Da Mayor did revoke, he thinks the Treaty a big fat joke."

Jack mumbled a string of curses. *So what else is new?* he thought. *The poor Venusians have been getting the short end of the stick ever since that skunk of a drunk Captain Ronnie Hubbard first landed on their planet two hundred years ago.*

He scowled and pushed the transmit button. "I hear you, old buddy," he said. "Hang tight. I'll meet you early Thursday morning in the clearing where that Medusa's nest used to be." The one they had rescued then-Princess Anya from, with the help of Rachel and Katie.

I never did understand how they appeared out of nowhere in the middle of the Venusian jungle, Jack thought.

5

We should have been back in Aphro-Port two days ago. We must be lost.

As a Crewman, Helia was never supposed to admit defeat or weakness of any kind. Especially not to an outworlder, one who was a child to boot. Her father Lonya had drilled that into her, along with a love of reading and a deep respect for hard work. But slogging through the Venusian marshland wasn't the kind of work a Crewman was supposed to be doing. Or at least, not a Po.

And she was so uncomfortable. Her bug bites itched, and she couldn't help flinching when moosquitos landed on her, even though she knew they were harmless, because they were so big and loud. She was hungry and thirsty, and the marsh water was disgusting even after you boiled it to kill at least the weaker native microbes.

Of course, I was supposed to be long dead by now. And I would be, if not for this strange outworld girl.

Helia wasn't sure how she felt about Sonya the Martian, or Earthling, or whatever she was. She should be grateful to her savior, she supposed, but mostly she was ashamed. Helia kept wishing Sonya would do something, anything, to justify ripping her head off. Like asking again why Helia had tried to drown herself, or complaining about the heat and the discomfort and asking when they were going to get back to the city already. But after the first day she had gone quiet, so quiet Helia sometimes had to glance around to make sure that blond head was still bobbing along beside hers.

"I'm sorry," Helia blurted when they stopped for a water break on a dry hummock of strawlike marsh grass.

Sonya turned her blue-eyed gaze on her. "What for?"

"I should have gotten us home by now. Your parents must be worried sick."

"Mike and Mary? They'll be all right, I guess. They're tough Texans. My sis, too." Sonya patted Helia on the knee, startling her. "You saved me, anyways. I would of drunk the marsh water straight and probably puked and pooped my guts out without you."

Helia grimaced. "Thanks for the image."

"How do you keep starting fires for boiling the water anyways, when everything's so damp?"

Helia sighed. "I tried to show you before—I use a *mokked*, a little plant with a sort of natural magnifying glass that focuses the sunlight. My father taught me that trick."

"What sunlight? It's all gray and cloudy all the time."

"Well, you know how you have to squint when you look up at the sky, like now? See, it's brighter out than you think—"

"WHAT THE HECK ARE THOSE?" Sonya wailed, and clutched at Helia with her left arm while she pointed her shaky right finger into the dense fog.

Helia peered in that direction but could see nothing at first. Suddenly, as if stepping out in front of a stage curtain, a row of strange creatures appeared. They were two-and-a-half to three meters tall and covered with soft purple scales, with heads like an English sheepdog and claws like an Earthly tyrannosaur, except that there were seven of them per limb.

Helia's heart had started pounding, but now she giggled with relief. "They're just Venusian natives, Sonya," she said, standing up and dragging the outworlder to her feet. "They won't hurt us. Usually they're quite friendly."

A spear soared through the air, catching in the tangled mess Helia's Afro had become and ripping a large hank of hair out.

She bit back a yelp. "Except of course, when they aren't," Helia gasped, and turned to run.

But there was no running through the mud that surrounded the hummock they'd been sitting on, not unless you were a Venusian with seven-toed feet that hydroplaned right over it. The ground heaved away below her, as one of them grabbed her and she caught a glimpse of Sonya struggling in another creature's grasp.

"*Anee neseechah me*-Aphro-Port!" Helia gasped, though the thing was crushing her chest as it regarded her calmly with large, chocolate-brown eyes. "*Toreed oh-tee mee-yad, oh sheh'anee aharog oat'chah—*"

"What's that you're speaking?" Sonya broke in.

"It's Venusian, of course! The N'Bialy dialect! We have the most contact with them! Stop interrupting when I'm conducting diplomatic negotiations!"

Their captors were taking them somewhere at a rapid clip.

Sonya rolled her eyes. "No it ain't! It's Hebrew! And you just threatened to kill them!"

"If you know it so well, why don't you try talking to them?"

"I don't really speak Hebrew so good. Rachel keeps trying to learn me 'cause she says I need to be Bat-Mitzvahed, which I couldn't give two kruckle beans about, only she thinks she'll be stickin' it to them Hasids in Noctis Labyrinthis who only Bar Mitzvah their boys …"

Helia shushed her. "I think I was wrong, actually. They're speaking a different language." An icy cold fear was clamping itself around her chest, which almost felt good in this steamy heat, but still …

The Venusian holding Sonya reached deftly into her pocket and pulled out a coin. Although it was about the same size as a familiar Venusian half-shell, from its dull red color Helia could see it had to be Martian.

"*Rivita min neereeg,*" it said.

"*Lah-mah?*" said the one holding Helia.

Sonya shook her head and whispered, "That sounds a little like Hebrew, but not really," as her captor glided over and held the coin up for Helia's captor to see. Heads was the Martian Queen Anya in profile.

The creature deftly flipped the coin over to display tails, which was a loaf of Martian kruckle-bean bread. "*Ha lach'ma Anya,*" it said.

At that, the forward motion of the herd ceased and Helia's captor began addressing Sonya in yet another language. Sonya looked it in the eye and replied fluently, to Helia's surprise.

"What's that you're speaking? Martian?"

"Nope. It's Polish, though in Rachel's crazy mixed-up world they call it 'Marpolski,'" Sonya said. She giggled, startling Helia. "Its grammar sucks, though."

In their time together Helia had learned that among Sonya's many strange outworlder ideas, the strangest was that she refused to take anything that happened seriously, since she thought the whole world had been made up by someone called Rachel.

Let it go, Helia thought. "All right then, could you ask these shaggy dinosaurs what they intend doing with us?"

Sonya spoke, and Helia's captor responded. From the look on the outworlder's face and the fact that the herd was moving again, Helia didn't even need to wait for the translation, though Sonya provided one anyway. "They're gonna hold us for ransom. They figure Anya will pay pots of money, and that your daddy must be rich 'cause they can tell you're a Crewman. Uh, what's a *behemah?*"

"Hmm?" Helia was furiously trying to think up an angle. "Uh, it's a kind of Venusian crocodile with hundreds of huge fangs. Why?"

"He says he is King Rawbaw, his people are called the Malchussei, and if you call them dinosaurs again, he's gonna cut you in four pieces with his claws and feed you to his pet *behemah.*"

At the sound of their name the creatures took up a chant, six syllables that matched their stride with a terrible rhythm.

"*Vi-yam'leech* Malchussei … *Vi-yam'leech* Malchussei …"

King Rawbaw stuck his face next to Helia's, his breath so strong with rotting swamp plants she started to gag. "Dat means 'Malchussei rule,' princessss," he hissed.

* * * *

Sonya couldn't decide what was the worst thing about being held captive by Rachel's ridiculous made-up monsters. The near-total darkness of the oversized thatched hut that was their prison? The heavy, sticky, close air that stank of the wet wool the Venusians' heads were covered with? The almost-Hebrew jabber of the beasts? Or the stuck-up stoicism of her cellmate?

Oh, Helia meant to be brave, and Sonya had to admit she had shown real courage. It was just that she was so annoyingly superior in how she showed it. For instance, when the Malchussei guards brought them food, Helia always said she wasn't hungry and Sonya should eat first. Which was no favor, since the stuff their captors brought them was so disgusting. All they got was slugs, bugs, grubs, and leafy slime that their guards growled was perfectly good food, so why are you retching all over the place, ungrateful alien monkeys?

"I could make a million overnight with 'the Malchussei Diet,'" Helia groaned, "if only it didn't involve so much throwing up and diarrhea! I must have lost three kilos already."

Sonya shook her head. "I know, Helia, but you have to eat something. Try some of these crunchy things."

"Those are megapedes, and all those legs are still moving," Helia pointed out.

"That just makes mealtime more interesting!" Sonya said, trying to ignore the strange crawling ache in her stomach. "Anyways, it's so dark in here, how can you even tell their legs are still moving?"

"'Cause I got so hungry I tried to eat some. They scratched my throat going down."

"I could bite off the legs for you," Sonya offered. She could just imagine the face Helia was making in the dark.

"No, thank you. This is ridiculous," Helia groaned, "we've got to get out of here!"

"How about we jump the next guard who brings us food?"

"I don't know about you, but I like the shape of my skull just fine the way it is. And even if we did manage to overpower one of them, there's a whole village of those monsters just outside the door. No, I'll have to try talking to them. Get an audience with their king."

This was easier said than done, since the guards wouldn't respond to Helia's attempts to talk to them in English or Hebrew, which Sonya refused to think of as "Solar" and "N'Bialy." A bialy was nothing but a kind of bagel with a filled-in hole that Sonya's dad used to bring home all the time from Greenwald's Bakery down the street, before the Germans made everybody move into the ghetto. Couldn't that stuck-up Rachel have thought of something more creative to call her aliens?

"I invoke my rights under the Solar Treaty to speak with your king!" Helia yelled at a retreating scaly back when mealtime rolled around again. "Dammit! Why won't they listen to me?"

"Because they ain't nothing but a bunch of scaly galoots," Sonya explained. "If you'd talk to them like galoots and not like lords and ladies, maybe they'd listen."

"I don't know what a 'galoot' is, nor do I wish to know," said Helia, "but you're welcome to try the next time one comes in. My head hurts too much to shout again, anyhow."

"Why can't I just pinch myself and wake up from this nightmare?" Sonya sighed.

"Not that again!" Helia clutched Sonya's arm a little too hard. "I know things are bad, sweetie, but you've got to stop that crazy talk!"

Sonya shook her off. "Says the girl who tried to drown herself."

"That is an *ad hominem* argument, and I shall ignore it."

"I know what that word means! My sister Katie told me! It means I'm attacking your snooty personality and not your logic. Don't take this the wrong way, 'cause I like you a lot, but it's a plain fact that you ain't real."

A stray beam of light revealed Helia clutching her tangled Afro as if her headache had spread all the way up there. "I wish I was a philosopher like my father, so I could talk you out of being a solipsist."

"I ain't *that*, neither, because I do *so* believe that other people besides myself exist. Such as Rachel. It just so happens that you ain't one of them, and neither is anyone else on this creepy planet. No offense."

"Guess you won't mind, then, if I say I'd rather be in prison here than free on your dried-up desert world."

"It don't offend me none, 'cause I'm from Earth, not Mars, like I told you." Sonya slumped against a wall and began to cry softly. "Why can't I wake up? I miss my parents … even my little sister Shoshie!"

Helia wrapped her arms Sonya and began rocking her like a baby. "Oh honey, I wish for your sake you could just 'wake up' from all this."

"Don't think I haven't tried," Sonya said. "Only I can't wake up, on account of it ain't my dream but Rachel's, and on account of I ain't got …"

She cried harder as Helia murmured and patted her back. But as nice as Helia was under the snootiness, she couldn't really help Sonya.

In the utter darkness there was nothing to distract Sonya from the memories that welled up. The ones she had carefully buried in the two Earth years that had passed since Rachel's beautiful double Anya had brought her instantly, impossibly to Mars.

I ain't got no one to go back to, if I did "wake up" back in Warsaw. And then the Germans would kill me, too.

There had been no warning when they came knocking on the door. Papa and Mama had told Sonya and Shoshie to hide under the bed, but Sonya was a little faster, and Shoshie's arm was left sticking out in plain sight of the SS man who grabbed it and flung her out the door, with her parents darting shrieking after her.

A moment later there was a fusillade of shots, and the screams of Sonya's family were stilled. She would've been killed too if the SS man had only bent and peeked under the bed, but he hadn't. Was his back bothering him? Was he in a rush? Or was he just lazy? Whatever the reason, Sonya was left on her own to try to survive as best she could in the abandoned slum, sneaking out at midnight to drink rainwater and scavenge for rotting garbage in the rapidly emptying ghetto.

If Anya had come a day or two later Sonya would have been dead too.

Sonya curled up in a tight little ball and wailed, remembering. *I didn't ought to have survived. I hid under the bed like a coward while them Germans murdered my family, 'stead of fighting back like Katie or Rachel or Helia here would have.*

"Listen, Martian girl or Earth girl or whatever you are," Helia said softly but intently in her ear. "I swear on my honor as a Crewman I'll get you home, whatever it takes!"

Sonya dried her eyes on Helia's sleeve. "Th-thanks, Miz Po. But I think we both know I'm the one what's got to rescue us." She could feel the older girl's body stiffening in surprise. "It's true," she insisted. "They *have* to listen to me. I'm the hostage that's worth something to them. They don't seem to care none about you, Crewman or not. I'm the one that's gotta talk to them."

"I don't like it, Sonya. If they hurt one hair on your head—"

Before her courage could fail her, Sonya stood up and yelled hoarsely for the guards, calling out in English and Polish till the door flew open.

"Why noise female-monkey?" demanded the monster who stood framed in the gray Venusian light. His Polish was terrible.

How can I be scared of him? I survived the Germans, this is just some stupid thing Rachel made up!

"Take me to your king RIGHT NOW, you overgrown lizard, or when I get home I'll tell Queen Anya you hurt me! She'll skin you alive and use your skull for an ashtray, and she don't even smoke!"

"You bad female-monkey!" the thing growled. "King Rawbaw eat you for snack!"

Sonya willed herself not to flinch as it advanced on her and grabbed her in both clawed hands. She braced herself to be flung against the wall, but instead the Malchuss (if that was the singular) tucked her under its arm and marched out the door, grumbling aloud as it went, for all the world like Mike Webb on one of those Martian mornings when a dust storm was a-blowing and nothing seemed to go right.

If she got nothing else out of this little adventure, it was exhilarating to be able to breathe fresh air and get a glimpse of the gray but strangely lush Venusian rainforest, the enormous unearthly trees growing right in the middle of the Malchussei village. All the "cottages" were more than four meters high, as tall as a tall man standing on another tall man's shoulders, and the doors and windows were sized accordingly. Not many of the giants seemed to be around.

Maybe they're hunting for more humans to kidnap.

After a few minutes the guard climbed a low rise topped by a building that had to be at least five stories tall, though it was made of the same crude thatch as all the other dwellings. Two guards flanked the entrance, and when the one carrying Sonya tried to push past them he was shoved back.

Sonya's head bobbed and she thought she was going to be sick, *which probably ain't a great idea when I'm going to meet the king.*

"*Mah aved?*" demanded one of the king's guards in that not-quite Hebrew they used.

"*Asirtah tzav-ah mechezey malkah,*" the beast holding Sonya replied.

The royal guard laughed, sounding like a bullfrog amplified by a million, and Sonya was reminded of the Yiddish curse, *Lakhn zol er mit yash'tcherkes—he should laugh with the lizards.*

"*Yiktiilah. V'af ant yiktul,*" the royal guard spat. That didn't sound promising, but he stepped aside.

Inside it was barely any brighter than in her cell, but there was enough light for Sonya to see an extra-large Malchuss sitting on a giant's chair, wearing a crown that looked like it had been forged out of rusty scrap metal. The king and the guard snarled at each other for a few seconds, then Sonya found herself falling to the floor, which hurt when she struck it more than dried mud had any right doing. Her guard stomped away, and she started to get to her feet.

"I didn't say ya could get up," the king said in Polish. "Respect, you not show da proper. *Yakruni!*"

At the king's roar in their own language, his guards saluted and chanted, "*Yisgadal shmei Rawbaw!*"

A guffaw bubbled up in Sonya's throat, and she fought heroically to swallow it back down and stay in her prone position.

What were these creatures doing chanting the Jewish prayer for the dead? Because that's what it was. She recognized it from Papa's prayers in synagogue after Grandpa died. The prayer didn't mention death, of course—that would be too logical—instead it went on and on about how great God was. "*Yisgadal shmei rawbaw*" meant "may His great name be exalted," but these silly monsters had turned it into, "May Rawbaw's name be exalted."

For that matter, "Malchussei" was supposed to be the word for the heavenly kingdom, not for a tribe of sheepdog-headed dinosaurs. And Helia wanted her to take this whole business seriously? What could she possibly say to this absurd monster, which was absently scratching its furry forehead beneath the crown?

Then she remembered what Rachel sounded like when she practiced for the times she had to substitute for Queen Anya. "Oh mighty king, I bring you greetings from your sister Queen Anya, and respectfully request that you let the poor, unworthy human girls who are your guests return whence they came."

Whence! If I'd only remembered that word last month, I would've passed that stupid vocab test!

The king laughed again. It was really not a pleasant sound. "Oh no, Erss girl, much gold you worss," he said. "Mars queen, she paying one million credits, but Da Mayor, he paying TWO million!"

Uh oh, Bellissini's found out where I am! But first things first ...

Thinking fast, Sonya said, "But nobody will pay you anything if we starve and die in the dark."

"Food not enough yummy for yiz guys?" the king inquired.

Why, I do believe the Malchussei have discovered sarcasm!

"Most respected king, your generosity is known far and wide," Sonya said smoothly. "Us filthy monkeys are not worthy to partake of your sumptuous repasts."

Mrs. Karpolsky would be amazed to hear me use all those fancy words in a sentence. And Rachel would just sit there like a big dummy with her mouth open.

"All we require is the junk our kind eat in Aphro-Port, and a little light to eat it by."

"Chutzpah you got," King Rawbaw observed.

Sonya wasn't even surprised that the alien ruler knew the homey Yiddish word for nerve.

After all, everything here came out of Rachel's imagination. And the prayer for the dead ... She shivered inwardly. *Well, death was all around us, in the ghetto.*

There didn't seem to be much choice but to take this ridiculous alien king on his own terms, so Sonya attempted to plaster a sincere look on her face, like that time she was trying to talk Mike out of spanking her for clogging up the toilet with thistlecat dander. It didn't work then, but it must have worked now, because the ruler's big sheepdog head swept from side to side and he shouted an order to his guards, who started to run around in a frenzy. Sonya braced herself to be flung around like a dog toy, but nothing happened to her.

"Why you still standing here then, Erss girl?" the king snapped. "Your wish, has be!"

Sonya tried to puzzle this out, and decided he was trying to tell her she was getting her way. So she bowed to him. "*Yisgadal shmei Raw-baw,*" she said.

"*Yam-leekh Malchussei,*" he replied, which was supposed to mean "His Kingdom shall rule," not "the Malchussei shall rule." Oh, well. "Beat it, kid," the alien king added in English.

I just hope we don't end up like the people you're supposed to say that prayer for, Sonya thought as the guards hustled her away.

6

Jim had a bad feeling about going back to Aphrodite Port for any reason other than buying a ticket to get the hell off the planet. The place was
so run down and sleazy compared with his admittedly hazy childhood
memories. When he was little Aphro-Port was the big city, the place you
went to buy Earth-made luxuries like flashlights and blenders from the
shiny, glamorous shops under the Dome.

The Flashes were homesteaders in the Delta region of what the human settlers called the New Amazon River, though all the aboriginal
tribes referred to it as the Yarden. Papa Gordon and Mama Cass had
cleared their property themselves using hand tools before their twins
were born, though they'd had an easier time of it than some of their
human neighbors thanks to their eccentric habit of befriending the aborigines and listening to their advice on farming.

"Treat the forest as your friend, not the means to an end," Papa was
fond of saying, quoting Karolla's grandmother Tarfona, the respected
elder or zikuna of the N'Bialy.

This meant that instead of chopping down all the erez trees on their
farm, they used the tall canopies to grow cloudlight-loving crops like
the leafy khassa, which tasted faintly of blueberries although it was light
gray, and the charcoal-colored toot berries, which squeaked when you
ate them. Jim and Jack had learned to climb almost before they could
walk, and soon came to spend more time on the leafy roof of the world
than they did on the ground.

To Earthly visitors the Venusian jungle looked dead, in its clothing
of ashy gray. But that was only because the permanent cloud cover meant
the native flora had never evolved chlorophyll, and the chemicals their
leaves did use to take advantage of the diffuse light and moist, humid air
gave them an unappealing cast to eyes expecting terrestrial greens.

When you grew up on Venus, you learned to distinguish many subtle
shades of gray, though of course N'Bialy or Malchuss foragers could
pick out many more, just as they could lend a deep, eerie undertone to the
singing of the "Delta Grays" music that no human, no matter how fluent
in the native languages, could ever quite match, though Papa came close
when he strummed his Venusian jithara at the end of the day. There was a

soft, lush beauty to the Venusian cloud-forests that had once covered the entire planet, a beauty Jim never stopped yearning for in all his years as a forced conscript in the Martian army, out in that cold, rust-red desert.

But coming back to Venus he had found the planet so changed he barely knew the place. The jungle was disappearing at a rate of thousands of hectares a year, but he still preferred it, even if he had to live in a smelly tent city, to the ugly, dingy, overcrowded capital.

You wouldn't think it possible that a town covered by a dome could be unplanned and jerry-built, but *inspector* in Aphro-Port slang was a synonym for bribe-taker, since Da Mayor handed out the jobs as rewards to low-level informers. You could hardly walk down the street without passing a pile of rubble that marked the site of another building collapse. Like the one Jim was walking past now.

But why was there a shady character loitering around it, his hat pulled low over his eyes?

Jim slowed his pace a bit and pulled down his own hat, a battered gray monsoon minishelter, until it covered most of his face on the left side, the side toward the shadowy figure. He'd been beaten up enough times in his life to recognize the stance of a man poised to attack.

Jim strolled on, not turning his head, and raised his right hand as if to stifle a yawn—the hand with the radio ring on it. He tapped it against his teeth, dot-dot-dot, dash-dash-dash, dot-dot-dot, praying that Jack would receive the SOS and detour away from the meeting at Adrian's Bar and Grill, which had to be a trap.

Four more steps and he passed behind a deserted, tumbledown shack. Then he broke into a run, his ears straining for the sound of footsteps behind him. He veered sharply left into an alley, jumped a low fence, dodged around a pile of rubble, and came out on a broad avenue busy with traffic. Luckily he knew this neighborhood well from his first few months back on Venus, and he remembered another alleyway passed behind Adrian's, which could be reached from the avenue where he was standing via a gap between two buildings.

After casting one more quick look around to make sure he wasn't being followed, he ducked into the narrow space, which was barely wide enough for him to squeeze through sideways. As he inched his way along, the oily black grime that covered the walls got smeared all over his face and clothes. That was good camouflage on a dark gray day like today, and it wasn't as though he cared about his ragged shirt and pants.

He was less than five meters from Adrian's back wall when he heard muffled shouts and a thump. It wasn't possible to flatten himself against the wall any more than he already was, but he stopped moving, held his breath, and flicked his eyes as far to the right as they would go. The alley was so dim it was impossible to see anything but flailing, hunched over figures.

"Unhand me, you—oof!" said a voice that sounded like Jack's.

A dazzling beam of white light seared across Jim's field of vision, leaving flashing purple afterimages in its wake. When he finished blinking the tears out of his eyes he saw a new gouge in the wall just above his head, extending halfway back to the avenue. Only a really powerful zap-gun could do that, one much stronger than most of the Venusian thugs and cops (the distinction was a blurry one) could afford to carry.

That has to be Jack's Annabelle, Jim thought. There was a loud crack, after which the scuffling seemed to die down. *Time to get moving.*

Back on the avenue Jim's coating of black grime attracted little attention. Except for the Crewmen, Aphro-Port's residents were not a clean or well-dressed bunch at the best of times, and the best of times had ended long before Mayor Bellissini came to power.

Jim shouldered his way through the crowds, keeping his head down as he headed westward toward the shantytown. Outside the dome, the steady flicker of lightning warned of the approach of a monsoon. Jim was willing to take his chances with the weather if it would keep him out of Bellissini's clutches.

In the tent encampment people were scurrying around getting ready for the oncoming storm. Those with non-monsoon-proof shelters were begging or in a few cases forcing their way in with their luckier neighbors.

Jim made a beeline for his shelter, only to find it crammed full of squatters. He shook his head at their greed and foolishness. Townies were such wimps. You could easily survive a Venusian monsoon out in the open if you just took a few simple precautions, but most of these folks were terrified at the prospect of having to face the storm without the protection of Aphro-Port's battered old bucky-dome overhead.

For Jim, though, the oncoming storm and even the loss of his shelter were blessings in disguise, because there was next to no chance of Bellissini's Bullyboy Bastards chasing him through the jungle during the storm. And once the rain stopped, he could track down Jack's friend Karolla and his N'Bialy tribe, whom he remembered well from their slightly late charge to the rescue when Jack had battled King Ares on Mars. With their help he'd have a much better chance of rescuing his big brother … and maybe even finding the Martian girl all the fuss was about.

Lightning was flashing every few seconds now, leaving jagged violet afterimages against the blank gray sky. There wasn't a moment to lose, and Jack began shouldering people out of the way in his haste to reach the freedom of the rain forest.

"Trampled by a panicked mob. I suppose I deserve it," groaned a familiar voice.

Jack turned and saw Mark Mahlett, who had a cut on his lip and the beginnings of a black eye.

"Mark? Why aren't you in that mini-bucky-ball Helia bought you?"

"There was a couple with three little kids just standing there hopelessly when everyone started running around. I couldn't just leave them out in the open to die, and there isn't room for six people in the shelter."

"That … that was mighty nice of you, Mark." *Nicer than I expected of him.* "Stick with me and you'll be fine. I know how to stay safe in the open during a monsoon."

It was like Mark didn't even hear him. He struck a pose and said, "Is it better for me to suffer? Or, by fighting back against my troubles, to end them?"

"Jeez, will you stop brooding?" Jack yelled. He grabbed Mark's hand. "Come with me! There isn't much time!"

"Maybe I should just lie down and die," Mark panted as Jim dragged him away from the encampment.

One, two. Jim counted. *Flash! One, two. Flash! That storm will break any second!*

He had to find a tunnel tree, so called because its roots were planted in the ground like the fingers of a giant's hand, forming a cozy and safe shelter under the trunk where animals, Venusians and people could take cover during a storm. But all he saw around him was a grove of stone-woods covered with tangled slither-vines.

"Yes, to die," Mark said. "To die, to sleep. Maybe to dream … dream I'm back home on Earth, safe in my bed."

"There!" Jim said, pointing. "Come on, Mark, run for it!" He gave him a shove. "I don't feel like sweeping up your ashes to give to poor Helia!"

When they were lying side by side, safe in the woody dark as a solid wall of lightning-lit water fell across the opening they had dived into, Jim said, "What was that about your home on Earth? I thought you were a Venusian native."

"What? A Venusian native? Of course I am," Mark said, but Jim had felt him shudder.

What's this strange kid hiding?

"Come on, Mark, we're going to be stuck here at least a couple of hours. And you know me a long time now. It's not like I'm working for Bellissini."

"Bellissini!" Mark snarled. "All right, I confess. I'm really from Earth. It was to escape Bellissini that I came to Venus in the first place. Don't look so shocked, he's an Earthling, too!"

"So how did he get here? How did you get here?" Jim heard himself ask.

The kid must've lost his mind. Everybody knows that Bellissini's as Venusian as a cloudy day. And Mark's accent is as Venusian as mine.

"I wrote myself into the story, I admit it," Mark said. "It was a lot of hard work, but I did it only at night, after all my homework was done, on the typewriter my parents gave me for my Bar Mitzvah."

Bar Mitzvah? Oh no, not another crazy mixed-up Jewish kid like Rachel! Though Rachel's a lot more likeable than this character ...

"You wrote yourself into the story? What story?" Jim asked, trying to keep his tone light.

"'Zap-Gun Jack Flash and the Dame-Eating Monsters of Venus,' of course!" Mark began to cry in hiccups. "And the school literary magazine, the *Chatham Crier,* printed it! But then I was stupid—I brought my copy of the book I found the original story in to read in gym class, and Mr. Bellissini stole it from me!

"I was so miserable I went to the school office and complained to Miss Fink, and she read my story in the *Crier* and told me how great it was, and, and, the room began to blur and somehow we both found ourselves here. And she seemed happy to be the mother I always dreamed of, but then BELLISSINI appeared and stole her from me!"

The constant lightning made the whites of Mark's eyes flash as he turned to look at Jim. "But you must think I'm crazy, right?"

Jim tried to think of something diplomatic to say, but it didn't matter that he couldn't because Mark was more interested in talking to himself.

"Crazy ... hey, what if I PRETEND to be crazy when I go see my mom? Then Bellissini will just laugh at me ... he might also kick me and put a trash can over my head now and then, but it'll be worth it to have my wonderful mommy Delores back!"

Jim's head swam. "Your mother is Delores Fabuloso? *The* Delores Fabuloso?"

"That's the one! I'm so proud of that name I gave her, it's so much cooler than 'Denise Fink,' don't you think?"

Jim was silent. In his experience mothers tended to name children and not the other way around. The luscious brunette beauty wasn't from Earth, she didn't look very much like Mark, and how could he have been the one who named her? Yep, there was no doubt about it—Mark was really insane.

Jim carefully patted his shoulder. "There, there. You don't need to pretend to be crazy. You've really got it pretty good, pal, for an outlaw. What about Helia?"

"I think she finally got sense and stopped coming around to see me. I haven't seen her in almost a week."

"Women. Who can figure 'em out, eh?" Jim said with a forced laugh.

Yeah, like why would a gal like that who has everything go out with a messed-up kid like you in the first place?

"But like I said, Mark ol' buddy, why don't you get your mind off your own troubles for a while? Come with me when this rain stops and help rescue my big brother Jack and a girl who is under the protection of the queen of Mars!"

"An adventure, huh?"

"You could call it that, yeah!"

"No thanks. Sounds awful."

This time Jim did grab the little twerp and shake him. "What's the matter with you, pal? You've got nothing to go back to now! You've lost your home, and your girl has run away!"

"And my mom loves Bellissini more than me!" Mark cried, and broke into fresh sobs.

Jim shook him again. "Exactly! So now's the time to start afresh! Come with me and meet the N'Bialy!"

"What do I need a thing that's like a bagel without the hole for?"

Jim gritted his teeth and said, "They're not pastries, they're aborigines! Natives of Venus. If you're really a native of Earth, you've probably never seen one before! They look like purple tyrannosaurs with the heads of sheepdogs. It'll be a new experience for you."

"A new experience," Mark sighed. "That's what my old mom back on Earth used to say before dragging me off to something she knew I wouldn't like, like a museum. But what choice have I got?"

"That's the spirit!" Jim said aloud, clapping Mark on the shoulder.

If all else fails, maybe I can chop him up for scorpion-bunny bait.

7

Rachel's first step on Venus in two years was an inglorious belly flop in the mud.

Everything was soaking wet after the monsoon. The water was spraying down so hard from the jungle canopy into the little clearing where she had landed herself and Katie with her magic Remington that for several seconds Rachel thought it was still raining, and raining hard. She certainly couldn't tell any different from the unbroken cloud cover, but then she remembered the constant lightning and thunder during the monsoon she had been through on her last visit and realized that the drenching she was getting was coming out of the Venus equivalent of a perfectly blue sky.

On the plus side, it was quickly sluicing the mud off her clothes. On the down side, she had just sneezed all over Karolla.

"So much time has passed, it's true. I am deeply moved to see you too," Karolla piped. The delegation of N'Bialy he headed nodded solemnly in unison.

Rachel nodded miserably and tried to wipe her nose on her soaked shirt sleeve. If the giant scaly creature thought sneezing was the human way of expressing affection, she wasn't about to correct him.

"Karolla, Katie is going to need some help," she began too late.

A *splutch* followed by a *splootch* let her know that Katie had tossed her opened wheelchair one-armed into the mud and sat down heavily in it. It promptly sank up to its axles in the mud. The fact that the local gravity was twice what they'd gotten used to on Mars wasn't making it any easier on either of the girls.

"Follow the boardwalk into town. A good idea, if you don't wish to drown," Karolla said.

"The boardwalk?" Katie said.

Karolla blinked. His eyes were a gorgeous blue. "Yes, Katie, you bet. In N'Bialy, we call it a *tayelet*."

"I didn't see no boardwalk when we were here before," she said.

"When you follow Zap-Gun Jack, attention to other things you tend to lack," Karolla said.

It was hard to disagree with that. But something else was bothering Rachel. She was getting a distinct feeling of *déjà vu.*

"What did you say the N'Bialy word for boardwalk is?" she asked Karolla as two of his little group of companions stepped forward and lifted a protesting Katie up on their shoulders, wheelchair and all.

"Come, let's go and dry off so you are no longer wet. Our boardwalk, we call a *tayelet,*" Karolla said.

"Funny, that's just what they called the boardwalk in Tel Aviv," Rachel murmured. "Mom always said she couldn't wait to have a cup of coffee there with me and Dad …" She started to tear up.

"I see you have paid a fearful cost, and your parents, you have lost," Karolla said, placing a scaly hand on her shoulder.

"You'd better cut it out, you big tyrannosaur sheepdog, or I'll starting bawling over you," Rachel said, tears streaming down her face as she followed him into the forest.

"*Ani mish'tattef b'tza'arech,*" Karolla said solemnly. "In N'Bialy, that means—"

"—you're sorry for my loss," Rachel said. She knew now where the feeling of *déjà vu* was coming from.

Karolla blinked at her. "You speak N'Bialy?"

"I think I do, Karolla. I might be a little rusty, though."

"When needs it must, you'll find your tongue will lose its rust."

"Thanks for your confidence in me, Karolla. Do you mind if I talk to Katie for a second?"

"It's best you ran, to catch her if you can."

Rachel saw what he meant. As soon as Karolla's friends had put her down at her loud insistence on the weathered strip of gray planks of the *tayelet,* she'd taken off like a wheeled rocket, and was now barely visible between the looming, dark tree trunks.

Rachel's legs were trying to drag her down in this awful gravity, but she ignored them and lurched up onto the boardwalk, with the heavy typewriter tucked awkwardly under her left arm, yelling for Katie to wait up. The wheelchair stopped its clattering progress right away, but by the time Rachel caught up she was soaked anew, this time in sweat. Her knees gave way and she clutched frantically at the wheelchair's arm rest to stop herself falling flat on the wooden boards.

"Land's sake, Ray, what's so all-fahr'd urgent?" Katie drawled.

"The N'Bialy—they speak—Hebrew!" Rachel gasped.

Katie's right eyebrow quirked up. "Do tell, Ray. Why, that's the most remarkable thing I ever did hear since I learned they speak Polish on Mars!"

"I guess this is my doing as well."

"Reckon it is. How well do you speak it?"

"Hebrew? I used to speak it pretty well. I was going to emigrate with my parents to Palestine, remember?"

"Uh huh. But I reckon you ain't had much practice, these past couple of years. Say there, Ray, you sure you're all right?"

Rachel wondered when Katie's wheelchair had sprouted that extra pair of wheels.

"Never better," she said, and fainted dead away.

* * * *

When she came to she was lying on a pile of soft gray leaves inside an enormous gray tent made of more such leaves, with the only light streaming in through the huge but ragged flap.

Katie scowled when she saw her eyes open and reached down from her wheelchair to help her sit up. "Darn it all, Ray, didn't I tell you not to overdo it when our weight was suddenly gonna double?"

"Well, I—"

"—ain't got no common sense, but you *did* have me warning you," Katie said. "Never mind. Leastaways you didn't break anything, near as I can tell." She propped her chin on her fist and gazed keenly at Rachel. "Explain me again how come you couldn't just write Sonya back home?"

Rachel sighed. "If we just snatch her back, Bellissini will know for certain that we've got a 'magic' typewriter of our own, and he could change the world before we could stop him. He could even"—she swallowed hard as the thought seized her brain—"he could even make Mars a dead planet like it is back where we came from, and we'd all suffocate and freeze in the thin atmosphere!"

"Then how come you didn't just magic his typewriter away?"

"I don't think that would work either. Not with an object from the 'real' world. Remember when we tried creating a canal on Mars with a 'Kosciuszko' typewriter made there? Nothing happened, and we had to use Johnny Marshall's old Remington instead." She reached over and stroked the keyboard with her fingertips, relieved that she hadn't accidentally smashed it when she fainted. "There's something special about people and objects that come from our universe, Katie. We have to be careful."

"Agreed. Well, your Israeli-Venusian-sheepdog-dinosaur pals are about to serve dinner. Don't know about you, but I'm hungry." She wheeled herself out of the tent, leaving Rachel scrambling to keep up.

On the way out Rachel took a closer look at the leaves that made up the tent. They were shaped like beech tree leaves on Earth, but were almost a meter in width and close to double that in length. They were a muted gray, like the boards that made up the *tayelet*, like the living trees themselves.

Unbidden the memory came to Rachel of tapping out the first sentence of "Zap-Gun Jack Flash and the Dame-Eating Monsters of Venus" (the title had NOT been her idea), in which she had described the Venusian landscape. That had been years and worlds ago in the Warsaw Ghetto, the typewritten fantasy little more than an attempt to ignore the wild beast of hunger gnawing away at her stomach.

"Venus is a gray world beneath everlasting gray clouds," she had written.

I must have been influenced by what I saw around me in the ghetto when I wrote that, Rachel thought. *Everything there was gray and horrible.*

But the grayness here was a fantastic palette of subtle colors, something she never could have imagined. The wooden walls and furniture were a rich, dark-grained gray. The permanently overcast sky wasn't a blank slate, it was a constantly shifting, churning kaleidoscope of delicate tendrils of mist and massive, bruise-colored thunderheads. The rugged bowl of deliciously aromatic fruit compote an N'Bialy was handing her, now that they had entered the even bigger dining tent, was a somehow scrumptious swirl of beige, though Rachel gobbled it down too quickly to appreciate its appearance or even its taste. She didn't even mind the lack of utensils or the fact that a good portion had ended up all over her face and clothes.

Mama would have been beside herself, she thought sadly.

When her stomach was full of compote, followed by a main course of roast scorpion-bunny, Rachel leaned back and listened to the conversation around her.

Katie was slumped over her own folded arms and was struggling to keep her eyes open, while the dozen-odd N'Bialy gathered in a loose circle were chattering away in rapid-fire Hebrew. Unlike Karolla when he spoke English, when speaking their own language the creatures didn't feel the need to make strained rhymes.

"These aren't like the other Earth invaders," said one.

"*Batei-chava kulam ganavim,*" snapped another N'Bialy. This one was unusually tall and had a bare patch on his forehead, where greenish-blue scalp peeped through. "The humans are all thieves. All they've done is steal our land from the moment that *mamzer* Elron Hubbard set foot on our precious soil. He would have put us in chains if the dark-skinned Crewmen hadn't stopped him. And even they were more than happy to uproot our precious klemeth vines, chop down the forests, and dump their trash in our pure, clean rivers and seas.

"What do we care if the Malchussei have two of their females? It's no concern of ours. Especially when the dark-skinned one is a descendant of Hubbard's crew of pirates and the light-skinned one is from Mars. Away with all the human invaders, I say! Let the Malchussei barbarians eat them if they want!"

Katie leaned over and whispered, "What are they saying, Ray?"

"It seems Sonya's been captured by another Venusian tribe, but the N'Bialy aren't really keen on helping us save her," Rachel whispered back.

Katie's forehead wrinkled up. "Why not? I thought you said the N'Bialy were nice."

"Yeah, but the humans here on Venus have been playing cowboys and Indians, with the natives as the Indians."

"Oh," said Katie. "Uh-oh."

The balding N'Bialy bared his teeth at them. "You spick, ehhh, secrets, human girls?"

As Rachel slowly turned red with embarrassment and frustration Karolla strolled into the room. She could tell it was him by his weird, loping gait.

"Stop this rude talk!" he growled, pointing at Rachel. "That female speaks N'Bialy!"

"What do I care about a human's feelings? Anyway it's impossible that she speaks our language. *Ee-ef'shar!*"

Rachel hopped carefully down from her chair and stood up straight. Her chin barely topped the table. "*Ef'shar*. It's possible, all right," she said in Hebrew/N'Bialy.

The N'Bialy all stared at her.

"Look, I'm sorry for how the human settlers have been treating you. It's a disgrace. But we're not from Venus, or Earth. We're Martians, and I," she swallowed hard, "I have the ear of Queen Anya. If you help us I'll see she officially raises your mistreatment with the Solar Council."

"What difference will that make? All Da Mayor has to do is say that it's an *internal affair*." Baldie spat those last two words in English.

Karolla came to the rescue. "Word is, the human females were running from Da Mayor. He must want them really badly. Do we really want to give that *mamzer* what he wants?"

"Again I say it's no concern of ours," Baldie insisted.

"I'm the chief!" Karolla said, thumping his chest. "And I say we help them!"

"You're human-Jack's little pet," Baldie sneered.

Karolla poked Baldie in the chest with one sharp claw. "I challenge you to a duel, Aditai," he said mildly. "After the next sleeping-time, in the lizard-grass field just east of town."

"It will be a pleasure," Aditai said, poking Karolla in return, "to lay low one who licks the humans' boots!" And he stomped out of the room, which shook with each footfall. Two shorter N'Bialy scurried out after him, if creatures so large could be said to scurry.

"I hope you like our humble food. I'm sorry Aditai was so rude," Karolla said in English, sitting down and picking up a plate the size of a car wheel. At that, the other N'Bialy also sat and began eating as if nothing had happened.

"But was Aditai right that the Malchussei are holding Sonya captive?" Rachel asked. "And just what are the Malchussei, anyway?"

"So that our food may not rot, a fit topic for dinnertime, the Malchussei are not," Karolla said.

Rachel exchanged glances with Katie. Only when he had gnawed his scorpion-bunny down to the furry carapace would Karolla speak.

Then he explained that the Malchussei were the hereditary enemy of the N'Bialy going back hundreds of years. The tribes had fought eight full-scale wars and too many skirmishes to count in the 196 Venusian years before Accursed Elron's arrival on the planet.

Venusians had seven fingers on each hand, so they counted in base 14, which made their "centuries" 196 Venusian years long. The Venusian "year" was only 243 Earth days long, however—the length of time the planet took to turn once on its axis, which was longer than the 225 Earth days it took to orbit the Sun. The four-month-long day followed by the four-month-long night was far more significant, to a Venusian, than their planet's orbital period around the eternally hidden sun. Rachel suspected even Katie would have trouble working out the math in her head that would be needed to match Venusian history to Earth dates.

Accursed Elron had shrewdly figured out how to exploit the tribes' antagonism, setting one against the other and grabbing the spoils for himself and his crew, though it wasn't really true, Karolla said, that the N'Bialy had sold the site of Aphro-Port for a box of claw sharpeners. The tribe had thought the human chief was joking when he made the offer.

It was too bad they hadn't heard him saying to his crew, "It's ridiculous for a genius like me to be earning a hundred lousy dollars per trip piloting a rocket. If a man really wants to make money, what he ought to do is found his own colony."

In the three hundred or so Venusian years since then, most of the other mayors had followed in Accursed Elron's footsteps, often stirring up one tribe against the other to ensure that neither was in any position to cause the Earthlings problems.

"Why don't y'all get together then and throw the humans out?" Katie asked. When Rachel eyed her oddly she said, "I think it's a fair question, don't you?"

"N'Bialy are honest and Malchussei cheat, and never shall the twain meet," Karolla responded.

Was there a hint of resignation in his voice? It might be risky to read too much into an alien's tone of voice, Rachel thought … if she hadn't made the aliens up in the first place.

"Besides," Karolla added, "the same language we don't speak, and they sound like a bunch of freaks!"

The Malchussei don't speak Hebrew? But then what do they speak?

"Karolla, do you know any Malchussei?" Rachel asked.

He actually turned up his nose, which looked pretty funny on a being with a sheepdog's head. Rachel reminded herself how sharp his claws were and managed not to laugh.

"Malchussei like to babble and sing, especially to praise their king. It doesn't sound like anything," Karolla said.

Triple rhyme! He must really hate them.

"But you do know enough to talk to them, right?" Rachel asked.

"The words in my mouth taste like scorpion-bunny when it's raw. When they praise their nasty king, they say '*yisgadal shmei Rawbaw,*'" Karolla said.

Katie was eyeing Rachel with amusement. "Know what that is, Ray?"

Rachel slumped in her chair, her feet dangling far above the floor. "Yes, I'm afraid I do. It's from the Jewish prayer for the dead, which is in Aramaic—the same language Jesus spoke. Those three words are supposed to mean 'may His great name be exalted.'"

"Uh-huh," said Katie.

"In Yiddish-accented Aramaic," Rachel explained.

"Of course, Ray."

"Why the prayer for the dead, though?" Rachel murmured, as if to herself. She shivered despite the cloying heat and humidity. "Does that mean we're doomed?"

"No more are we creatures of the air, than Malchussei-speak is any kind of prayer!" Karolla protested.

Katie tugged on Rachel's arm. "What-for did you make up such ridiculous aliens?" she demanded in a whisper. "And what's all this about 'Accursed Elron?' I don't remember none of that from your original story about Venus!"

Rachel rubbed her temples and sighed. "A lot of this stuff seems to come from my unconscious mind," she said. "That was Freud's term— er, Sigmund Freud, a Viennese psych—"

"I *know* who Freud was, Ray! But why-fore would you be thinkin' of aliens who chant the Jewish prayer for the dead? Or some nasty Earth man named Elron lordin' it over the natives? I thought you was a big pinko socialist!"

Rachel clenched her fists in frustration. "I don't know, I don't know! Only, only, death was *everywhere*, in the ghetto, and if you think it's so easy to dream up a perfect society without anyone taking advantage of anyone else, *you* try it!" She got to her feet and addressed Karolla. "Look, don't ask me to explain how, but I think I can understand a little of their language. That ought to help in the negotiations."

"Talking to them is useless, they deserve a good smack," Karolla said. "Anyway, we have to wait for Zap-Gun Jack."

"That may be a long wait," said a new voice. Everyone turned to see Jim standing in the doorway with a teenage boy who stared at the floor. Jim smiled wearily. "Hello, Karolla, hello, ladies. Jack's managed to get himself captured again."

8

Being captured was a familiar experience for Zap-Gun Jack, and he always did his best to use it to his advantage. Even if the bad guys weren't quite as helpfully talkative in real life as they usually were in books, you could still learn lots about them from the way they acted and the kind of prison they threw you into.

The Pyromaniacal Pirates of Pluto, for instance, had tried to live up to their name by putting Jack in what they thought was a wrecked space-ship and launching it from their home base on Charon with its engine room on fire. Unfortunately for them the ship, and its weapons system, was quite salvageable for a man of Jack's dexterity, and it was their base that ended up a smoldering ruin.

So he had high hopes when he regained consciousness with a head-ache no worse than his usual Sunday morning hangover and found him-self bound tightly with clothesline and hanging upside down like a bat from the high ceiling of Da Mayor's throne room, with the great man sitting there looking mighty pleased with himself. If it became necessary, Jack knew he could free himself from the ropes in under ten seconds.

They aren't running a very sophisticated operation here on the Planet of Love, are they?

"Hello, Mr. Flash! I'm so glad you're awake!" Da Mayor said, cross-ing the room in a few quick strides. "It's great you could take the time to hang out with me!" he exclaimed and struck Jack on the shoulder, setting his body swinging.

"My ship's computer makes better puns than that with half its vacu-um tubes burned out," Jack said through gritted teeth.

Da Mayor boxed Jack's ears hard, leaving them ringing. "Where your sense of fun, man? I mean, I know you're a Martian spy and I'm going to have you killed painfully, but that's no reason we can't have a laugh."

"Yeah, bloodthirsty dictators are a barrel of chuckles," Jack snapped. "You're ruining our beloved planet, Beppo!"

"You're entitled to your opinion, unless I decide to Correct your mind, but the 99% of the vote I got in the last election shows you are truly on your own, traitor. I am truly in my people's hearts—"

"—because you'll rip theirs right out of their chests if they pull the wrong lever in the voting booth," Jack snapped.

Bellissini boxed his ears again. Jack's skull rang like the Liberty Bell—he could see the cracks spreading through his field of vision, and he struggled not to black out.

"—so I feel I owe them some excellent entertainment, when I'm obliged to slaughter their enemies and mine."

"Only a coward would beat on a bound man, Beppo!" Jack said.

Bellissini swung his right arm and fetched him such a blow on the side of the head his whole body began to spin, twirling around and around until the clothesline he was hanging from was twisted in knots, whereupon his rotation slowed, stopped, and reversed itself.

"You'll pay for that, Mr. Mayor," Jack said quietly, but the effect was ruined when he had to swallow to keep his lunch down.

"Nah, I don't think so," Bellissini said. "Now, as I was starting to say, I have just the thing for you. Back on old Earth, there was a fun little game the kiddies used to play in gym class called dodge ball. Ever heard of it?"

Jack, who was now spinning clockwise again, made an inappropriate suggestion about this sport, and Bellissini kicked him in the throat. He started to wonder whether it was time to wriggle free and lunge at the dictator, who had a sneer plastered all over his face.

"Don't make me remind you about your language again, Mr. Zap-Gun, or I might have to do some real damage to your windpipe. Now please stop gagging so that I can finish my explanation ... That's better.

"Now, in dodge ball two teams form up on either side of a line and toss a red rubber playground ball back and forth, trying to hit the kids on the other team anywhere except their heads or their privates. Anyone struck is out, as is any sissy little girl who makes such a wimpy throw that someone on the other team can catch it. The last team with one or more players left standing wins. A simple, fun little game, wouldn't you agree?"

He grinned at the lack of response. "Of course, those innocent rubber playground balls sting like a mother if you put a little force into your throw. Which got me thinking, how's about if the ball was rigged with explosives? Nothing very powerful, you understand. Just enough to make a colorful flash—you ought to appreciate the irony, Mr. Flash—and blow the body part the ball strikes to bits. A clever change to the rules, I think you'll agree. And a way of ensuring that sissies who won't play manly sports don't survive to mess up the gene pool." He grinned toothily.

From Jack's upside down perspective it looked like the grimace of an attacking shark.

"I'll make sure you have plenty of teammates from the sissy scum of Aphro-Port's jails. You can meet them right now, in fact."

Bellissini reached up and pressed a hidden switch. A motor rumbled and squealed to life somewhere and Jack found himself moving backward out of the throne room.

Maybe now's the time to break free of this rope cocoon, he thought, but the knots were too tight and all he could do was thrash around uselessly as his body was winched along slowly but steadily, like a passenger on a ski lift. He passed down a featureless corridor and then sharply right, through a heavy steel door, which a grinning, catcalling pair of guards opened for him.

"Hey, fresh meat!" they called. "Hope you have fun with your buds!"

The door slammed behind him and, still hanging trussed and upside down, he moved down a stone staircase into a dimly lit dungeon where a milling, silent crowd of prisoners watched his arrival. Abruptly the motion stopped and he was dumped on his head onto the stone floor, as if he was prize in a claw machine at a county fair. Jack's head pounded as rough hands grabbed him and stripped away the ropes, but he knew he'd been lucky; if he'd fallen a few feet further or at the wrong angle he might have broken his neck.

"Thanks," Jack said to the man who'd untied him.

"Don't mention it." He stuck his hand out. "Po Lonya, at your service. Call me Lonya."

As they shook Jack looked him over. It was hard to tell in the dim light, but the guy looked to be about forty, and was strongly built with a muscular torso and ropy runner's legs. He had pleasant, open features framed by sideburns that were just starting to turn gray. The fact that he was black meant he was probably a Crewman, but he didn't seem to be putting on airs.

Jack decided to trust him, at least for the moment.

"What are you in here for?" Jack asked.

"I work in Customs at the spaceport, and I wouldn't take bribes."

Jack whistled on a descending note. "That makes you pretty unusual, but why'd they throw you in here for it?"

"If an inspector won't take bribes, his boss, and his boss's boss all the way up the chain to Da Mayor himself, don't get their cut. Plus, it makes everybody look bad."

"Under a government which imprisons any unjustly, the true place for a just man is also a prison," said Jack. "Thoreau wrote that in his essay 'Civil Disobedience.' On the other hand, I'd rather break out before we end up starring in Bellissini's game of Death Ball."

"No one's ever escaped from Aphro-Port's dungeon," said another prisoner, a squat, balding white guy dressed in rags.

"No one's ever tried very hard," Jack said. "Usually you can bribe your way out of here."

"Not lately," said the short guy. "I slipped Siggie, the big beefy guard, a hundred solars, and he didn't even give me better swill at dinnertime."

"It's kind of urgent that we organize a breakout," Jack said. He explained briefly about the upcoming explosive sports match. "I don't know who exactly Bellissini has it in for, but everyone in this prison may be in danger."

Lonya stroked his chin. "What did you have in mind?"

9

Sonya couldn't understand more than one word of a hundred of the Aramaic spoken by these chimeras Rachel had dreamed up, but she didn't need to be a Biblical scholar to sense that something was up. For one thing, she and Helia had been given clean if bizarre clothing. For Sonya, there were slightly oversized dungaree overalls, and for Helia a man's pinstriped suit with a white plastic carnation in the front pocket.

When Helia complained the guard laughed at her, a grating sound like gravel pouring down a tin sheet. "Ha! You *bat-chava* has wearing what we gives yiz. Or *ulai* yiz wants to go naked?"

Helia snatched the suit from the creature's dangling claw with a growl. "When I am restored to my people you'll pay for humiliating a Crewman like this!"

"I kinda like these overalls," Sonya said, pulling them up over her filthy rags by the shoulder straps. "Thanks, Mar Bar Yallai!"

The creature turned and stomped out of the room while Helia gave Sonya a dirty look. "That's some serious sucking up you just did."

"Oh, I do know how to be polite when I feel like it," Sonya said with a rueful chuckle. "But I guess it don't really matter, cause those ridiculous bigfeet are getting ready to let us go. Queen Anya must have ransomed me. Course I won't go unless they let you go, too."

"Don't be ridiculous. It won't help me one bit if you stay here with me to rot."

"Ain't nobody going to rot." Sonya stamped on the dry mud floor. "I won't stand for it!"

Before Helia could think what else to say to convince Sonya not to be silly, heavy footsteps sounded outside the door.

Sonya stood up. "That must be them now."

The door banged open and several Malchussei stomped in, with King Rawbaw, unmistakable in his absurd scrap-metal crown, leading them. "Yiz is coming with us," he said.

"Why? Where are you taking us?" Helia demanded. Another Malchuss reached down and picked her up.

Sonya tried to walk out under her own power, but she was scooped up too. She forced herself to relax. *What does it matter? This must mean*

Anya has ransomed us and we're both on our way home! At least I hope so...

But when they got outside, there was no welcoming party waiting for them, only a long and bumpy trek through the jungle. Thanks to the creatures' long strides, they soon left the huge huts of the Malchussei village behind. The creature carrying Helia ignored her demands that he tell her where they were going, except to clout her on the side of the head once.

When she looked up her eyes were a little unfocused. "Sonya? Where are you?"

"Over here, Helia. They didn't really hurt you, did they?"

"Dunno. I'm seeing double." Helia swallowed and began to cough.

Sonya started to get mad. *They don't need to be so rough, when they're so much bigger than us.*

"You understand their horrible jabber a little," Helia managed to say. "Where are they taking us? Back to the city?"

"Can't be! Anya must've outbid Bellissini for us!"

But the creature holding her snorted like a horse, and panic seized her. She began to scream and scratch and bite until an arm the size of a log smashed into her head.

When she came to, she too was seeing double and Helia was yelling at King Rawbaw. "Where are you taking us, you oversized varmint?"

"Dat's KING Oversized Varmint to yiz," the king said, swiping at the side of the Crewman's face with a large, sharp claw.

She screamed and clapped her hand to the side of her head, trying to stanch the bleeding.

"Whoever you're giving us to ain't gonna pay if we arrive dead!" Sonya yelled.

King Rawbaw stepped in front of the Malchuss carrying Sonya and breathed in her face. The rotten egg stench made her gag. "Worry not, liddle Erss-girl. We keeps yiz nice and safe until we stomp da N'Bialy."

"T'foo, t'foo!" the other Malchussei yelled. Which was the same expression Sonya's grandmother back in Poland always used back before the war whenever anyone mentioned Hitler, or Stalin, or the young things in Warsaw who were wearing scandalously short skirts these days, or that no-good grocer Kagan down the street, or anyone else she didn't like.

Sonya started to giggle, but it turned into coughing.

"Yiz be nice and quiet when we talking to da feel'tee N'Bialy," King Rawbaw said, when Sonya had stopped coughing. "Or we kills you nice and quick, unnerstand?"

"Yeah, we got it, you scaly horror," Helia said hoarsely.

"Goot. Yiz helps us beat da N'Bialy. *Vi-yam'leech* Malchussei!"

"*Vi-yam'leech* Malchussei. *Yisgadal shmei* Rawbaw!" his followers bellowed.

Sonya's heart began to pound at the sound of the mangled prayer for the dead. The way things were going, she was going to need that prayer said for her by the time this day was over.

Another hour went by, and another, as the Malchussei carried their captives through the unending, gray Venusian jungle, under the unchanging gray light from above. When Sonya had complained that their captors never turned off the little square light set high over their heads in the wall of their prison hut, Helia explained that it was a skylight, and since Venus took 236 Martian days to turn once on its axis (a Martian day was just forty minutes longer than an Earth day, Sonya knew), they'd have to wait several Martian days for the sun to set—which it did in the east—and night to come.

"And then we'll have to wait one hundred eighteen Martian days for it to come up again, and the beasties will probably drag us into some cave because they hibernate the whole time, so let's hope we're rescued before then."

Now Sonya wished night would fall, so the Malchussei would have to stop walking and put her and Helia down.

As if her thinking it made it happen, Rawbaw gave a sharp order and his followers stopped walking. Sonya's and Helia's captors put them down with surprising gentleness, though maybe that had been part of the Venusian chief's command. They drank from canteens cleverly fashioned out of a tough, thick kind of gray leaf and shared the water with their human captives, who gulped it down gratefully.

When her thirst was slaked, Helia straightened her ridiculous clothes and patted her tangled Afro. "Wish I had a mirror. Actually, maybe it's better I don't, after the way these barbarians have been treating us."

Rawbaw, who had sunk down on his foreclaws with a sigh, twitched his tail. "Barbarians? As in, barbarian invaders? Yiz ain't da natives, Erss-girl!"

Helia shook a long, graceful finger that ended in a broken nail at him. Sonya almost laughed aloud, but what she was saying wasn't funny. "Smile when you say that, barbarian! I was born right here, and so was my father, and my father's father, going back ten generations! I've never even been to Earth!"

"And none of my forefadduhs done invaded da Erss," Rawbaw pointed out. "Nor none of da stinkin', shrinkin' N'Bialy, neidduh. We was mindin' our own bidness, fightin' da odd war or twosies, when Accursed Elron and his crew of pirates landed!"

"My ancestors were not pirates!"

"Land t'ieves, den. Call it what you want, Erss-girl."

"Well, I'm from Earth, by way of Mars," Sonya said, "and I got a question for you, Mister Big-Shot. Why ain't you fightin' against Bellissini and his Bullyboy Bastards, 'stead of the N'Bialy? Can't you see that Bellissini wants to keep you Venus natives fightin' each other, while he takes over everything?"

"I hope you ain't implyin' dat da Malchussei are stoopit," said Rawbaw, swiping a claw casually at Sonya's right ear—she ducked but still felt a sharp pain in the earlobe.

Hey, I want getting my ears pierced to be my own decision, thanks very much!

She clamped her right hand to the ear to stop the bleeding, almost missing the Venusian king's closing remark: "Da Mayor may t'ink he's a-playin' me, but iss me dat's playin' *him*." And with that he stomped away, not bothering to look back to check if his tribesmen had grabbed their captives and followed him. Which of course they had.

At some point Sonya noticed the ground was rising and the trees were getting shorter, until the Malchussei overtopped them. The forest gave way to tall grasses with sharp-looking blades. The grass was gray like everything else.

Couldn't Rachel have added a little color? This is getting boring!

There was movement on the other side of the clearing, and Sonya suddenly saw that she could complain to Rachel in person, because there she was, standing with Katie and two human guys among a group of Venusian natives who looked just like the Malchussei, except that none of them wore a crown and one of them had a sling on its right arm. The Malchussei let out a long, low, spine-tingling growl that the other group of Venusians imitated. Obviously the other group had to be the N'Bialy.

Before any of the humans could speak, King Rawbaw stepped forward and addressed the N'Bialy with the injured limb. Speaking English, he sneered, "Wossa madduh wiss yer arm, Karolla? Hurt it picking fruit?"

"If my elbow makes you cry, you should see the other guy," said Karolla.

"He almost killed him in a duel," Rachel said. "Don't mess with Karolla!"

Katie pointed at the creature holding Sonya. "And don't mess with my little sister, ya big galoot! Put her down right this second if you know what's good for you!"

Sonya's heart felt like it might burst as she looked at Little Miss Know-It-All in her wheelchair.

"Or what? You'll run over our toesies?" King Rawbaw taunted.

Katie actually started rolling herself forward and Rachel had to reach out and grab the wheelchair handles to stop her.

"You may be our mortal foe, but the human girls you shall let go," said Karolla.

"What, for free?" sneered King Rawbaw, "*La*, we won't. If yiz wants dem dat badly, you gives us da Whispering Wood for dem."

There was a cry of outrage from the N'Bialy. If Rawbaw had been human Sonya was sure he would have been smirking. Karolla silenced his tribe with a bright-eyed glance at each in turn. "The price you ask, you know is high," Karolla said, "Perhaps we divide the woods, in a tie."

"Two-ssirds, my final word," Rawbaw said.

Sonya wondered if he was mocking Karolla with the rhyme.

"The N'Bialy, you cannot bribe. I must speak with my tribe," Karolla said.

"Take all da time you need. If da price too high for yiz, we see what price Da Mayor pay," Rawbaw said, baring his teeth.

Sonya struggled in her captor's claws and began to choke when he squeezed her neck. Darkness was closing in around the edges of her field of vision when the creature loosened the pressure enough for her to breathe. Her head lolled loosely on her neck, and as she gasped for air she saw the N'Bialy standing in a huddle, with their human companions squeezed in among them.

They should be paying closer attention to the Malchussei, Sonya realized in a flash, and opened her mouth to shout a warning at the same instant Rawbaw glanced at his tribesmen and pointed his claw at the enemy.

"*Vi-yam'leech* Malchussei!" they bellowed, and charged across the field.

Sonya lunged for her captor's thumb and sank her teeth into it. He dropped her with a roar, and she scrambled to her feet, desperate not to be trampled by the rampaging Venusians. They were battling hand to hand, or rather claw to claw, which made for a brutal fight. As she darted around between their feet she saw one Venusian jab its claws deep into the eye sockets of another, which screamed piercingly and batted at its own face, from which greenish-blue blood spurted. Sonya shuddered and veered sharply left, dodging a giant foot and a huge spear that whizzed by right in front of her face. She scurried here and there, like a rat under raging dinosaurs' feet.

And then, just as suddenly as it had begun, the battle was over. For a dizzy moment Sonya didn't know who had won, but then a man grabbed her and held her tight. She clung to him as he shouted, "I've got her! Sonya's all right!" A ragged cheer went up.

Sonya looked up and her heart skipped a beat, thinking that she had just been rescued by Zap-Gun Jack. But then she saw his haunted, sad eyes and knew that it was his brother Jim, the one who had been kidnapped and tortured all those years in the bad old Martian Army. She gave him a quick extra hug before taking a good look around the battlefield.

Four or five Venusians were lying still on the ground with terrible gashes in their heads and bodies. One was sitting with a paw over its right eye, groaning as greenish-blue blood leaked out between its claws, while the others fussed around it. Another of the creatures was writhing on the ground while three more sat on it and a kneeling Katie tied a makeshift tourniquet around a spurting, jagged stump of an arm. There was a metallic tang in the air, mingled with something rottenly sweet.

Sonya jumped when Jim spoke, though his voice was quiet. "This is the glory of battle that my officers back on Mars were always going on about. Take a good look and a good snootful, honey."

Something else was bothering her though. *Where is everybody?* Apart from her sister and Jim, the only human Sonya saw was a stranger, a teenage boy who was staring wide-eyed at the alien carnage.

"Where's Rachel?" Sonya said loudly. Katie looked up from her attempt at alien first aid. "Where is she?" Sonya said. "Rachel? Rachel! And where's Helia?"

"Who?" Jim said.

"That Crewman girl the Malchussei were holding hostage with me … Where are they?"

"My arm, never mind, I no longer bleed," Karolla said faintly from the ground. "Find Rachel and the other human, they are in need!" He repeated the order in Hebrew for his followers, and they rushed to obey.

Sonya blinked at the sight. *Looks like not all the Venusians are alike, any more than human beings are,* she thought as she joined the search through the high grass.

The blades of grass, it turned out, didn't just look sharp, they actually *were* sharp, leaving long, shallow cuts on Sonya's bare hands as she ran. She hardly noticed, she was in such a frenzy to find Helia and Rachel.

What if they're hurt? What if they're lying bleeding on the ground? She didn't even want to form the thought, *what if they're dead,* as if thinking so might make it come true.

Then someone grabbed her from behind. *The Malchussei! They're back!* She struggled and kicked, but it was only Jim.

"Sonya! Take it easy! I just don't want you to hurt yourself! You have to know how to get around in *desheh* grass. Let the rest of us do the looking."

"Huh-uh! I want to help find them!"

"All right then, stick with me and let me beat the grass down first." Jim used a thick stick, which naturally was gray, to flatten the grass as they trudged forward, calling Rachel's and Helia's names. The N'Bialy were also calling, and with their greater height they could obviously see much further than any human, but Sonya and Jim kept up their bush-whacking, Sonya hoping against hope that being closer to the ground she'd spot something the others couldn't.

After a hot and sweaty hour most of the grass in the clearing had been flattened by the N'Bialy or the humans, to no avail. Karolla, who was propped up against Katie's wheelchair, delivered the grim verdict. "Sonya and Helia were only bait. For Rachel, the Malchussei lay in wait!"

10

Rachel had been taken captive on three planets—Earth, Mars, and now Venus—and she could say one thing with certainty: being a prisoner sucked, no matter where you were.

The Malchussei had left three dead on the battlefield, and four walked away with a variety of greenish-blue gashes. But King Rawbaw was in a wonderful mood, leading his followers in chants of, "*Viyam-leech* Malchussei!"

Rachel thought if she had to listen to this excruciating version of the prayer for the dead one more time, she'd be ready to die herself. But she wasn't exactly captain of her fate at the moment. Rawbaw himself held her tightly in his scaly clutches, her arms pinioned to her sides, and bounced her around as he led his followers through the jungle.

"Do you sleep in a bed, perchance, Your Majesty?" Rachel asked sweetly, in Hebrew, just as the king was enjoying a rousing chorus of "*Yisgadal shmei* Rawbaw—Rawbaw's name is mighty!" from his excited followers.

He scowled at his captive and said in English, "I don't speak barbarian N'Bialy babble, *bat-chava.*"

"*Shtu'yot*, stuff and nonsense, oh mighty king. If you speak Aramaic, you understand Hebrew well enough. I asked if you sleep in a bed, Your Royal Highness."

"I sleep in a bed made of the finest rushes in the swamp!" the king said in decent Hebrew.

She felt a tiny spark of triumph. "Oh, mighty king, I wish you may have a room with a hundred beds!"

"A hundred beds? That sounds nice. With an extra-scaly female or two in each, I assume?"

"But of course," said Rachel, repressing a shudder.

"Why, thank you, Earth-girl—"

"And you should have a hundred such bedrooms, oh king of all kings!"

"A hundred bedrooms?" Rawbaw's chest swelled as he thought it over, the additional pressure half-suffocating Rachel. "And why not? Am I not about to become the mightiest emperor Venus has ever seen?"

Not if I have anything to do with it, you blowhard. "No less of a palace would befit you, oh ruler of all rulers! And once your tribe builds you this palace, with the last gram of stone on the planet, the last newton of force they possess, and the last milliliter of their sweat ..." Rachel lowered her voice dramatically as she spoke, and the king had to bend his sheepdog's head closer to hear.

"Yes?"

She managed to wrench her right hand free, and used it to lift the king's floppy left ear, which was covered with shaggy gray fur. Its edge had been torn a bit in the fight and was seeping blood the greenish color of copper rust.

"You should walk from room to room," she crooned into the creature's ear, which was full of the nastiest, grayish-green ear wax she had ever seen.

"Yes?"

"And climb into bed after bed," she whispered, trying with all her might not to gag at the stench of the wax, which stank like rotting potatoes.

"Yes?"

"AND NEVER GET A WINK OF SLEEP, YOU MISBEGOTTEN SON OF A LIZARD!" Rachel roared directly into the king's ear canal. The king howled and clapped a paw to his ear, as Rachel wriggled free and landed on the ground with a thump. Before she could take two steps another Malchuss grabbed her and choked the life half out of her.

When the king recovered, he took Rachel back and growled at her in English, "Was dat worth it, Erss-girl?"

Rachel tossed her red curls as dramatically as possible, given the limited range of neck motion she had, and said, "You may kill me if you wish, O Mighty King. Nothing builds a royal reputation like the torture and murder of the helpless."

"Oh, you ain't so helpless as all dat, Rachel Zzzzilber."

Chills ran down her spine. "You know who I am?"

"We ain't blind and stoopit on Venus, Erss-girl. You're famous ssru'out da Solar System as Queen Anya's friend and double."

Rachel went as limp as cooked pasta. All this time, she'd been hoping for anonymity as Anya's friend and confidant. If everybody knew her name, they'd start asking a lot of awkward questions about how it was that she was almost the Martian queen's twin—though Rachel would never believe she was anywhere near as beautiful as her finest creation—and somebody might look a little closely for comfort into all the strange goings-on around Anya's miraculous ascent to the throne.

If they find out about the magic typewriter Katie and I "inherited" from Johnny Marshall, we're sunk. Especially if this character knows and he tells Bellissini. She was going to have to change the Venusian king's mind.

"What are you planning on doing with us, O mighty King?" she said, willing her voice not to quaver.

"Cut a deal," Rawbaw said bluntly. "I already done told dat udder Erss-girl, da liddle blond one, Bellissini will give more for your hides den Anya will."

"That's not true! If you just let me get a message through to her—"

Rawbaw shook his sheepdog head, and Rachel had to fight back an impulse to reach up and pat it.

"It don't matter, Rachel. We hafta live wiss dat pirate Bellissini. Anya is millions of klicks away in space."

"But don't you see, he's using you, Bellissini is! He wants to keep you Venusians weak and fighting among yourselves—"

"I made the same argument, Martian girl," Helia called wearily, where she slumped in another Malchuss's grip. "Apparently these lizards are too dim to grasp the concept of 'divide and rule.'"

Rawbaw swiped a paw in her direction, almost dropping Rachel again. He chuckled nastily when Helia flinched. "Ya know, dat's just rude. I t'ought yiz Crewmen was sposta have good manners and all. Doncha even know better dan to do *lèse-majesté*, leastaways when you at King Rawbaw's moissy?"

"*Yisgadal shmei Rawbaw!*" his subjects chanted in unison.

I can't believe these weird aliens I made up know the French term for insulting a king! Rachel thought. "Your Majesty is most wise, and merciful," she said aloud. "But the question still stands. Why are you letting the tyrant Bellissini take advantage of you?"

"Girlie, we hasta survive," Rawbaw said. "Bellissini gots more power now, so I plays along and try to t'ink up my own angle. Good enough for yiz?"

Before she could respond, he pitched her headfirst into the same hut where Helia and Sonya had been held prisoner before. Helia followed close behind, but she landed on her butt.

11

"Nice going, Martian girl," Helia said into the darkness of the prison hut some time later, as they both sat nursing their bruises.

"I'm not a Martian. I'm from Warsaw, on Earth," Rachel said. She bent over, ignoring her various aches as she studied the seam between the walls and the floor, trying to detect any hole she might enlarge.

"Funny, that's what the other Martian girl said."

"Sonya? She can be annoying sometimes, but she's telling the truth about being from Warsaw."

Helia blinked in the darkness, her eyes seeming to glow like a cat's. "Well, she saved my life. And now I get to formally meet the famous Rachel Zilber." She stood up and attempted to curtsey.

Rachel turned to look at Helia, whose dark eyes gleamed in the faint light from the skylight. The black girl's arms were crossed. "I'm not famous, and I don't want to be, but yeah, like King Rawbaw said, I'm Rachel Zilber."

"The one who dreamed up the whole universe, and everyone and everything in it."

Why can't that little brat keep her mouth shut? "Sonya has some strange ideas," Rachel said cautiously.

"She also said you're best friends with Queen Anya, and that the reason you look just like her is because you made her up, based on yourself."

"I'm lucky enough to have Anya as a dear friend, but that's all," Rachel said, cold sweat trickling down her spine.

It was bad enough when Jack, Anya, Gun, and Eddie all knew that Katie and Sonya and I come from another universe. What do we do now that everyone on this whole PLANET seems to know? And if you tell people in a dream that you're dreaming, don't you usually end up WAK-ING UP?

"She has a really active imagination," Rachel said.

"But she saved my life," Helia said. "And she seems very intelligent, you know, in a street-smart kind of way. Not really the dreamy type."

Rachel squeezed her eyes shut, layering darkness over darkness.

If only I had the typewriter with me, I could fix this mess. But, no, that wouldn't be right—brainwashing people and making them act against their nature is what dictators do, not writers.

She sighed, opened her eyes and took Helia's hands. "All right, I'll level with you. But you have to promise not to tell anyone."

"Who would I tell?" Helia said with a nervous chuckle. "Our scaly friends?"

"That's—that's really racist, Helia. The N'Bialy are Venusians too, and they're my friends. And even the Malchussei are just doing their best to survive in a bad situation."

"My heart bleeds for them. So what's your big secret?"

"Sonya, Katie, and I come from Earth—but in another universe, another version of history, one where Venus and Mars are lifeless worlds and people are divided up into dozens of warring nations, all stuck on the one planet."

"That seems … far-fetched."

Rachel was trying to think what to respond to that when the door of their prison swung open with a rustling of thatch so loud it sounded like the monsoon, and the biggest Venusian Rachel had ever seen strode in and swept both girls up, one under each arm.

"If anything you try, I make you suffer before you die," the creature rumbled, in English.

"Fee, fi, fo, fum," Helia said feebly.

Oh great. This creature's another rhyme-master like Karolla.

"We'll be good girls," Rachel gasped. "Just please don't break my neck." The creature shifted its terrible grip down far enough Rachel was afraid her stomach would explode. "That's much better, thanks," she groaned.

King Rawbaw was waiting outside the hut with a small entourage. "I hopes yiz enjoyed my royal hospitality."

"I appreciate the effort to bring us human food," Helia said. "but we usually like a little less gray mold."

"Not that we mean to be ungrateful or anything," Rachel said.

The king stepped toward her and pinched her cheek, drawing only a little blood.

He's actually trying to be nice, Rachel thought, gritting her teeth and willing herself not to cry out. When she had been writing about *other* people having adventures, she hadn't really considered what that felt like: all the tiny discomforts and indignities, the larger pains, and the grinding, constant terror. *If I ever write another story,* she promised herself, *I'll remember to put all that in. Along with the long, steamy walk through the jungle, the sweat beading on my forehead and under my arms that doesn't cool me off, the bugs as big as rats hovering in front of my face, Helia trying to keep her face and body still ...*

But the prospect of being turned over to Bellissini's tender mercies made it hard to think about anything else. *Should I tell Rawbaw what's really at stake? But if I do, won't that just make things worse?*

Rachel decided to compromise. "Your Majesty, I know you're trying to do your best for your people, but you're making a terrible mistake!"

"*Shekket,*" the Venusian snapped in Hebrew, "quiet, Earth-girl. We have made our decision and we aren't about to change it."

"I know a secret that Bellissini can use to wipe out all the Venusian natives, N'Bialy and Malchussei and anyone else!"

"What are you talking about? What secret?" Helia asked, in English. *Damn, she understands Hebrew too!*

Rawbaw stopped walking, and his people stopped in unison. "Yeah, what secret?" the king asked, in English.

Rachel hesitated, and the king snorted. "Nice try, Erss-girl!" he said, still in English, and resumed marching through the dense foliage as if it was a smooth pavement.

Helia caught Rachel's eye and mouthed, "I'm going to make a break for it!"

Rachel shook her head violently, not wanting to see the regal Crewman torn limb from limb.

Luckily the rest of their journey was short and mostly chant-free. They emerged in a marshy clearing, with Aphro-Port's dully gleaming dome visible in glimpses through the trees on the far side. Ranged against those trees, facing the Malchussei, was a small group of beefy men. Most were young, dressed in beige camouflage and toting laser rifles, but Rachel's eye was drawn to three unarmed figures who stood in front of the others.

There was a short, squat, balding man, with arms that looked long enough to wrap around a typical Venusian jungle tree, and muscular enough to snap the trunk in half. His hair seemed to have migrated down his forehead and parked itself over his eyes, in one long, dark strip. There was a striking young woman with jet-black hair that stood out against creamy pale skin, her delicate features set in a sardonic grin. Between them stood a man of slightly above average height and average build, with iron-gray hair and an unpleasant smile. Da Mayor, no doubt.

"I see you brought the redhead," he said to King Rawbaw. Then he spotted Helia and his smile broadened. "And an extra gift for me—a Crewgirl!"

"Smile when you call me that, usurper," Helia growled.

As she had during her misadventures on Mars, Rachel caught herself admiring the hauteur of an aristocrat despite loathing the whole concept in principle.

"I *am* smiling, Miz Po," said Bellissini. "Not only are you a tasty dish, but marrying you will shut up all those snobs who think I don't deserve to be mayor."

"I'd sooner marry a Malchuss, you—"

But Bellissini had turned his back on her to address King Rawbaw. "Well done, my scaly pal. My secretary, Miss Morgan, will give you the deed to the Whispering Wood as soon as you give the gals to me."

The woman grinned and waved a piece of paper just out of King Rawbaw's reach.

"Yiz forgotting da honor due me," the Malchuss chief said stiffly. "If you want dese girls, *yakruni*!"

"Ya gotta be kidding me," Vito muttered.

Bellissini elbowed him and whispered in his ear. The unibrow shot up, then settled back down. Da Mayor and his two associates took a step back, clenched their right fists and struck their chests. The soldiers guarding them copied the motion, then they all straightened their right arms out, palms down, and chanted, "Hail, King Rawbaw!"

Rachel shivered. *It's the fascist salute!* she thought.

But it must have satisfied the king, because he stepped forward, snatched the official paper from the secretary's left hand, and crooked a claw at the Malchuss holding her and Helia, who unceremoniously dumped them both on the ground. By the time Rachel could scramble to her feet two soldiers had her by the arms, and two more had Helia in their grip. They were frog-marched out of the clearing, through the trees and up to the gate of Aphro-Port, which opened wide to let them in, people scuttling out of the way to let the official procession pass.

"Make way for Bellissini's Bullyboy Bastards!" the soldiers chanted in unison.

The town looked little changed since the last time Rachel had been there, at the start of her otherworldly adventures two years ago. It was hard to be sure since they were being marched along so quickly, but the shabbiness and sleaze seemed a little worse. Men and women cutting crooked deals in alleyways ducked out of sight as the procession passed by, while children in ragged clothes stopped playing and stared openly.

There was one thing missing, though it took Rachel a moment to figure out what it was. "Where are the Venusians?" she asked.

Bellissini smiled. "I banned those weird aliens from entering Aphro-Port. Any time we catch them hanging around here, we throw them in jail and make 'em do slave labor."

"But *we're* the aliens on *their* planet," Rachel protested as they were hustled into a gleaming marble-fronted palace complete with cheesy fake-Doric pillars.

Bellissini turned on his heel and faced her so abruptly the guards almost shoved her into him. Then he leaned over and whispered something in her ear that made ice run through her veins. "Let's face it, sweetheart, those dinosaur dogheads aren't one of your better creations."

Everyone had come to a dead stop in the huge, echoing lobby when Bellissini halted. He straightened up and addressed the guards holding Helia. "Tell that sissy of a dressmaker to fit her for a wedding gown."

"If you think I'm going to marry you, dirtbag, you've got another think coming!" Helia snapped.

Bellissini showed his teeth. "Oh, I think you will." He snapped his fingers and more guards appeared out of a side door, dragging a short, stocky black man with a swollen face.

"Dad! What have they done to you?" Helia gasped as she struggled unsuccessfully to free herself.

The secretary shook her head. "It was most unfortunate, Miss Po, but your father *was* caught trying to escape. We do our best to treat all prisoners with respect and dignity, but your father had to make things hard on himself, and he really shouldn't have listened to that smart-aleck Martian spy. Of course we knew all about their little escape attempt ..." She shrugged and lowered her gaze.

Rachel felt as if someone had kicked her in the stomach. Was Jack dead?

Bellissini tsk-tsked and said to the guards, "I hope you didn't rough them up too much. I was counting on the Death-Ball tournament to celebrate my nuptials with the noble Helia."

"They should still be able to play, sir."

"Good." Bellissini grabbed Rachel's left wrist in a grip that might as well have been steel handcuffs and turned to address Vito. "See that Miss Morgan and I are not disturbed until we're done with this prisoner. I expect the skybox to be ready for the wedding as soon as the Death-Ball match is over."

Vito bobbed his head. "Yes sir, Boss-Man!" He leered at Rachel, but the secretary elbowed him hard.

"Don't get any funny ideas, Vito," said the black-haired woman. "She's another dangerous Martian spy, and we need to interrogate her."

"Yes ma'am," the Neanderthal said, and skulked away as Bellissini dragged Rachel across the gleaming tile floor, his shoes squeaking with each step.

She went numb as it sank in that Da Mayor and his mysterious girl-friend knew her secret.

Soon the three of them were alone. The room Bellissini had dragged Rachel into was paneled in dark brown cherry-wood imported from Earth, with a matching desk and chairs. Da Mayor sat down behind the desk with a satisfied sigh and put his feet up, while his secretary perched on the edge of the desk, her arms folded across her chest. Bellissini waved Rachel to a low, uncomfortable looking chair of gray native wood.

"Have a seat, darling. And shut your mouth, you'll let bugs in. As you know, you really don't want to swallow one of those Venusian su-perbugs you made up."

He chuckled as Rachel's knees gave way and she sat down with a gasp.

"If you put your filthy hands on me, you'll be sorry," Rachel said, her voice sounding shaky in her own ears. "Why don't you maul that secretary of yours and leave me alone?"

The black-haired woman rolled her dark eyes. "I have a name, sweetie. It's Cherie. And I'm not Beppo's girlfriend. We've had a busi-ness arrangement, ever since I read his story and we both got 'trans-ported' here from Earth."

Rachel's head swelled up. "HIS story? *I'm* the author of 'Zap-Gun Jack Flash and the Dame-Eating Monsters of Venus,' and don't you ever forget it!"

Cherie quirked an eyebrow at Bellissini. "Really, Beppo? You're not only a power-mad putz, you're a plagiarist, too?"

Bellissini jumped to his feet and shook his forefinger at Cherie, who didn't even blink. "Am not! That story 'It Takes a Strong Man to Rule the Woman's Planet' is my own work!"

"Changing the title does not—"

"It's my own story!" Bellissini cried, pounding his fist on the desk. "All I got from this Raggedy Ann doll, here, is the idea to set it on Ve-nus!"

"I don't know what a Raggedy Ann doll is, but I'm sure you stole more than that from me!" said Rachel, who was also on her feet.

Cherie chuckled, pushed herself away from the desk, and put a hand on Rachel's shoulder. "Don't worry, Rachel, I won't let Beppo here steal all the credit from you. Mind you, nobody's going to know but the three of us, but I'll make sure he never lives it down."

"Thanks a lot, Cherie," Bellissini growled. "And I told you to stop using that name for me! I'm master of this whole planet now, in case YOU forgot!"

"Only because I've been at your side this whole time … though not TOO close to your side, Beppo. Yech, you really need a better cologne!"

Da Mayor sniffed his left armpit suspiciously. "But I thought this stuff is nice and strong!"

Rachel and Cherie's eyes met for just a moment. *At least we're in agreement on one thing.* Rachel shook her head. *I've got to pull myself together.*

She folded her arms and turned her green-eyed gaze on Da Mayor. "What is it you want with me, then? And how did you even figure out I was the author of the story you STOLE from me?"

Bellissini started to shake his finger at her, then thought better of it. He forced a grin. "Well, it was a good piece of detective work on my part. The author of the story was anonymous, but someone had to have written it. And then, soon after I got here and assumed my rightful position, I began hearing strange stories from Mars. Stories about how the queen had an identical twin who wasn't even related to her. Stories about the strange way the previous king had come to power, and the even stranger way he got tossed off the throne and into a lava pit. And I started wondering whether I was the only one who had come here from the real world. So I sent Cherie to the Red Planet to check things out."

Cherie rolled her eyes again. "You didn't 'send' me, Beppo, it was *my* idea to go, because I'm the one who put two and two together about that weird stuff happening on Mars."

"No, you're wrong, it was me who—"

But Cherie wasn't talking to him anymore. She was looking at Rachel, who didn't like the gleam in her dark eyes. "Imagine my surprise when I saw the Elysian Canal appear out of thin air."

Rachel put her head in her hands. "Oh, no."

"Oh yes."

Katie had been right, she shouldn't have taken the risk of breaking out Johnny Marshall's typewriter to write the canal through Elysium Planitia into existence. But millions of people had been threatened with starvation due to the drought, and the digging crews couldn't work fast enough to prevent it.

Yes, she had sworn she wasn't going to monkey with reality anymore, but, well, this wasn't changing anybody's personality or God forbid *erasing* them or anything like that, this was just creating something to benefit lots of people. So she had gone out on the flat, dusty volcanic plain with Katie, and as she rolled each page out of the typewriter Katie read it aloud, and the canal magically snaked its way across the parched landscape as if it had always been there. Apparently the Earth-woman had been hiding behind a boulder watching the whole time.

"It was good work Cherie did," Bellissini said, patting her on the shoulder. She flinched and glared at him. "When she told me what she'd seen, I sent men to find out all about you." He chuckled and rubbed his hands together while Rachel shrank back in her chair.

The creep hasn't laid a finger on me, and it's almost worse than if he had!

"Of course I was concerned about the competition. There's only room for one god in this little world you made, and that god is me."

"Not just you," Cherie said quietly. "We're a team, Beppo, don't you forget it."

Rachel stared at them in sick fascination. She and Katie had spent two years running away from their terrifying power. They both wanted nothing more than to be normal girls living a normal life. What kind of man wanted absolute control over the world and all the people in it?

A madman, that's what kind. And Cherie's even worse, since she seems so rational! Hmm, seems so rational ...

Rachel decided to ignore Bellissini and speak only to the woman, who seemed to have more brains than him anyhow. "Why does it have to be a competition? You and your boyfriend can run this planet, and I'll run Mars." Even making such an offer sickened her, but she had to get away.

"I told you, honey, he's not my boyfriend. Oversexed gym teachers really ain't my type."

"Tell that to Delores Fabuloso and all those girls from Botticelli Island! They seem to find me plenty masculine! All the girls do, except for you and that Jenny Dauphin chick!" Bellissini growled. Both women ignored him.

Cherie was shaking her head sadly, making her thick, shiny black hair bounce around. "I wish I could let you do your own thing on Mars, honey, really I do. But there's a little bit of a problem."

"The fact that Beppo's a maniac?"

"Nah, I can handle him."

"HEY! You little—"

"Shut UP, Beppo, I'm talking. You see, a little problem started on Venus at the very moment you were using your awesome powers to dig a great big ditch."

"A ditch? It saved—"

"YOU shut up too!" Cherie advanced on Rachel, who flinched in her chair.

There was something scary about her, even though she wasn't very imposing, physically. Nor was she dressed like a sex toy, as Rachel had to admit Beppo's girlfriends likely were. She was wearing a subdued pastel business suit and low heels, and as she approached Rachel she didn't raise her fist or shake her forefinger or anything so obvious. In fact she lowered her voice so Rachel and Beppo both had to lean forward to hear her.

"Something strange appeared out of nowhere, right here in Beppo's office. Completely trashed the place."

"Yeah, and I had just had a new shag rug—"

Cherie raised a warning finger, topped with a violet nail. Bellissini quieted down. "Luckily, it didn't get any bigger, and we were able to contain it and even rebuild his office in the room right next door. Want to have a look?"

"I really don't see what this has to do with—" Rachel stopped with a startled yelp as Cherie grabbed her by the arm and hauled her to her feet.

"Ooh, catfight!" Bellissini said.

"Don't be disgusting, Beppo," Cherie said as she marched Rachel into the far corner of the room and opened an unmarked door she hadn't even noticed before.

It was like an oven in there, if someone had decided to use a large office to incinerate plastic at a temperature hot enough to melt lead. Everything was dark as a cloud of black ashes, except for the nearest part of the walls, which glowed a dull red. Rachel gagged, then started to hyperventilate.

"Enjoying the smell?" Cherie said, shoving Rachel's head forward.

Her throat burned and she started to cough uncontrollably until Cherie yanked her back into Bellissini's office and slammed the door. Rachel fell to her knees, clutching at her throat.

Cherie smirked down at her. "That stink is actually just the burned remains of the stuff that was in this room when the vortex appeared. I had the walls lined with steel so the whole palace doesn't burn down."

"Vortex?" Rachel croaked.

"Whatever you want to call it. What it is, Rachel darling, is a big hole the 'real' Venus is poking through. A hole that *you* opened by messing with this universe after you already formed it! Luckily it hasn't been getting any bigger, I guess since you haven't been magically digging any more canals!"

"How do you know it was me who caused it, especially when it was here that it appeared?" Rachel's voice sounded raspy in her own ears. A thought struck her and made her smile slowly as Cherie looked away. "You made a dumb mistake, didn't you? You left the typewriter here, with Beppo, while you went to Mars, and he did something stupid with it."

"I had to use it to Correct a customs agent who was raking a little too much off the top for himself, not that it's any of your business." Bellissini stepped forward, his fist clenched, and said, "And maybe I ought to Correct YOU, make you nice and docile!"

Rachel gasped, but Cherie shoved Bellissini away without even looking at him. "Point is, this was YOUR fault, Rachel. And I won't have you smothering us all because you want to be a do-gooder, any more than I'm gonna let Beppo kill us all because he wants to be a god instead of a dictator."

"But I created this world," Rachel said in a small voice.

Bellissini snorted. "It's not like it was really all that original. My favorite thing my men found out about you was that you first got interested in science fiction because of your cousin Abe Rapaport in New York sending you all those magazines."

Rachel blinked, remembering those lost prewar treasures with their garish covers and cheaply printed pages full of wonder. "So what?" she wondered aloud.

"Your goober of a cousin used to pick fights with me when we were kids, that's what! Rotten kike, always getting in the way when I was just having fun beating up some little twerp who had it coming." Bellissini's florid face turned a darker red as he spoke, but then he smiled. "And you look just like him—an ugly yid girl version of him, that is. It'll be a pleasure to pay you back."

Rachel stood up and squared her shoulders. "I'm not afraid to die. And I'm certainly not afraid of the likes of you! Good for Abe, that's what I say!"

"Oh, I'm not going to kill you. That'd be letting you off too easy," Bellissini said.

"But we can't exactly let you go and try to write us out of the story, now, can we Rachel?" Cherie said. "Be reasonable." She made a sign with her left hand, and two soldiers came through the door and grabbed Rachel's arms.

Bellissini raised his voice, as if making a speech. "I am going to make sure you never touch a typewriter, or so much as a scrap of paper, ever again. And that you never, ever, lay eyes on another human being." He leaned forward and made kissy noises with his lips. "You're gonna die a very, very old, lonely woman."

While Rachel was trying to think of a comeback the soldiers tied her up with thick clothesline and strung her upside down from the ceiling. A faint mechanical whining sounded and the floor of Da Mayor's office began to slide away before her eyes.

She found her tongue just in time. "Neither of you has the imagination to keep this up!" she shouted. "If you try and take over my story, that vortex will swallow you all anyway!"

"We'll take that chance, Rachel," Cherie called after her.

What Bellissini's response was, if any, she never found out, but for a moment she thought she sniffed a faint whiff of sulfur as she slid down a chute into darkness.

12

It was quiet in the N'Bialy village, so quiet that Katie, idly rolling herself around its outskirts in her wheelchair, could hear how the Whispering Woods had gained their name. Growing up in the barren Texas Panhandle, Katie hadn't had a lot of experience with forests, but she knew from reading stories that the wind was supposed to sigh and make the leaves rustle as it passed through. But there was something peculiar in this wood, something that made the wind seem as if it was speaking words that could almost be understood—almost, if she just concentrated a little harder.

Which didn't seem worth the effort. It had been a long day and Katie was content to enjoy the quiet sounds and the ripe smell of growing things on the damp air. In what she had come to think of as the Meeting Hut, Karolla and the other warrior N'Bialy were sleeping—the wounded Aditai among them, she marveled to see. Poor Sonya had barely managed to stagger in with them before collapsing, snoring loudly with her head pillowed on Karolla's shaggy gray mane. Her sister had taken quite a shine to the Venusian chief, who had reacted with his usual fierce affection. That strange boy Mark Mahlett who had arrived with Jim was also asleep in there. The N'Bialy women and kids were all gathered inside too, in a giant pile with their menfolk ranged protectively around them.

Yeah, it's primitive, but it seems kind of cozy.

The sound of a guitar drifted to her on the wind. Curious, she wheeled herself into the forest, but was stopped by a gnarled root several inches high.

There's no way I can roll over that thing.

Cursing under her breath, she climbed out of the chair and pulled herself along the forest floor with her hands and an occasional weak kick until she found a stick sturdy enough to lean on. Then she climbed to her feet, grunting with effort, and hobbled deeper into the forest toward the source of the music.

It sounded less and less like a guitar the closer she got to it. It was a stringed instrument of some kind, she was sure, but the sound was deeper and richer than a guitar. As she approached Jim's fine tenor joined it, and she tried to make as little noise as possible with her staff and her clumsy feet, hoping not to startle him.

In a little clearing behind a stand of charcoal-gray trees with pale beige leaves she found Jim sitting on a log, his eyes closed and his face tilted up toward the soft gray clouds as his fingers picked out a tune on a bulky black instrument, which looked like a viola that had swallowed an isosceles triangle and got it lodged in its throat.

> *My maiden fair left me, she's gone clear away*
> *I'd not wound my pride, if I asked her to stay*
> *But her heart's spoken for, and it's no longer mine*
> *It belongs to a pilot of the Earth-Luna Line.*

Jim played a closing chord and stayed as he was, nose up in the air as if sniffing the wind. Without turning or opening his eyes, he said, "Hello Katie, can't sleep either?"

"I can't never fall asleep when it's still light out," she admitted, willing herself to cover the final few steps till she could sit down on the log beside him.

He turned and smiled at her, but his dark eyes were sad. They were always so sad. "I reckon that might be a problem for you, Miss Katie, 'cause sunset ain't for another couple of weeks. Anyways, you're welcome to stay and listen to me plink away at my jithara."

She studied his face closely for any sign of mockery in that "reckon" and that "ain't."

It's not there, she decided. *You might just as well ask a Venusian to bleed red, as ask Jim to be mean to anyone.*

She thought how Rachel had written in "Zap-Gun Jack" about the years of torment Jim had endured "at the hands of cruel Martian military men, ever ready with their swagger sticks and their fists and their jackboots." And then the horror Rachel had felt at the thought that her words had meant real suffering to the real Jim.

Katie had never known how to say it to her, but she didn't think Rachel was responsible. The suffering was already there; her friend had only described it. And now the redhead was being held captive somewhere.

"It's really 'cause of Rachel I can't sleep," Katie said. "And that other poor girl Sonya told us about, the Crewman. That Bellissini character is a nasty piece of work, no better than Johnny Marshall." When Jim looked blank, she added, "The jerk who called himself Ares III."

"Oh, him." He looked thoughtfully at the little patch of gray sky visible through the gray trees. "I guess the difference is Da Mayor doesn't want to conquer the Solar System. He's content to bully everyone here on Venus. Not that that's any better, if you happen to live here."

He sighed and put his mutant viola carefully on the ground, propping it up against the log they were sitting on. "I left Mars and came back here partly because this was where I was born, and I had a happy childhood here with my parents and Jack … but mostly because I wanted to get as far away from those power-mad Martian bullyboy soldiers as I could. But sleazy Venusian bullyboys are almost as bad. So where does that leave me?"

Katie wanted to chase the sadness out of Jim's dark eyes, if only for a moment. She thought kissing him on his stubbly cheek—just a quick surprise peck—might do it. But when she leaned toward him he turned unexpectedly and she found herself kissing him on the lips.

On the lips. And it was *nice.* She didn't want him to stop. And then he was holding her, and she was holding him, and they were putting their hands other places. And that was even *nicer.*

Suddenly Jim pulled away.

"What is it?" Katie gasped. "What's wrong? Did I do something wrong? Did I hurt you when I—"

Jim shook his head and put his finger to his lips. "The trees," he said, so softly Katie had to lean forward to hear him. "Don't you hear them?"

"Hear what?" The wind was moving the branches, lashing them into a frenzy. *But—there's no wind!*

Living wood collided with living wood, and small, dense nuts like acorns began to rain down around her. Katie cried out and covered her head with her hands. These woods weren't whispering, they were screaming. *Screaming a warning!*

Before she could react, Jim had leapt to his feet and covered the distance to the clearing in three long bounds.

Shucks, I couldn't have done that without tripping even when my legs worked right, flashed through Katie's mind.

But quick as he was, Jim was too late. The trees on the far side of the clearing erupted with roaring, stamping Malchussei and shouting, zap-gun wielding thugs wearing the beige uniforms of Bellissini's Bullyboy Bastards. Katie staggered to her feet, determined to pull Jim back out of danger, but found it wasn't necessary.

"I know a hopeless fight when I see one," he whispered to her as they hid behind a stand of wild joowallah plants. "I was in them often enough on Mars." His eyes were wider and more haunted than ever.

Katie put a finger to his lips and shook her head. *Don't blame yourself,* she wanted to tell him, though she knew he would because she felt the same helpless rage as they watched the raiders roust the N'Bialy from their makeshift campsite.

The male N'Bialy struggled hopelessly while the adult females threw themselves over the children. Karolla raised his remaining claw and slashed a Malchuss across his shaggy face, and was clubbed to the ground for his trouble. The melee seemed to go on forever, amid the triumphant roars and shouts of the attackers, the desperate cries of the defenders, and the mewling of the frightened children.

But in fact it was all over in minutes, as the attackers herded the defeated N'Bialy away, with one enormous Malchuss carrying a feebly wriggling Mark under his tree-trunk-sized right arm. Two N'Bialy lay dead in the ruins of their camp, an adult male whose head lolled on a broken neck and a baby who had been trampled and lay bleeding greenish blue.

Jim staggered into the clearing, silent tears running down his cheeks, with Katie leaning against him for support, holding back her own tears— not because she thought it was shameful or that Jim ought to be ashamed of crying, but because she wanted to be strong for him. They knelt beside the Venusian corpses in silence for a long time.

"We ought to bury them," Jim finally said. "They deserve a decent burial, and none of their people is here to give them one."

"We ain't got no shovels," Katie pointed out. "Nor the time. I'm sorry, Jim, but we've got to get out of here before the bad guys come back."

Jim nodded absently. "Wouldn't matter if we did have shovels, Katie. The roots of plada grass are so tough, the N'Bialy and Malchussei use them to haul heavy loads. Least I can do is chant the N'Bialy prayer for the dead, though, if you don't mind waiting."

"Course not, Jim," Katie said softly, her eyes blurring with unshed tears. If she hadn't fallen in love with him yet, she was doing it now.

She watched as he squeezed his eyes shut and began chanting in a haunting tenor, "*El malei rachamim ...*" *O Lord full of mercy,* he told her it meant.

When he was done they walked back to their hiding place. Jim folded up Katie's wheelchair and hoisted it on his left shoulder, along with his jithara, while she leaned on his right shoulder.

"Where do we go now, Jim?" she asked.

"Only one choice I can see, and that's to head back to Aphro-Port. Maybe we can hook up with other people there who also don't like the way things are going, and figure out how to help the captives. O'course, if my brother was here, he'd solve everybody's problems in a jiffy."

She tilted her head back and looked into his eyes.

He frowned and said, "You all right, Katie? I can carry you if …"

"I'm a-doin' fine," Katie said, though sweat was pouring down her face and her back and legs were on fire. "You listen here, James Tiberius Flash, and you listen good 'cause I'm only goin' to say this once. Your brother is a fine man, everybody loves him, 'specially the beautiful, perfect Queen Anya of Mars. He's brave and smart and funny and gosh-darn handsome—like his brother—but he ain't half the hero you are."

Jim flushed. "Beggin' your pardon, Miss Kaitlyn, but you're talking nonsense. Do I look like the man who took on the Pyromaniacal Pirates of Pluto single-handed, in a burning spaceship, and won? Who fought a zap-gun duel with Thomas the Tittering Tyrant of Titan, the fencing champion of the entire Solar System, and left his right arm a smoldering ruin? Who stood up to the Murmuring Myrmidons of Mercury and—"

"You hush with all that alliteration now, Jim. I said he ain't *half* the hero you are, and I meant it. You were kidnapped and press-ganged into the Martian Army when you were barely knee-high, and you didn't never let them turn you into a brutal bullyboy. Back where I come from, we call that courage and character. Now me, I ain't much to look at—"

"—beg to differ, Miss Kaitlyn—"

"—but I don't lock lips with just any guy, my Ma and Pa didn't raise me like that. There's only one flaw I can see in you, and that's self-pity. It ain't befittin' a *man* like you. Do I make myself clear?"

Jim looked at her for a long moment. "That means a lot, coming from a hero like you, who dared insult Ares to his face on planet-wide TV and paid for it so dearly."

"Don't you embarrass me like that, Jim." She took a deep breath. "Now, there's just one small favor I do have to ask of you."

"Anything, Miss Kaitlyn."

"Please, PLEASE call me Katie."

"That's it? You want me to call you Katie?"

"No, that AIN'T it, though I surely do want you to call me Katie 'cause everybody else does. I want you to go over there," she pointed, "where that heap of nasty gray Venusian palm fronds is, and fetch a wooden crate that's hidden under it. I'm afraid you're going to have to carry it, too."

"No problem, Miss Kait—I mean, Katie—but would you mind telling me what's in the crate?"

"A superweapon that'll bring that no-good Bellissini to his knees, soon as we can free Rachel."

Bless Jim, good little soldier that he is, he ain't asking no stupid questions, Katie thought as Jim tromped off through the jungle. *Which is good 'cause I ain't no storyteller like Ray and I don't know how I'd explain why he has to carry a heavy old typewriter through an alien rainforest.*

She slumped against a tree trunk and dozed till he got back, then tried to make out like she hadn't been sleeping.

"What took you so long, Jim? Let's git goin' while the goin' is good."

Which it wasn't, not by a long shot. The air was muggy, hot, and close even for Venus, more suitable for drinking than for breathing. Every step Katie took, even with half her weight on poor Jim's shoulder, sent lightning arcing up the base of her spine. And the way wasn't easy, not with moosquitos moaning as they flew around her head and klemeth vines underfoot all tangled up with various critters that were perfectly camouflaged as leaf mold until you stepped on them. Katie bit her lip so hard to keep from crying out that blood was soon dribbling down her chin.

Then her knees gave way and she sank to the ground, nearly squashing some humongous bug the size of a rat that buzzed right by her ear like a miniature helicopter. She didn't even react.

Jim crouched down beside her, but Katie couldn't make out what he was saying over the roaring in her ears. She didn't need to hear the words, though.

"I'm fine, you big lug, just let me rest a second," she gasped through clenched teeth.

He shifted the crate onto his shoulder, then bent down and gripped her under her arms with his strong hands.

"Don't you dare pick me up, Jim!" she groaned. "I'm—I'm not some helpless little baby!"

Tears of pain rolled off her cheeks as he cradled her to his chest. The smell of his sweat was exhilarating, like a whiff of the ocean. She tried to wriggle free but her body wouldn't obey her, and then she blacked out.

13

The darkness around Rachel was a close physical presence, as if she was wrapped up in a canvas bag. No, she decided, it was more like she was floating, weightless, inside a giant's cupped hands.

It had taken her what felt like hours to work free of her bonds, but in retrospect that had been a welcome distraction. Now she was all alone in this cell with nothing to do, just as Bellissini had promised.

Nobody replied when she called out, and her voice echoed flatly from somewhere very close at hand. Eventually she got up the courage to stand up and take a few shuffling steps forward, hands out in front of her. After seven or eight little steps she bumped into a wall. The material was rough to the touch, like concrete.

She edged along to her right until she came to a corner, where she turned right and kept going. In this way she paced the whole perimeter of the pitch-black cell, which she estimated at just over two meters on each side—barely big enough for her to lie stretched out on the floor, if she had dared try that. A toilet in one corner that was nothing more than a hole in the floor announced itself by smell. There was a bare cot whose springs groaned loudly when she sat down on it.

She put her head in her hands as the damp, filthy mattress sagged so low under her weight it almost touched the ground. When she'd been feeling her way along the walls she'd found no trace of a door—nothing but blank concrete wall. This place was a concrete-lined hole in the ground, an oubliette with no way in or out but the ceiling she'd been dropped through.

Maybe Bellissini means to starve me. He may have promised I'd live to be a very old woman in here, but who can believe the promises of a dictator?

On the other hand, the stinky floor toilet seemed to signal that prisoners stayed down here indefinitely. In which case, food and water had to be dropped down from the ceil—

A scraping noise broke the silence and light blazed down for a brief moment. Rachel gathered her wits just in time to scramble off the cot before something fell on it with a thump. Blinking away glowing purple afterimages, she got up on her knees and felt around on the cot until she found something round. It was about the size of a grapefruit, soft and mushy when she pressed her finger into it. Cool liquid welled up from the spot.

I can't even see what color it is. What if it's poison?

But her throat was scratchy and raw, and if she was going to die, it might as well be sooner than later, so she took a cautious sip. It tasted like lemon juice mixed with ashes, and she almost spat it out. But she needed the liquid, so she slurped it greedily, pushing and squeezing the fruit again and again until it had no juice left to give. Then she devoured the pulp. It was full of seeds as big as cherry stones, one of which she was sure she'd cracked a molar on, while another almost choked her to death.

After that she spat the remaining seeds into the toilet, wincing at the crack they made when they hit the wall instead.

I can't even spit in a hole without missing! Pathetic ...

Lying on the cot afterwards with her arms behind her head staring at nothing, she tried to remember if she'd mentioned a lemon-and-ash fruit in her short story "Zap-Gun Jack Flash and the Dame-Eating Monsters of Venus," but she doubted she could have come up with anything so disgusting. Deprived of any sensory input, her mind began to drift, painting softly glowing pastel billows on the walls and ceiling.

"That looks like a herd of electric sheep," she said aloud, and began to giggle. "I wonder if robots dream about them, too?"

If only someone, anyone was here for me to tell stories to!

Katie would be perfect, of course—if she were here, and they had the typewriter, the story wouldn't just be a story, it would be a way to escape this dungeon—not just in her imagination, but in reality. Which was why Bellissini had made sure she was trapped here all alone. The man was a devil in human form, and that Cherie woman was even worse— how could anybody be so smart and seemingly reasonable, and yet help a power-mad lunatic like Bellissini? Rachel's eyes began to swell and sting.

I'd better find something to occupy my mind, fast!

Well, sheer hatred was better than nothing.

"Bellissini, you *mamzer* of a *choleria*," she said aloud.

If Dad and Mom were still alive, they'd be aghast hearing their precious, expensively educated daughter babbling in *zhargon*, the ridiculous Germanic dialect of lower-class Polish Jews that they refused to dignify with the name "Yiddish."

But what does it matter? It's not like I'm ever going to get my university degree now!

She remembered how her grandfather used to go on, inventing imaginary tortures for Hitler and all the other enemies of the Jews, and drew inspiration.

"May you stuff yourself on delicious strudel until it chokes you! May the most beautiful women in the Solar System come into your bed, and point and laugh when they see what's inside your shorts! May your ships conquer all the planets and bring back a disease that makes your eyeballs swell up until they burst—and may you drown in the goo that runs down your cheeks!"

That was a good one. But Rachel was just getting warmed up.

"May your air conditioning get stuck so you freeze as solid as the Heart of Pluto! You should snort a miniature black hole up your nose, one just a few angstroms across that eats your malicious little brain, molecule by screaming molecule! Your mother was a *khurveh* from Callisto and your father was a toadstool from Titan! You should mistake an airlock for a toilet and flush yourself into the void, and the void should *spit you out*!"

She went on for quite a while like that, not forgetting to condemn Cherie to slow suffocation and roasting in a spaceship hurtling unstoppably toward the Sun, until she was gasping for breath and her throat was almost as raw as it had been from crying. A gray depression settled over her then. What was the use? She would never see or speak to anyone, ever again. She would spend endless years down here until she withered away and died, and when she did they'd probably leave her here to rot.

Maybe that's what they did with the previous prisoner!

Once that thought entered her mind, it refused to go away until she got down on her hands and knees on the cold concrete floor and checked every square centimeter of it, from wall to wall, not neglecting the space beneath the cot and around the rim of the toilet-hole, until she was sure she wasn't sharing the space with a skeleton. In the process she found the seeds she had spat out that had missed the hole.

For want of anything better to do she gathered them and lined them all up between the mattress and the metal cot frame. There were only six or seven, but if they kept giving her lemonash to eat, maybe she could collect enough to make a game.

Though I stink at checkers. If Katie were here she'd beat me at every game. Though she'd call it "whupping your bee-hind."

Which made Rachel giggle, which turned into a full-throated laugh, which turned into hiccups and then sobs. She cried herself to sleep on the filthy, reeking mattress.

When she woke it was to the sound of water dripping somewhere. *Oh God, no! I'd better find that leak and stop it somehow, or I'll go crazy and bash my brains out against the wall!*

The sound was coming from somewhere down low, so Rachel got on her hands and knees and crawled around the cell slowly, hoping to feel cool water on her skin. But when the noise grew loudest, in a far corner of the cell, she felt nothing and every surface she touched was bone-dry.

She stopped moving and strained her ears. Tap, tap, tap.

It's not dripping water, she realized, her heart leaping up into her throat, *it's somebody on the far side of the wall deliberately making noise!* She frantically started scratching at the wall, but the only result was a broken fingernail. *Whoever's there won't hear that! I need something to hit the wall with!*

But what could she use? The cot was bolted to the floor. As she clutched her head, the tapping stopped. *Oh, no, they'll think there's nobody in here!*

Just as she opened her mouth to scream in frustration the tapping started up again. She had to respond in kind, but how?

Remembering the lemonash seeds she'd spit out, she retrieved her collection from the bed, clutching them tightly in her left hand. But how could she use them to communicate?

Plain tapping would tell whoever was on the other side that she was here. It would have to do for now. She squeezed a seed between thumb and forefinger and banged it against the wall three times with such force her biceps tingled.

The other tapper paused, then started up again.

It's a pattern of some sort, Rachel realized. *A code, like Morse code. But how would you tell the difference between the long and short dashes?*

Sitting back on her haunches, she listened carefully to the noises. They came in clusters: two taps, short pause, six taps, long pause; two taps, short pause, three taps, extra-long pause; three taps, short pause, seven taps, long pause; two taps, short pause, six taps, extra-long pause; and then the pattern started over from the beginning.

As Rachel squatted in the dark, racking her brains, a ghostly, bearded face seemed to float in front of her. She'd know those haunted, dark eyes anywhere: they belonged to her Uncle Shloimie, her mother's much older half-brother, a communist who had run away to Russia when the revolution of 1917 broke out. In the early 1930's, when Rachel was a little girl, he returned home to Warsaw a broken man, having been sent to prison and then Siberia as a "counterrevolutionary." But why was she remembering him now?

It came to her in a flash a few minutes later, time enough for the maddening pattern of taps on the wall to repeat itself several times over. Rachel's parents had warned Uncle Shloimie over and over again not to talk about what had happened to him in Russia around her—she was only six or seven the year he lived with them while he was getting back on his feet—but the man couldn't seem to help himself, and visions of frostbite-blackened toes breaking off with a snap in the Siberian snow haunted her dreams for years afterward.

But that's not why I'm remembering Shloimie now.

When the Russians held prisoners alone, half naked and freezing in forgotten cells with thick stone walls in the depths of the infamous Lyubyanka prison in Moscow, he had told her, they sometimes communicated by tapping on the walls of adjoining cells, using the "prison alphabet." Each letter held a place in an imaginary grid, so that the letter C, for instance, would be represented by one tap, for the first row, followed by three taps, for the third position in that row.

That's what the person on the other side of the wall is doing now! Only, which alphabet is he using?

If it was a similar system to the one Shloimie had told her about, the other prisoner was sending two words of only two letters each. Try as she might, Rachel couldn't think of a message that short that would make sense in "Solar" (English), or "Marpolski" (Polish). Hebrew, on the other hand …

The N'Bialy spoke a version of Hebrew, a much more compact language to begin with and one the Venusian natives had further simplified by combining both of the letters that made a "T" sound into one, for a total of just twenty-one letters, or three rows of seven letters each, as she had seen back in their encampment, leafing through handwritten books made of actual leaves. Her Hebrew was a little rusty, as she'd told Katie, so she wished she had paper, pencil, and light to see by, but the message was short enough that she could remember it and work out what it meant:

מי שם

ME SHAM?
WHO'S THERE?
She gripped the lemonash seeds extra tight and tapped out:
IT'S ME, RACHEL FROM MARS
There was a pause, then an explosion of tapping.
SLOW DOWN! Rachel responded. **WHO ARE YOU?**
The reply was so long in coming Rachel was starting to wonder if the other prisoner had given up.
I AM ADITAI OF THE N'BIALY

The one with the bald patch who hated humans, the one Karolla had almost killed in the duel. Just great. Rachel thought furiously, then tapped out: **HOW MANY OTHER N'BIALY ARE HERE?**

Aditai seemed to hesitate. **A DOZEN. THEY ARE ALL IN THE CELL WITH ME.**

She had a feeling he was lying. **ADITAI, YOU CAN TRUST ME**, Rachel replied. **I AM A MARTIAN, NOT AN EARTH-HUMAN.** Which was pretty much true. She didn't live on Earth anymore, and Anya had granted her and Katie noble titles along with Martian citizenship.

The pause this time went on and on. **FINE. I AM ALONE HERE, SINCE MIOR DIED OF HIS WOUNDS.**

Rachel had been afraid of that. **WE HAVE TO BREAK OUT OF HERE, ADITAI.**

REALLY. HAVE YOU ANY IDEAS?

How could anybody tap on a wall sarcastically? Rachel shook her head.

I'M SORRY, NO. I WAS HOPING YOU COULD THINK OF SOMETHING.

WHY DON'T YOU THINK OF SOMETHING, MARTIAN?

I can think of something. I could think of everything, *if only Katie were here with that typewriter!*

But what could a klutzy Earth girl and a bad-tempered Venusian aborigine do with their bare hands against thick stone walls?

Another hour of exploring and comparing notes established that the stone blocks were held together by crumbly mortar. Given enough time, and if Rachel could sharpen her fingernails until they resembled Aditai's claws, they might be able to dismantle enough of the wall between their cells to join each other—if they could keep their tunneling hidden from their captors. Then, perhaps, Rachel could climb on Aditai's back and ambush whoever brought their food when the trap door in the ceiling opened.

But all that might take years. Long before that happened, Jack would be dead, and Helia forced to marry Bellissini.

Rachel shook her head, dismissing the thought, and began scraping her fingernails across the stone wall to sharpen them. The action sent up a spark small and dim as the hope she had left.

14

"It was a good plan. It should have worked," Jack said for the hundredth time, his breath whistling through the new gap in his front teeth.

"It wasn't your fault," Lonya said wearily, also for the hundredth time. The Crewman somehow managed to retain his dignity even though his eyes were swollen almost completely shut and his face was lumpy from the beating he had received at the hands of Bellissini's henchmen when the two of them were captured at the street opening to the dungeon's ventilation shaft.

Jack could still taste the ozone tang of the outdoor air—well, Aphro-Port under-the-dome air—beneath the coppery taste of blood in his mouth. They'd been so close!

He and Lonya were caged in a windowless room with concrete walls, floor, and ceiling, not very different from the oubliette where Rachel was imprisoned except that they had each other to talk to, a naked light bulb overhead, and a regular if imposingly heavy steel cell door with a flap in it through which they had been given a prison breakfast of stale, moldy bread and plain water. They did not, however, have any cots, which meant that in the long, empty hours since their capture they'd taken turns sitting up against the walls drowsing.

Lonya raised his head and looked at Jack. "On second thought, maybe it *is* your fault, Jack," he said.

Jack bolted away from the wall he'd been leaning against, as if it had suddenly turned red hot. "What's that?"

"I said," Lonya climbed slowly to his feet, "maybe it is your damn fault, you damn hero."

Jack blinked at him. "I'm going to put that down to a lingering after-effect of being kicked in the head."

"I haven't got a concussion, Mr. Big-shot Zap-gun. This has to do with your escape plan." He poked a finger at Jack's chest.

It was all Jack could do not to flinch. Any other man who did that to him would have already found himself flat on his back with a boot on his chest. But he'd thought Lonya was his friend and ally.

"I didn't hear any clever plans from you," Jack said as coolly as he could.

"You're supposed to be the one with the clever plans! You're famous throughout the Solar System! So when Zap-Gun Jack says we're going to break out through a ventilation shaft, I figure he must know what he's doing! Even though everybody knows he escaped from not one, not two, but three prisons the exact same way!"

"Your count is off," Jack said. "I only broke out of two prisons through ventilation shafts. The captain's cabin on the *Frosty Friday* wasn't a prison, the Pyromaniacal Pirates of Pluto just locked me in there and melted the door latch, and what's your point, anyway?"

Lonya leaned so close Jack could see the sweat droplets oozing up around his neck stubble.

"Don't you think the bad guys ever learn anything, Jack? I mean, that ventilation shaft trick was old school back in the twentieth century!"

"I'm old school," Jack said, taking a step backward. "And it's always worked for me."

"Yeah, but this time they were expecting it. So what d'you have up your sleeve now, Mr. Zap Gun? Grabbing the light fixture for leverage while you kick the door in? Because I don't think the wire that bulb is dangling from can support your weight!"

Jack licked his lips, trying to think how to protect his own dignity without starting a pointless fight. He was saved from the trouble by the sound of stamping footsteps echoing down the hall. There was a jingling of keys and the cell door swung open, narrowly missing Jack. The prisoners winced in the harsh white light from the corridor.

Standing in the doorway with an armed Bullyboy Bastard on either side, Bellissini beamed at his captives. "Hello, peeps!"

Lonya spat on the floor, narrowly missing the Maximum Leader's gleaming black boots.

The dictator clucked his tongue. "Where are the famous manners of the Crewmen we're always hearing about?" he said as the Bullyboy on his left took one step forward and slammed his fist into Lonya's gut, knocking him into the far wall.

"You have to admit, our treatment hasn't exactly been up to Solar standards," Jack said mildly, eyeing the Bullyboys' guns. He decided he didn't like the odds, not with Lonya doubled over groaning.

Bellissini, who was watching Jack very carefully, slowly smiled. "Good for you, Mr. Flash!" he said, clasping his hands behind his back and starting to pace the cell like a professor lecturing a class.

Could Bellissini have been a teacher before? Jack wondered. *But that doesn't make any sense. Why would anyone so mean become a teacher?*

"I would be disappointed if my men, here, have to blast you so you can't take part in our friendly game of Death Ball. But I do have to thank you for discovering the rather obvious security flaw in my dungeon."

"Not at all," Jack snapped. "Always happy to help out a power-mad lunatic such as yourself."

"Oh, it was a great help, all right. I had that ventilation shaft closed off so none of the other prisoners could try to climb up it. And I had the little barred window on the door sealed up nice and tight, too."

Lonya got on his feet. "And the chute you drop new prisoners down closes tight as soon as they fall," he said, "so how are all the people down there supposed to breathe?"

Bellissini just stood there grinning.

Lonya tensed himself to lunge, but his eyes flicked to the guards and he slowly relaxed. Then he grinned, displaying perfect white teeth. "See, I'm guessing you didn't check that mass murder with your ball-and-chain, Mister Mayor."

Bellissini's face flushed. "I have no idea what you're talking about!"

"Don't you though? Everyone knows you don't make a move without the approval of your girlfriend."

The dictator snorted, but his face was still brick red. "Delores? She's a nice piece of ass, but she doesn't tell me what to do."

"Don't play dumb, Mister Mayor, good as you are at the role. Everybody knows you'd just be another greedy businessman without the mystery woman Cherie. Though why she'd want to help a creature like *you* …"

Da Mayor snarled and lunged at him, while Jack and the Bullyboy guards eyed each other. The zap-gun hero could've sworn one of them raised an eyebrow just fractionally and made the tiniest of shrugs.

When the dictator was finished swinging wild punches at the Crewman, who dodged the blows as best he could but didn't bother fighting back, he took a deep breath and turned on Jack. Clamping a hard hand on Jack's right shoulder, Da Mayor growled, "I'm really looking forward to your performance in the match. And not just because I'm going to make sure your big-mouth friend here is on the other team."

He wants me to ask him how come he's looking forward to it so much, Jack thought. *I'm not going to give him the satisfaction.*

Bellissini must have read his mind, because his smile broadened and his grip on Jack's shoulder tightened, so much he couldn't stop himself from wincing, since his right arm had been twisted half out of its socket by the Bullyboys who recaptured him. "A normal Death Ball match is a challenge for an ordinary man to survive for as long as three minutes," the dictator said, "but not for a man as brave and dexterous as you, Mr.

Flash. And I wouldn't want to insult you by giving you a *sissy* challenge."

One of the guards snickered. Bellissini's grin was so wide, Jack wondered how his jaw stayed attached to his head. Jack bit his tongue so hard he could taste his own blood.

"So when you go out there," Bellissini said, "you'll fight with both hands tied behind your back. You too, Crewman. How does that sound? No, no," he held up his hand, "please don't answer. If my men have to hurt you guys any more, you may not be in good enough shape to make the match interesting. And that would be a real shame."

"The real shame," Jack said, "is that you're still breathing the air here on Venus. Unlike all those men you smothered for no reason."

"I always have reasons for the things I do, even if they don't make sense to people like you," Bellissini said. He said something else, but Jack couldn't hear it because the same Bullyboy who had beaten Lonya was pistol-whipping him.

"How hard did I just get hit?" Jack groaned after the cell door swung shut behind the dictator and his flunkies. "I could swear that goon said something about the ancient Greek philosopher Plato, but I must have been hearing things."

"I wish he'd crawl back into whatever cave he climbed out of," Lonya sighed.

15

Jim was still snoring heavily when Katie woke up on their fourth day alone in the jungle. She got up on her hands and knees and began rummaging around in their pitiful supply bag, trying to make as little noise as possible so the poor man could sleep. They would already be starving if Jim didn't know the jungle so well from his childhood, but as it was his battered backpack was stuffed full of a nasty-tasting but nutritious fruit called lemonash.

Eating them reminded her of the time she'd put her tongue on the contacts of an antique 9-volt battery, but the stuff was keeping them both alive. Mixed in with the fruits were a few shelf fungi about the size of her hand, mottled gray like everything else on this planet, that tasted not too different from earthly mushrooms.

Jim gallantly insisted she have them to herself, as a break from the lemonash that he claimed was like mother's milk to him, even though his handsome face turned into a mass of wrinkles every time he bit into one. But that was Jim: endlessly chivalrous and self-sacrificing, speaking not a word of complaint as he *schlepped* her along (*schlep*: that was a Yiddish word Katie had learned from Rachel, which she loved since it sounded so much more descriptive than plain old "drag").

He kept saying it was less trouble for him to simply carry her (as well as the crated-up "superweapon," and his jithara, and their backpack) than for her to stubbornly try walking but have to lean on him every few steps, and it might even be true.

They were making agonizingly slow progress, that was for sure. If they had covered more than three klicks since escaping the ambush, Katie would be surprised. And the irony was, they were heading straight for Aphro-Port—or rather for the outlaw tent encampment outside it. Jim said that was their only hope of finding allies, and news of what had happened to their friends.

He sat up suddenly and silently, tossing aside the blanketlike covering of huge gray leaves that had served him as a bed.

"Oh, Jim honey, I'm so sorry, I didn't mean to wake—" Katie squealed in surprise as Jim clamped his hand over her mouth.

He brought the index finger of his other hand up to his lips, then crept away through the foliage, leaving Katie frozen with fear, her heart pounding. Several seconds later someone yelped and there were noises of the dense foliage being trampled and kicked aside. Jim burst back into the clearing, his arms around a struggling Sonya.

Katie's relief and joy turned quickly to annoyance as the little pest began shouting at Jim.

"Leggo ya big galoot, you *gorgel-shnaider*! What for a big *shtarker mensch* like you has to go 'round grabbin' a little girl like me!"

"Try not sneakin' up on people, you blond terror!" Katie snapped. It took an effort not to lunge and swat Sonya in the butt as she so richly deserved.

"I wasn't sneakin' up on you nor nobody else, ya big *nudnik*," Sonya retorted, once her feet were safely back on the ground. If Katie had been the one holding her, she would have dumped her on the ground without a second thought instead of lowering her as gently as if she was a raw egg. "I was only tryin' to keep away from them stoopit monsters what Rachel dreamed up!"

A throbbing ache was starting in the bridge of Katie's nose, like it always did when Sonya was in one of her moods. "I don't know how many times I done told you not to go 'round saying the Malchussei and the Martians are imaginary!" she hissed. "Folks'll think you're crazier than a blanket full of bedbugs drunk on white lightning! And I done *told* you, the Malchussei and the N'Bialy are chimeras, not monsters!"

"You're darn tootin' them things are *cholerias*. Specially the one that grabbed me this time round. I bit it right between its two thumbs and it done dropped me right quick." Sonya's chest swelled with pride. "I wasn't about to let them nightmares take me captive again."

Jim was looking quizzically from one girl to the other. He shook his head. "I'll leave you two sisters to sort yourselves out while I look for some wild Venusian bananas we can eat. Try not to kill each other." He pushed off through the dense underbrush, leaving Katie and Sonya looking at each other sheepishly.

"I'm sorry, sis," the blond terror said after a moment, sticking out a muddy hand. "Friends?"

"Okay, but you're the *nudnik*," Katie said, pulling her into a hug. "I was so worried about you!"

"Then stop strangling me now!" Sonya's voice was muffled.

Katie let her go. "I'm glad you found us. Though at the rate we're going, it'll take us weeks to get to Aphro-Port!"

"Why? Don't Jim know where he's going?"

Katie clenched her fists at her sides. "Of course he knows! It's these gosh-darn legs of mine!" As she said that, an idea began to take hold in her mind. She tried to push it away, to drown it, but to no avail. "Sonya ... do me a favor and bring that-there big wooden crate over here."

"This one?"

Katie nodded.

"Whatchya got in here, sis? Martian sandstone, in case you get homesick?"

"Smart-aleck! No, it's this," she said, carefully lifting the Remington out and placing it on a relatively level patch of ground.

"A typewriter? What do you need that for?" Sonya blinked, then her eyes widened. "Oh no. You don't mean ..."

"Yeah, I *do* mean. Just this once, seein' as how it's an emergency and all. But, sis," Katie grabbed Sonya's arm, "you got to promise never to tell Ray about this. Nor nobody else, of course."

Sonya solemnly spat in her palm and shook her hands with her.

"All right, then." Katie found her arms streaming with cold sweat in the fierce, sticky jungle heat. "Right—"

How would Rachel say it? Her fingers came down on the keyboard, slow but sure:

```
After the sisters' joyous reunion, energy surged
through Katie's body and the older girl suddenly
found that two years of painful exercises were
finally paying off! She could stand and walk and
run just like anybody else.
```

Katie turned the knob on the right and took the typed page out, handing it to Sonya, who read it aloud slowly, reverently, as if were a passage from the Bible. As she did, Katie climbed slowly to her feet. the cold sweat cascading down her back.

"I'm standing up," she mumbled, looking down at her legs. A whole passel of pins and needles was tumbling down there, but there was none of the liquid fire she was used to every time she tried to take a step, and only the vaguest ache in her back. "I can walk, Sonya! Sonya, it worked!"

But Sonya wasn't looking at or listening to her. Her eyes were wide. "What in tarnation is that!" she cried, pointing a shaking finger over Katie's shoulder.

Katie spun around so fast she almost skinned her palms on the tough Venusian vegetation. She barely noticed. Between two trees was a gaping, pitch-black maw with a ragged edge.

It was almost big enough to swallow them both when she laid eyes on it, and it was spinning clockwise rapidly and expanding as she watched. A hot, stinking breath came out of it, something like broiling chalk, far worse than the taste of lemonash. She scooped up the typewriter and began to run, shouting at Sonya to keep up. Katie twisted around so she could see what was going on and narrowly missed being hit in the head by the falling trunk of the tree that had stood to the left of the hole in the air. She yelped as a sullenly burning leaf brushed against her bare arm.

It's a black hole! No, that can't be right, a black hole that big would've sucked us in and crushed us up in a microsecond, followed by the whole rest of the planet. And why's it so hot, and that smell—

At first she thought she'd run into a tree trunk, but it was Jim, and he grabbed her fast to keep her from falling. "Katie! You're, you're walking—running ... but what's that smell in the wind—?"

"FOREST FAHR!" she shouted, her accent thickening in her panic.

"What? But the Venusian jungle is so wet, it never burns, not even when lightning strikes!"

"Never mind that! Just run! Sonya's right behind us!"

But if that thing is growing, we won't be able to outrun it for long ...

Suddenly she knew what it was, and the knowledge filled her with nausea, because it was all her fault for doing the very thing she and Rachel had sworn never to do again, after they averted the drought on Mars. If only being burned to death in a forest fire was really the only danger they faced!

Jim nodded. "Follow me," he said as a wild-eyed Sonya burst into the clearing where they stood. Both girls did their best to match his footfalls exactly, as he dashed nimbly through the undergrowth, never once stumbling.

With every step Katie's dread grew that it was all for nothing, that darkness and burning heat and choking gas were about to overwhelm her and Jim and Sonya. But the only burning she felt was the air rasping in and out of her overworked lungs, and the muscles in her legs and back and the arm that clutched the typewriter screaming from being stretched to their limits.

As if he sensed that she couldn't go on any further, Jim stopped abruptly atop a small rise where no trees grew. Katie dropped the typewriter and doubled over coughing, her hands on her knees, sparks swimming before her eyes.

This is the end. I'm going to die on the 'real' Venus, hacking up bits of my lungs in the acid atmosphere!

But nothing happened except that Sonya bumped into her, whimpering, and Jim embraced them both.

"Well, there's good news, girls," he panted, pointing ahead. "Just look at that!"

Katie peered down the slope and saw a ragged collection of tents and mini-bucky domes huddled up against the enormous, scratched-up plastic dome of Aphro Port. But the dread hadn't left her, and she turned around slowly, as in a nightmare, expecting to see an onrushing wall of darkness swallowing the jungle behind them.

Instead she saw a ragged, ugly black cloud that crouched like a giant monster waiting to spring. It wasn't moving and it wasn't getting any bigger.

Jim followed her gaze and his eyes widened. "I grew up on this planet, and I've never seen anything like that! What is it?"

She took a deep breath, feeling his gaze and Sonya's boring into her. *What can I possibly tell both of them?*

"Yeah, I think I do know what that smelly, broiling darkness is. It's what Venus is like in the universe Sonya, Rachel and I were born in. Thirty years after she wrote her stories, way back in the twentieth century, America and Russia sent robot ships near the planet, and they found out those clouds that reflect all the sunlight back into space and make it so purty and bright in Earth's morning sky are made of sulfuric acid. And the surface is as hot as a kiln and as dark as Beppo Bellissini's heart. Ain't nothing livin' on the surface, now nor ever."

"That's … that's unbelievable," Jim said, looking around at the wild jungle, gray though it was and scarred by the Crewmen and the other humans of Aphro-Port. "Venus, a dead planet? And even if that's so, how and why can it be breaking through here?"

"The how I don't really understand, but I sort of do get why," Katie said, and pointed at the mud-spattered Remington. When Jim raised an eyebrow, she said, "It's not just a typewriter …"

What did Rachel call it, that time on Mars?

"There's an interdimensional wave differential generator hidden inside the little bell that rings when you reach the end of a line. When I program the keyboard, it sets the space-time coordinates. But now it ain't workin' like it's supposed to, on account of interference from the generator that Bellissini has."

Sonya was slowly shaking her head over crossed arms. Katie felt like punching her, but all she did was glare silently and hope that Sis was smart enough to get the message, *Play along for now, okay?*

She took a deep breath and turned back to Jim. "See, Rachel and I think Bellissini comes from our home universe, and that he got here using the exact same kind of machine we got. That's why he had Sonya, here, kidnapped—he figgered out we had ourselves one on Mars, too, and he hoped to hold her for ransom, and only give her back if we gave him our, uh, interwave dimension generator."

"That ain't what you called it a second ago," Sonya snorted.

"It don't make no never mind, Sonya! The point is, we have to turn the tables on Bellissini and snatch his device from him, on account of it can mess with reality and even change people's personalities! That's why the people here, and the Martians back when Johnny Marshall a.k.a. King Ares had himself one, took to calling them things 'Correctors'—them lunatics like to use them to 'correct' people who stand up to them!"

"Well, whatever your machine there does, it's getting awful wet and muddy without that crate you brought it in," Jim said. "I'll go find some tent-plant leaves to keep it dry, and klemeth fibers to tie it all up pretty as a package."

"I'll come with you," Katie said.

Jim shook his head. "Uh-uh. I think you'd better take it easy, give your body time to adjust after the workout you just gave it, right after recovering. I remember once, when I had to run with a pack on my back after this sergeant beat the crap out of me—beggin' your pardon … Anyhow, my back still hurts me nights from that. So I'm not just bein' a Jewish mama when I tell you not to overdo it."

Katie rolled her eyes. "Yeah. I got Rachel to take care of all that for me. Or *will* have again, soon as we rescue her. So let's not waste time standin' here jawin'." She breathed a silent sigh of relief as Jim got a machete out of his pack and walked away into the dense foliage.

Which left Katie alone with her sister. "What'd you lie to Jim for?" Sonya said tartly. "Y'all been telling me ever since I joined your family how lyin' is the worst thing there is."

"Yeah, but sometimes you got to tell a lie to protect people," Katie said. "Nobody but us is supposed to know that we can change the world just by writin' about it. Can you imagine how much trouble we'd be in, if everybody knew that?"

Before Sonya could think what to say Jim came back with his arms full of useful plants. He wrapped the typewriter up faster than it takes to tell and shouldered the rest of what supplies they had left after fleeing the vortex.

"Hey, let me carry something!" Katie exclaimed.

Jim shook his head. "Nope. Maybe later, when we see how you're doing." When Katie frowned, he added, "Look, I might as well get some use out of these muscles the bastard Martian Army gave me. They're all I have to show for those years."

Not true, Katie thought as she followed after him and Sonya. *The way he worries about everyone who's weaker than him, because he knows what it's like to be helpless—being tortured in King Ares's horrible army gave him that, too. Although it couldn't have, if he wasn't a sweet guy to start with.*

16

Katie couldn't get over it. She was walking, really walking on her own, for the first time in the better part of two Earth years. She felt as if she might float away through the trees like a balloon, so happy was she, even though she was walking through a jungle on a hostile planet, into a possible trap.

C'mon, concentrate, Katie!

She watched the people walking around down below in the outlaw camp. Everyone looked so ragged and muddy, she figured they'd fit right in. But when she started down the slope she walked right into Jim's outstretched right arm. When she looked up he was holding his finger to his lips.

"The camp must be lousy with Bellissini's agents," he whispered to her and Sonya. "We're going to have to disguise ourselves."

"Disguise ourselves how?" Katie whispered back.

Jim bent down beside a gnarled medium-gray tree trunk as thick around as his waist and plucked a spray of leaves growing out of a stem that sprang from a large knot. They were spade-shaped with serrated edges, about the size of a man's palm, and almost as dark as charcoal.

When Jim crushed them in his hand they yielded a sludgy syrup with a sharp but not unpleasant odor. He dipped his forefinger into the mess and spread it all around his face. "Jack and I used to streak our faces with this stuff when we were kids and pretend we were 'wild Indians' from old Earth," he explained.

"Cowboys and Red Indians! I loved playing that with Shoshie before we had to move to the ghetto," Sonya said.

Katie rolled her eyes. "My friend Kevin when I was growing up was part Comanche, but he was real quiet," she said. "And he wasn't no redder than me, 'ceptin when he was sunburnt."

"Yeah, well. We were only kids," Jim said. "Smear some of this stuff on your face. It'll disguise you well enough to keep us safe."

"Won't people stare?" Katie asked.

"Nah, you can see even from up here how everyone in the camp is covered with mud all the time. That's what you get, living in an area that should be jungle, but with all the trees cut down."

"Give me some goo too!" Sonya said.

"Nah, we were gonna let 'em catch you," Jim said. "Of course you can have some!"

"It'll only improve your looks," Katie said, nimbly dodging Sonya's attempt to swat her on the arm. *Just an hour ago I would've been a sitting duck!*

After applying their face-paint the three fugitives strolled right into the sprawling outlaw camp. "Look at those crowds! There must be twice as many people there as when I left," Jim said, shaking his head. "If Bellissini kicks many more people out of the city he's going to have no one but his own Bullyboy Bastards to lord it over."

"Which would suit him just fine," Katie said.

"Nah, he needs workers too," Jim said, lowering his voice. "Slaves, more like. Now don't go slinking around—just strut casually, like you have every business being here. Otherwise you're sure to attract attention."

Katie eyed Sonya's blond hair and sighed. "We're sure to attract attention anyways. Ain't there some kind of hair dye plant in this stinky jungle?"

"I could whip something up, but there wouldn't be much point, when a monsoon's due to hit in the next few minutes," Jim said, glancing up at the sky. "Come on. We'd better back up into the forest and find a tunnel-tree with roots we can hide under."

"Aww, but we just got here," Sonya complained, adding in a whispered aside to Katie as they ran after Jim, "Couldn't you have done something about the climate, while you was remakin' the world?" Her reward was a sharp elbow in the ribs.

But some of the crowd from the outlaw camp seemed to have similar ideas to Jim. Anyway, they were no longer alone in the forest.

After days of isolation, it was startling to be among so many people, all of them running in different directions to take shelter from the approaching storm. Katie found herself enjoying elbowing people back and asking them if'n they'd been raised in a barn.

"No, missy, I was raised in the bucky-dome of Aphro-Port," said one wild-eyed girl not much older than her. "I ain't used to being outside in a Venusian monsoon. Nobody is, ya dumb outworlder! Take shelter or drown, spacerat!"

"I'm from Texas, don't mess with it!"

"Ain't no such planet!" the girl cried, elbowing her out of the way.

Just then Katie heard a familiar voice calling over the tumult.

"Hey guys! Over here!"

"That looks like Mark, standing in front of that huge tunnel-tree!" Jim said, pointing. He and the girls made a beeline for him.

When they were safely under cover snacking on crumbled shelf-fungus, Katie said, "You got away too! How'd you do it?"

"Damn if I know," Mark said, shaking his head. "We've got to save the others, but how?"

The discussion had to wait because just then the monsoon burst, bringing with it an unending roar of thunder and the hammering of iron-hard rain on the thick roots above their heads. Only when the storm ended forty minutes later—very short for a Venusian monsoon, which could go on for the better part of an Earth day—was it possible to hold a conversation.

"Where are the N'Bialy being held captive?" Jim asked.

"I don't know," Mark admitted, his eyes downcast. "I've got no sense of direction in the jungle, or anywhere outside Long Island, actually."

"Lawn Guyland?" Sonya said, mimicking his pronunciation. "Where's that?"

"It's on Earth. I'm from there, but I ended up here—well, you wouldn't believe me how."

"We might, at that," Katie said, exchanging worried glances with Sonya.

"And that sucker Bellissini is from there, too! He used to be my gym teacher! I was trying to get away from bullies like him, but no sooner do I get here and get both the mom of my dreams AND the girl of my dreams, than HE shows up! It's like a nightmare!"

"Helia's the girl of any red-blooded boy's dreams," Jim said, glanced at Katie and cleared his throat, "but whaddya mean, 'the mom of your dreams?' Don't you have a mother back on Earth?"

"I do, but it's complicated. She was all mean to me. Not like the school secretary, Miss Fink! That's why I brought her with me, to be my mother! But now she's Bellissini's girlfriend. I can't understand it."

"I still don't get how—" Jim began.

"Never mind," Katie said hastily. "This is good information, that Bellissini used to be a teacher on Earth. Maybe we can use it against him somehow."

"Not even a real teacher, a gym teacher," Mark said. "That must be where he got the idea for those 'Death Ball' games. On Earth, it was called 'dodge ball' and it only made you *wish* you were dead."

"And Miss Fink went for Bellissini, as soon as he came here? Just forgot all about you?" Katie asked.

"She's called Delores Fabuloso here, but yeah. I got so upset when Bellissini kicked me out of my own house. Even Helia couldn't cheer me up. That must be why she tried to drown herself." He covered his face with his hands.

"Which is how I met her," Sonya said, "out in the swamp, when she was trying to drown herself. She was singing some stupid song while she was doing it, too. You must of driven her crazy!"

Tears started leaking through Mark's fingers. "I think maybe you're right! Oh, my poor Helia!"

Everyone looked away from him. But something about what Mark had just said was tickling at the back of Katie's brain. What could it be? She couldn't figure it out, and suddenly she felt very tired.

Jim was saying something about nosing around in the outlaw camp to see what he could find out about their captured friends, but that everyone else should stay put because there was too much of a risk they'd be recognized. She knew she ought to talk him out of risking his own neck, but staying put sounded too tempting, as long as it meant she could sleep. The excitement of walking normally and almost without pain for the first time in almost two years ... it was too much. She slumped down against a fat tree root and shut her eyes.

Just for a second ... can't leave Sonya unsupervised ...

Katie dreamed she was sitting alone in the front row of a darkened auditorium. The air was cold and stale. When she turned around in her hard wooden chair, she saw no one else, though there was seating for hundreds. Turning around again to face the stage, she saw a heavy maroon curtain rising on invisible pulleys.

A spotlight came on, focusing on a tableau of three still figures—Rachel, dressed in purple royal robes like Queen Anya of Mars; Jim, who looked so ridiculous kneeling in a suit of armor Katie laughed aloud; and another man dressed in a white tunic, his face hidden in shadow. Rachel was frozen in mid-gesture, her arms high as if holding a large beach ball. No, something weightier, a watermelon maybe.

Katie wanted to ask her what she was doing in that silly royal getup, a pinko socialist like her, but she couldn't get her voice to work. Her friend suddenly unfroze, thrusting her arms out as if throwing away whatever she'd been holding.

"Alas," she said in a squeaky falsetto, "for sorrows stepping on each other's feet! Your brother's captured, Jimmy my boy!"

Jim looked up at her, his face a mask of anguish. "Captured? But how!"

"He did fall in the weeping brook," Rachel wept, "his coat spread wide, and, billowing around him, let him float, while he sang snatches of old show tunes."

"Alas! He cannot sing!" cried Jim. He stood and drew his sword. "Where is he now? I'll slay the knave holding him!"

"I think not, thou wretch!" said the man with the shadowed face, drawing a bigger, shinier sword. They fought, their swords striking one another hard enough to throw off sparks, but without making a sound.

Rachel stepped to the edge of the stage, raised her green-eyed gaze to a spot somewhere far behind Katie, wrung her hands and then opened them, revealing a tangled string and two honeybees that flew away, buzzing loudly.

"Pay heed, for this is what Jack sang: 'Two bees, or two knots? That is the question!' *Oy vey iz meir*, for I hate riddles!"

The shadow-faced man raised his sword arm and drove the blade deep into Jim's chest, penetrating the armor as if it were paper. Maybe it was, because it fluttered around the stage in sparkling shreds.

"Alas! I am slain!" Jim cried, falling to his knees.

"And I will take my prize," snarled the man in the tunic, stalking up behind Rachel. He reached for her with one arm while lobbing the bloody sword at Katie with the other. At last Katie could see his face—it was Bellissini—but she was powerless to move as the blade spun through the air, closer and closer …

"SHAKESPEARE!" Katie bellowed, leaping to her feet so fast she almost hit her head on a root.

"What!" exclaimed Jim, striding up to her and grasping her shoulders with both hands. His pants were spattered with mud from his outing.

Katie wanted nothing more than the comfort a smooch from Jim would bring her after such a nightmare, but she twisted free. "I said, Shakespeare! You know—Willie the Wonderful, the Bard, greatest writer in the history of the English language?"

Jim frowned. "I think I did hear of him, yes. My unit back on Mars had to take a culture class once, taught by a dried-up old captain. He said Shakespeare was a sort of second-rate Earthly version of Carl 'Craters' Cerozetsky, far as I remember. Though I never did care much for that warlike old Martian playwright."

"What about you, Mark?" Katie asked. "Ever have to read Shakespeare in school, back on Earth?"

"Sure, we had to study Shakespeare for two whole boring months last spring," Mark said.

"Last spring? How long have you been on Venus, Mark?"

"Umm … never mind. What does Shakespeare have to do with anything?"

"Maybe nothing … only maybe quite a lot! Didn't you say your Venusian mama ran off to be with the head honcho bad guy Bellissini?"

"Yeah. Thanks for reminding me."

"And your girlfriend tried to drown herself?"

"Who can blame her, you jackass! Ow!" Sonya yelped as Katie stepped on her foot.

"What's her name, again? Your girlfriend, I mean."

"Helia," Mark and Sonya said together.

"Is that her whole name?"

"Well, her family name is Po. So what?" Mark said.

"So her full name is Helia Po?" Katie felt weirdly disappointed.

"Crewmen like her put their family names first. It's considered more refined," Jim said.

"Po Helia," Katie said, rubbing her chin.

"And her father's name is Lonya. Po Lonya," Mark said.

"Sounds an awful lot like Ophelia and her father Polonius—characters in one of Shakespeare's plays. What?" she said when everyone stared at her. "You think we can't read, out in the Panhandle? Ain't nothin' to do but read, when it's stormin' out."

"It's a funny coincidence, Katie, but so what?" Jim asked.

"Well, I'll tell you so what, Jim." Katie turned back to Mark. "What's *your* family name, Mark?"

"Mahlett."

"Like a hammer? Spell it." When he did Katie said, "Ah-HAH! I knew there was something funny goin' on here! You're not 'Mahlett,' you're HAMLET. And that ought to worry you, 'cause things didn't turn out so well for that dude."

"Shows what you know," Mark said, folding his arms. "I haven't been haunted by my father's ghost. Or anybody's ghost, for that matter." Katie was just about to admit he had a point when he added, "And I don't see that jungle turning into marching soldiers, or three witches cackling over a cauldron."

"That's 'Macbeth,' Mr. Know-It-All," Katie snapped.

"I still don't know what difference it makes, Mark and his girlfriend and her dad having names out of some old play," Jim said.

But Katie looked at Mark, who looked at Sonya, who looked back at Katie. She'd be willing to bet the others had the same thought as her: *We'd better rescue Rachel soon, before a lot of people get stuck with swords.*

17

Rachel had been chipping away at the mortar on her side of the wall, and Aditai from his side, for what felt like days, but of course there was no way to be sure how much time was passing when there was no window to the outdoors and no light whatsoever in the cell except when the trapdoor opened and someone threw food down. But it *seemed* logical to assume that event happened once an (Earth) day or so, and that's how much time it *felt* like she had to endure between meals. At least, her stomach complained loudly enough by the time it received more food for a full twenty-four hours to have gone by.

Aditai wasn't much help in figuring out the passage of time. The closest period of time the Venusians had to an Earth day was the amount of time between sleeps, but Rachel wasn't sure how long that was because she'd never written about it (she'd never even thought about it when she was making the N'Bialy up, she had to admit to herself), and she'd only spent a couple of Earth days with the tribe before being captured. She had a vague idea the Venusians needed less sleep than humans, because Karolla always seemed to be awake when she went to sleep, when she got up again, and even once when she woke during the "night," and in fact she'd only seen him lying down after his duel with Aditai.

Which reminded her she hadn't asked Aditai if his wounds were healed. He'd had a long ugly gash on the side of the neck after the duel, which Katie had bandaged with a leafy plant the N'Bialy told her about that looked and smelled like rotting lettuce.

I AM WELL, came the tapped reply. **N'BIALY WARRIORS ARE STRONG.**

I was trying to be nice! You don't make it easy!

There was really only one other topic of conversation, though. **HOW FAR HAVE YOU DUG?** she tapped.

YOU ASKED THAT TWICE ALREADY SINCE I LAST SLEPT. EARTH-HUMANS HAVE NO MORE PATIENCE THAN A ZVUVIT.

A tiny fly, that would mean in real Hebrew. Rachel ground her teeth in annoyance. On her side she hadn't scooped out enough mortar to fill a teacup, leaving a dent no deeper than her fingernails. Perhaps Aditai had made more progress with his sharp claws, though if he'd gotten very far he surely would be boasting about it.

WELL KEEP GOING. WE HAVE TO SAVE THE OTHERS. THERE ISN'T MUCH TIME.

GOOD YOU SAID SO. I WAS PLANNING ON MAKING THIS CELL MY HIBERNATION-HOME. Where he'd sleep the length of the Venusian night, one hundred twenty—

OH YOU WERE BEING SARCASTIC.

GOOD I WAS STARTING TO WORRY HUMANS DON'T UNDERSTAND THE CONCEPT.

* * * *

Meanwhile, Helia had not been giving her captor an easy time of it. When the dressmaker came to measure her for her wedding gown, she gave him a black eye. When he nevertheless produced a gorgeous white confection that looked like a cross between a snowflake and a towering Earthly cumulus cloud, she tore it up, jumped on the shreds, and flushed them down the toilet, making it back up all the way into the hallway outside her locked suite. She kicked the plumber sent to fix the toilet in the shins, grabbed a wrench out of his hands and was winding up to brain the hapless man when the guards finally tackled her.

So she was not in the best of moods when Delores Fabuloso, paramour to Beppo Bellissini and mother to Mark Mahlett, came to see her. The fact that the guards had found it necessary to tie Helia to a chair bolted firmly to the floor and gag her wasn't improving her mood any.

Delores shut the door behind her, sighing at the mess the Crewman had made of her formerly luxurious quarters. She clacked over to Helia in her high heels and short crimson skirt, planted her fists on her unnaturally slim hips and tossed her head, making her elaborately piled and sprayed, glossy brown hair bounce like a coiled spring.

"Well, this is a fine fix you've gotten yourself into, Helia. I'd like to discuss your situation with you, if you'll promise not to scream like a crazy person."

When Helia nodded Delores produced a pocketknife (*where does she hide it in a skirt that tight?* Helia wondered), sliced away the damp cloth and wiped her hands on her low-cut, sequined blouse. Then she produced what Helia had always thought was an absent-minded smile when she visited Mark at home. Now Helia had to wonder.

"That's better!" Delores said. "Now, it is my understanding that you are to join me in blissful matrimony to Da Mayor next Wednesday, at the conclusion of the Death-Ball match your father is taking part in, am I right so far?"

"No, you are wrong so far," Helia replied in her snootiest Crewman accent, "in that in preference to marrying *Mister* Bellissini, I would rather be wrapped in a cocoon of the Greater Venusian Medusa's finest, strongest silk, dissolved extra-slowly by its stomach acids, and fed screaming into its hideous maw!" She shuddered, and added, "Besides, don't you think it's a bit creepy that we're both going to be married to that maniac, when I'm Mark's girlfriend and you're his mother?"

"I grant you it's not ideal," Delores said. "The problem, though, is this. If you don't cooperate with these proceedings, what do you think will happen to Mark—not to mention your father?"

"Since my poor dad is being forced to take part in something called a 'Death-Ball' match," Helia snarled, "I think the question answers itself!"

"Helia, do you WANT your father to be blown up by a red rubber playground ball packed with high explosives?"

"Of course not! But he's going to be in that grotesque game anyway, whatever I do! Mark, too, I'm assuming."

Delores sighed. "And people think I'm dumb, just because I'm pretty and I'm Beppo's girlfriend. Well, I do admit to encouraging that perception for my own purposes. Didn't it occur to you, Your Most Excellent Excellency, to try to get what you want from Da Mayor instead of fighting him every inch of the way?"

"You call my dad Most Excellent Excellency, not me. He's a duke," Helia snapped. "As a duchess, you call me Most *Radiant* Excellency. Don't they teach you Earth women anything?"

Delores's face froze. "How do you know I'm from Earth?" she said after a long, interesting pause, in a very different tone of voice.

Even though the ropes were cutting off her circulation, Helia began to feel a glimmer of hope that she might actually gain some control over the situation. "I'll be happy to tell you, if you cut me loose."

Delores took a half step back. "Helia, I'll be happy to untie you, but you have to promise not to jump me. I just got my nails done for the wedding. Do you like the color?"

"Yeah, scarlet suits you perfectly," Helia growled. *Like the tramp you are,* she did not say aloud. "Now let me loose! I give you my word as a Crewman, not one little chip in your perfect manicure shall I make. Untie me!"

Delores thought for a moment, shrugged, and cut through the ropes with surprising deftness.

Helia stood up shakily, wincing at the pins and needles shooting up and down her arms and legs. "It's your accent, Mrs. Mahlett," the Crewman said without missing a beat. "You're doing a passable job, but nobody born on the third planet can get those *s*'s soft enough."

She took a step toward Delores, who licked her lips and took a half step back.

"My name's not Mrs. Mahlett. It's not even really Delores Fabuloso—it's Denise Fink. I'll be happy to explain if you keep your word like a good little Radioactive Excellency. Or do I have to call the guards back in?"

Helia held her hands up, palms out. "I have no violent intentions toward you, ma'am—whatever your name really is. As far as I'm concerned, anyone who'd go out with 'Beppo' is already being punished more than enough."

"Ma'am," Denise echoed, a distant expression on her face as she found a straight-backed chair of native gray Venusian wood gilded with fake gold leaf and sat down facing Helia. "Nobody's called me that since I left Earth all those months ago and got turned into a hot young babe."

"Since you— What are you talking about? You're as crazy as your son!" Helia exclaimed.

"Mark, you mean? He's not really my son. Oh, don't look so shocked. I don't have any kids of my own. That's why I liked working as a secretary in his school so much—it let me feel as if I hadn't missed the chance to have a family of my own.

"Imagine my surprise when I found out Mark felt the same about me, even though he already *had* a mother! The shy, hopeful look on his face when he brought me a copy of the *Chatham Crier* with that silly little story of his in it … Of course I knew right away the mother in the story was supposed to be me, and I'd already decided to talk to the guidance counselor about it the next day. But when I finished reading the story and told Mark politely how great it was, the room started spinning around us and we found ourselves on another planet!"

Helia suddenly felt dizzy and groped around behind her for the chair she'd just been freed from. "Now you sound just like Sonya," she said, sitting down heavily.

"Who, that Martian girl Beppo had kidnapped?" Denise frowned, tapping a lacquered forefinger to her lips. "I thought he just did that to annoy the Martian queen, since she's fond of the girl for some reason."

"Well if you believe Sonya, she's not a Martian at all. She's from Earth, although not the Earth from 'this-here made-up universe,' whatever that means." Helia rubbed her eyes hard enough to make sparks float in her field of vision. "Maybe I should have become a doctor after all, like Dad wanted. It seems I've discovered some kind of brand-new psychiatric disorder here."

Denise snorted. "If Sonya and Mark and I are crazy, so is Beppo himself. Yeah, that's right! Instead of sitting there looking like a meteor just hit you, hear me out. After I got over the shock of moving overnight to another planet, I started enjoying it. Thanks to Mark, I had an office all to myself over at Half-Shell High School, a much bigger salary, and a home of my own that I only had to share with him. Like I said, I always wanted kids of my own, so it was perfect.

"But then Beppo showed up! He was always a rude, butt-pinching, sniggering little jerk. Even if he hadn't had B.O., I would never have gone out with him back on Earth. But then he showed up here, wearing a nice suit and smelling of some really strong cologne, and somehow I, I couldn't keep my hands off him. Worse, my memories were all messed up and it seemed like I'd already been his girlfriend for, like *years*. And that all that time, I'd loved dressing up like a tramp for him. Though part of my mind remembered different …

"So the best I could do was figure out how to manipulate him to get what I wanted—to get him to leave Mark alone, to be satisfied with only half of Aphro-Port's wealth, to let people be if they didn't challenge him openly. And I came in here to urge you to do the same."

Delores, or Denise, or whoever she was, produced a shaky smile. Helia thought if the Earth woman hadn't been sitting down, she might have fallen over.

"But you don't feel that way anymore, do you?" Helia said quietly.

It was as if Denise hadn't heard her speak. Her eyes were focused on a spot millions of klicks away, on Earth or maybe even farther.

"Filling the role Mark wrote for me. Filling the role Beppo wrote for me. Even back home, I always felt like I was doing what someone else told me to." She clenched her fists on the arms of the chair, the knuckles white. "What would it be like if I wrote my own role?"

Great. I'll do myself in now, while she's away visiting the planet Cuckoo-Brains. Dad would rather die than see me dishonored by marrying Beppo Bellissini. And so would I.

A small corner of Helia's mind cried out in protest as she got to her feet and tiptoed across the room toward the gaudy bathroom she'd glimpsed while she was turning the bedroom suite upside down. Wouldn't it be more honorable to fight to the last newton of her strength rather than do herself in by her own hand? Weren't her actions now being dictated by an *invisible* hand, jerking her around on wires, as if the Earth woman's crazy talk was actually correct?

She tried to drown her doubts, just as she was about to do with her body, as she walked calmly into the bathroom, shut and locked the door behind her and began running a bath. There was an assortment of bath gels to choose from. Soothing Swamp Salts jostled with Lavender Lunar

Lullaby and 'Allo Very Very Venus. But she chose Brashly Brilliant Bubblegum.

"Sweets to the sweet," she murmured, emptying the whole bottle into the bath and dipping a toe into the foaming suds, which were just short of scalding. "Ah, just right!" She climbed in, ignoring the pain, and began to sing in a high, delicate voice as she slid lower and lower:

"How should I your true-love know from another one? (*glub glub!*)

By his cockle bat and staff and his sandal shoon (*gurgle gurgle*)."

Why am I doing this? cried that lost corner of her mind. *I don't even know this song, and what's a cockle bat or a shoon?*

There was a rattling at the door, followed by shouts and a pounding fist. Helia inhaled water as deeply as she could, sneezed most of it out, forced more down her disobediently spasming throat.

I'm not going to let Bellissini take me, I'm not! I am a Po, dammit! A direct descendant of Po Vesham, the first man to set foot on this planet!

She knew just what he looked like from the faded old photograph in her father's den, and she could see him smiling, reaching his hand down to her where she lay drowning in the bath, the world going dark around his broad, friendly brown face. His hands were so strong! But there was something wrong with them, they were turning so pale. Did he have leprosy?

She opened her mouth to scream and vomited sudsy bathwater all over the bed where the Fabulous Fink had thrown her. Now Bellissini's brassy brunette rolled her onto her back, straddled her and began pushing down on her chest, making her cough up more soapy water. Who knew the skinny little witch weighed so much! It was like being run over by a car.

"Enough, enough!" she spluttered. "You'll crack my ribs!"

"Oh yeah? A minute ago you didn't seem to care about drowning!" But Denise climbed off the bed, eyeing Helia warily.

Her hair was a mess, though it took Helia a few moments to realize why: there were bobby pins scattered on the floor and one hanging out of the keyhole in the bathroom door.

She wrecked her perfect hair to save me! How's that for dedication?

"Why does everyone keep trying to rescue me?" Helia moaned. "Just let me die in peace!"

Denise grabbed Helia under the armpits and hauled her to her feet. She was unbelievably strong for such a skinny thing. "Why did you try to drown yourself?" she hollered in her face.

"I'm a Crewman! We believe in death before dishonor! And Bellissini's perverted wedding, with YOU at the same time, would be the ultimate dishonor, no offense!" Helia broke out into a cold sweat as Denise stared at her without saying a word. The rebellious corner of her mind was shrieking like a siren. "What? Why are you looking at me like that?"

"I'd think 'death before dishonor' would mean you'd go down fighting, not try to do yourself in, dear," Denise said at last. "The only reason I can think of that you'd do such an out-of-character thing is the same reason why I'm running around dressed like a pole dancer ... fictionitis!"

"Who-zee-whatsis?"

"Someone's been pulling your strings, dear." Denise grimaced. "And I think I know who it is! What's your last name again? And what's your dad called?"

"Huh? I already told you, I'm a Po. Po Helia. My father is Po Lonya."

"Po Helia ... Ophelia! Po Lonya ... Polonius! Now you're staring at *me* funny, but I had to teach Shakespeare to a class full of rowdy eighth graders last fall when Mrs. Forester was out on maternity leave. We did 'Hamlet.' Ring any bells for you?"

"Shake ... spear? You gave spears to a bunch of rowdy eighth graders and let them wave them around? You're lucky nobody was killed!"

Denise covered her face with her hands for a moment. "Never mind. Of course you've never heard of the Bard. But I'll bet anything your dad has a habit of giving really annoying unwanted advice, right?"

"He's the worst," Helia said, grimacing. "'Neither a bribe-taker nor a briber be.' But this is all too crazy to be true ... except, you're right, I didn't really want to drown myself, I just felt like I had to, you know?"

"Just like I had to put on this skimpy outfit and drape myself all over Beppo. No more! I'll keep you away from large bodies of water if you keep me away from Beppo, all right?"

Helia smiled uncertainly.

"Good girl!" Denise exclaimed. "Now, the dressmaker's coming back, accompanied, so I'm told, by a squad of Venusian Marines. Here's what we're gonna do ..."

18

Maybe wandering around out here in the Venusian jungle on my own wasn't such a hot idea, Katie reflected as she stepped over a tangled knot of klemeth vines. *But I had to clear my head so I can figure out what to do.*

She hadn't told Jim she was heading out into the jungle. Not only was there no way he would have let her go, it wasn't what she had originally planned. She only meant to talk to the other "outlaws" to find out if anyone had heard where the prisoners were being held, or when exactly the Death Ball match was to take place. Which was just stalling, really, because she was terrified to use that nuclear bomb of a typewriter inside its leafy wrappings in the tunnel tree hideaway.

What if I mess everything up and kill everybody on Venus, or everybody in this universe? What if I turn into a power-drunk maniac like Johnny Marshall and Beppo Bellissini? But what if I do nothing and Rachel dies?

Sonya and Mark seemed just as scared of the typewriter as she was—Mark had left his own machine back on Earth, it seemed. But now Jim was catching their nervousness although he didn't quite know why. So it was a relief to step out of the claustrophobic den under the tree roots into the muggy, smoky air of the camp.

But as soon as Katie did the back of her neck started crawling, the tiny fine hairs doing that prehistoric dance called *there's-a-lion-behind-you-about-to-pounce*. If Bellissini's men really were tailing her, she didn't dare lead them straight back to the tunnel tree so they could round everyone up and grab the typewriter. Better to slip away into the jungle and hope they wouldn't follow.

There ain't nothin' too dangerous out here, right? she reasoned. *We just had the monsoon, and them Greater Venusian Medusa monsters Ray dreamed up in her story need a clearing to spin their webs, not dense foliage like—*

Stumbling over a thick, gnarled root, Katie looked up and saw the trees had fallen away around her and she was stepping on a cable as thick as the ancient, dead telephone wires her family used to collect back in

Texas for the copper. She yelped and jumped back toward the safety of the trees, leaving her left shoe stuck in place.

Alerted by the motion on its web, a dark blob the size of her daddy's prize heifer Joe-Bob skittered toward her. Katie turned and began to clamber away as fast as she could through the dense gray leaf mold, kicking off her remaining shoe when it threatened to slow her down. She could hear the medusa gaining on her, a thrashing, crashing tumble as if a buffalo had decided to jump on a pile of autumn leaves.

If Ray and I both survive this misadventure, Katie thought as she scrambled up the nearest tree with branches sturdy enough to bear her weight, *I'm a-gonna open up a big ol' can of whupp-ass on her skinny Polock butt! Good thing I ain't in a wheelchair no more or I'd be Medusa chow by now ... though if I was still in a wheelchair, I wouldn't be in this pickle in the first place!*

Climbing a tree to escape a predator was another instinct left over from prehistory, but *Earthly* prehistory; she could hear the Medusa just below her, clacking its mandibles as it prepared to feed on the exotic Texan treat. "The medusa's mandibles were sharper than a Parisian chef's steak knives," Ray had written—the text seemed to swim mockingly in front of Katie's eyes. "They could pierce human flesh, impaling the unwary colonist just as easily as they skewered Venusian love-grubs."

At that moment, Katie broke through the canopy and found herself staring up at the churning gray swirls of the Venusian sky. There was nowhere further to climb. She hugged the swaying treetop and squeezed her eyes closed, waiting for the end.

The thing's feelers were already tickling her arm when she heard a deafening *crack* as the branch the medusa was balancing on broke, and the branch Katie was holding began to sway. She clutched it in a death grip, sobbing as her pursuer fell bellowing through the lower limbs, landing with a *whump* on the boggy ground. As the motion of the branch she was clutching slowed, she opened first one eye, then the other to get a good look at the medusa lying on its back far below her, waving in the air a dozen legs, each as thick as her torso.

"Ha! How you like them apples, you dang stupid monster!" she hollered at it. But how to get rid of the thing? "Wait a sec ... what did I just say ... 'how you like them apples,'" she murmured. "Well of course! If only I had me some hard fruit to throw at it, like Gregor Samsa's daddy in Kafka's 'The Metamorphosis' ..."

She craned her neck, but the damaged tree she was holding onto didn't seem to be fruit bearing. Just out of reach behind her, though, was the top of another tree, one laden down with charcoal colored lumps.

Lemonashes, unmistakably. Did she dare to deliberately rock the branch she was holding onto so she could grasp them?

Well, I've got to come down from here sometime, some way ... slow or fast, easy or hard. Then down will come Katie, medusa and all! So here goes!

The wood groaned as Katie rocked it up and down more and more energetically, till finally she was able to reach out her left arm—she pitched a mean southpaw—and break a fruit off to hurl at her tormentor with such force she almost lost her grip.

"Take that, you nasty beastie!"

It hit with a satisfying thump, making the medusa roar with rage. The legs, which were jointed with sharp corners and speckled with hairlike protrusions, like scaled-up spider legs, waved frantically as the creature tried to knock the weight away. One leg finally made contact and the lemonash hit the trunk of Katie's tree with a splat. The juice dribbled down and the medusa shrieked as loud as a siren when the liquid touched it.

Katie wished there was some way to cover her ears, but all she could do was rock her branch again till she could pick another fruit to lob at the medusa. This one missed, but was impaled on a stick so its juice also dripped onto the struggling monster, yielding more unnerving yet satisfying shrieks.

Only one more lemonash was in reach after Katie rocked her branch so hard the wood started to splinter in her hands. *Better make this count!*

WHAM, this time she hit the creature dead center with such force the lemonash disintegrated. The creature howled like a person being tortured and waved its legs increasingly feebly. When it seemed to have stopped moving Katie cautiously began to climb down, hampered by the aches in fingers and arm muscles that had been clamped in one position for too long. Reaching terra firma, she leaned against the trunk of her poor wounded tree for support, hawked and spat on the dead medusa.

"That'll teach ya to mess with Texas!"

"Well done, Earth girl," a voice said.

Katie spun around and beheld a six-foot-tall black girl dressed in a torn-up wedding gown.

"Helia, I presume," Katie said.

The Crewman curtseyed, causing a large patch of white to flutter down on her left, exposing yet more of her leg.

Katie stifled a giggle. "I'm a-guessin' the groom ain't none too pleased."

"I don't imagine Beppo will be," Helia said. "And the dressmaker likely up and quit after I knocked him cold, this time. Of course, that was after the Fabulous Fink lured the Marines out of my room by telling them a coup was under way, and I imagine *they* won't be any too pleased when they find out otherwise. So we'd better act fast. Take me to your secret weapon, now!"

"I don't know what you're talking about," Katie stalled. "I am just a poor Earth tourist on this world."

Helia rolled her eyes. "Spare me, oh short and sassy one. I know you brought a 'Corrector' just like Beppo's all the way from Mars. And I know how it works, too. The Fabulous Fink told me all about how Beppo Bellissini and Mark Mahlett messed with her mind, and mine! I aim to correct all that, with your help or without it."

"Secrets just ain't all that secret anymore," Katie sighed. "There's just one small problem—if you use the power in the 'Corrector,' the world may come to an end!"

"It would be worth it to take Bellissini down!"

"In that case, follow me."

When they arrived back at the tunnel tree, it was to find Jim standing outside looking at the sky. "There you are!" he exclaimed when he saw Katie, adding a little bow when he saw Helia. "Your Radiant Excellency. Let's get inside right away. The monsoon's going to start up again any minute."

The space under the roots reeked of sweat, and as if that wasn't bad enough Sonya almost bowled Helia over cannoning into her, calling her name and crying. Then she spotted Katie and flung herself on her, knocking her into the Crewman.

It's like she's shootin' pool, Katie thought as all three girls sat up and tried to disentangle their limbs, *the white ball goes rolling straight into the black one.*

"Are you all right, Katie, Helia? That stinker Bellissini didn't hurt you none, did he?" Sonya demanded, wagging her finger at the Crewman.

"I WAS all right, till someone slammed into me. Oh, hello, Mark."

"Helia," Mark gulped, "I, I'm so glad you're all right, there's so much I have to say to you—"

"Save it for later. Right now there's a lot we have to—"

The monsoon broke with a tremendous crash of thunder. While Jim sealed the opening with a giant waterproof beige leaf and lit a candle, Helia yelled in Katie's ear, "Where's the Corrector?"

Katie pointed at the crate. Helia lifted out the typewriter and set it up on top of the upended crate.

"How does it work?" Helia shouted over the stony drumming of the rain and the constant peals of thunder.

Sonya and Mark watched, wide-eyed, while Jim shouted questions that everyone ignored.

"Just write what you want to happen, and I'll read it."

"That's it?"

"That's all."

"Pardon me, Your Radiant Excellency," Jim bellowed, "but now is hardly the time to—"

"Be QUIET! Please, Jim," Helia said, when the younger Flash brother blinked at her, his mouth open. "And bring that candle a little closer!"

Katie took a deep breath as Helia sat cross-legged on a knot in the roots, her fingers poised in proper home-key position. The Texan girl only knew hunt-and-peck, herself. But then, she'd never considered herself a writer.

"I think we'd better save your friend first!" Helia shouted over her shoulder, when the rain let up a little.

"But we don't know where Bellissini's holding Ray!"

"Oh, everybody on Venus knows about the oubliettes!"

"Ladies, I don't see how you're going to—" Jim began.

"QUIET, sweetums!" Katie said, and kissed him on the lips. Sonya put her hand over her mouth and rolled her eyes.

The typewriter keys smacked into the paper. Though the rain was coming down harder again, Katie thought she could hear each keystroke as Helia typed:

```
Rachel let out a surprised yelp as her desperate
scratching at the stone wall
```

19

Rachel let out a surprised yelp as her desperate scratching at the stone wall suddenly dislodged a massive block, which slid into the next cell with a thump. The cell's occupant gave out with a howl of pain.

"Sorry, Aditai," Rachel said, "I wasn't expecting that!" She cringed, thinking he'd surely attack her with his thick claws. But all he did was slump against the far wall, holding his right foot in both hands and rocking back and forth just like a human being would.

"I had no idea you Earth-humans were so strong!" he mumbled.

"We're not! I swear I had no idea that was going to happen. Here, let me see that foot—my asteroid miner friend Gun taught me a thing or two ..."

The trap door in the ceiling of Aditai's cell didn't fit its frame perfectly, so she had enough light to see by. After scrutinizing the green-blue blood oozing out of Aditai's big toe and the broken-off toenail which resembled a small scimitar cracked in the middle, and very carefully probing the whole foot with her fingers, Rachel pronounced it unbroken.

"You can walk, Aditai. Come on and help me with the wall you're leaning against. Maybe all the monsoons have soaked the mortar, I don't know."

"Ridiculous, Earth girl! This is solid stone," Aditai said, thumping it for emphasis.

It slid away at his touch, and the stones above it teetered. The Venusian jumped to his feet and pushed Rachel out of the way as the wall crumbled almost the entire way up to the ceiling, sending heavy stones thumping down everywhere.

Somewhere above their heads came shouts and running footsteps. Rachel looked at Aditai, Aditai looked back at her, and they both bolted through the gap in the wall, clambering over the fallen stones to reach a dim tunnel that turned a sharp corner, then divided in two. Aditai ran down the right fork.

"Why are you running this way?" Rachel shouted, pounding after him.

She hoped it was some sixth Venusian sense, but he shouted back, "No reason, I'm just right-clawed!"

"Oh great," Rachel panted, "great choice then, slow down, would you!"

"I think the tunnel is sloping upward!" he called back, then roared as he went over a cliff's edge.

Rachel stopped running, but blundered over the edge anyway, screaming as she tumbled down a steep, rocky slope. Instead of hitting her head on stone and being knocked out, she collided with a surprisingly soft, yielding hump that was covered with purple scales. It was Aditai's chest, and he said *oof!* just like a human would. Rachel started to apologize but the N'Bialy shook his great furry head and pointed with one long, sharp claw at the cave mouth they had just fallen from, where the noise of pursuit could be heard. Rachel gulped and tried to scramble to her feet, but Aditai was faster—he scooped her up and carried her under one arm through the gray jungle.

A pelting rain was falling, and there were men out there trying to kill her, but in the Venusian's scaly arms Rachel felt oddly warm and comfortable.

Well of course I like the beasties, I made them up, didn't I?

But suddenly Aditai tripped over something and fell forward, cursing in Hebrew as Rachel screamed and put her arms over her head. The ground was hard and woody, and her forearms took the force of her fall. She bit her lip hard to keep from screaming at the pain, though it felt like her forearms were merely skinned and she hadn't suffered any broken bones. Staggering to her feet, she blinked at the darkness and the candle-light floating in the midst of it. She could hear people breathing.

"Who is it? Who's there?"

"Careful, Ray, you're bleeding all over the typewriter," said a very familiar voice.

With a cry, Rachel threw herself on Katie. "Now you're bleeding all over my shirt," the Texan complained.

"I can't believe it! I can't believe it actually worked," Helia said, standing up from the typewriter and ducking her head so as not to bump it on the low ceiling.

Poor Aditai couldn't stand up at all in the tight space and crawled out into the rain, grumbling as he shook off the shreds of Jim's leafy tarp. The rain was tailing off, and now that it was possible to be heard again everyone started talking at once.

"Quiet!" Helia boomed. "That's better. Now that we know the secret weapon works, I say we use it to overthrow Bellissini and rescue our friends who are still in captivity."

"More human plotting," Aditai complained in Hebrew.

"Nobody's plotting against you, sir," Helia responded in the same language. "I only said we are going to rescue all the captives—including your tribesmen—and get rid of Bellissini."

Aditai stood up straight to his full impressive height right outside the tunnel tree. Rachel stared at him.

He must be three meters tall!

"I want the honor of tearing the human tyrant limb from limb," the N'Bialy snarled. "Transport me at once to his chambers that I may expose his miserable guts to the air!"

"*Lo kol-kach pashoot,* it's not so simple, Aditai," Rachel said, flinching at the murderous glare he turned on her. "I promise, we're going to get rid of him, but he's a human problem and we need to do it our way." She turned to the others and said in English, "We have to do this carefully."

Helia stepped out into the open and folded her arms. "I don't see what's so complicated," she snorted, "I'll just sit back down in front of that infernal machine and write ol' Beppo a nice heart attack."

"That's too good for the likes of him," said Sonya. "Howzabout he gets locked in his bedroom with all his guards and flunkies, and a fire breaks out?"

Rachel shook her head. "This is exactly why I never wanted to take the typewriter out of hiding in the first place," she said. "Nobody should wield such terrible power!"

Katie bit her lip. "We got a worse problem than that, Ray. Every time we use it, we risk destroying this whole world … or at least, bits of it."

Rachel's heart sank as Katie, Sonya and Jim told of their narrow escape from the vortex in the jungle. She told them in turn about the vortex that had destroyed Bellissini's old office.

"But he himself escaped without a scratch."

"Naturally," Katie sighed.

"I guess Cherie really was telling the truth," Rachel said. "You can't have two different interdifferential wave-generating dimensionifiers working at the same time, or you punch a hole in the universe."

"That's not what Katie called that old typewriter," Sonya said with an evil grin. "Her name for it was—"

"Never mind that," Katie said firmly. "I guess we was lucky this time, when Helia sprung you from jail. I say we push our luck just this once, Ray, if you've got a surefire idea for how your, uh, wave thigamajizer can help us get rid of Bellissini."

"I just might," Rachel said. "But if we're going to take this awful chance, we have to make sure that somebody just as greedy and power-hungry as Da Mayor doesn't take over after him, and that the people of

Venus don't just think that's business as usual. No, we have to bring him to justice so that everybody understands."

"That sounds good, Ray," Katie said, "but what does it actually mean, and how are you going to do it? Conjure a court complete with judge and jury out of thin air?"

"We've never even had juries on Venus," Jim said. "Captain Hubbard thought they'd get in the way of his authority. So he just shot anyone who he accused of plotting against him, but even after he was overthrown in the Great Mutiny, the mayors who followed him liked to do all their judging themselves."

"That's exactly my point," Rachel said. "We have to stop a power-mad maniac without becoming maniacal ourselves. And I think I know a good place to start—with someone who's known Beppo since they both were kids. My cousin Abe."

"All right, Ray, summon him up," Katie said. "Strike while the iron is hot and let's hope Bellissini ain't also using it." As Rachel sat down and rolled a fresh piece of paper into the platen, Katie murmured as if to herself, "I wonder what deviltry Bellissini was up to when that vortex opened in the jungle?"

* * * *

Cherie watched Bellissini's rage smolder as he regarded the smoldering remains of his office. *That's a good one*, she thought, *which of them will burst into flames first, the dictator or his throne room?* She wasn't surprised when it was her former neighbor who proved far more combustible.

"What is that girl, some kind of red-haired witch? She ruins my dungeon and my office at the same time, and she didn't even have her typewriter with her!"

"Keep your voice down, Beppo," said Cherie. "Everyone thinks you have a fearsome Corrector, not an IBM Selectric. Just be grateful I was able to rescue it when the vortex expanded." She glanced at the singed piece of paper and her upper lip curled. "I see why you thought it was so important. You just got confused and thought you were ruler of Jenny Dauphin's mound of Venus rather than the *planet* Venus."

"Gimme that!"

Cherie clutched the typewriter with all her strength, and Bellissini had to satisfy himself with just the piece of paper on which he had been typing his latest sex fantasy.

"Really, Beppo, I don't understand why you do it. There are enough girls on this planet with so little self-respect they'll sleep with you willingly."

"You obviously don't understand politics like I do, missy. It's not just about Jenny Dauphin. If you let ONE Botticelli girl turn you down, soon everybody will be laughing at you!"

They are anyway, thought Cherie, who had heard some of the jokes. The one about Venus's shining glory was especially filthy. *Focus, Cherie.*

"I told you, you can't take the risk of 'Correcting' anybody or anything until we find Rachel's typewriter! Then you can be as nauseating a pig as you like!"

Bellissini wouldn't meet her gaze, and Cherie had a sudden realization: he'd tried to make her "fall in love with" him but it hadn't worked, since she was from the "real" world just like him. Still, for a while there she had had a strange urge to kiss him and hold his flabby body close. Probably poor Jenny had had a similar experience.

Ick. I better make sure to keep the typewriter away from him. Plus, his spelling is atrocious.

The dictator took a menacing step toward Cherie, who stood her ground. "You better remember who's in charge here, you little tart. And it's not like you know everything. I used my magic powers just a few hours ago and nothing bad happened!"

"To do what, Beppo? Or whom?"

Beppo just folded his arms and smirked.

That proves it, Cherie thought, *he tried to control me!*

"All right, Mr. Great Dictator. I'm locking your Corrector away until we have the other one. No more monkeying with reality until then." And she stalked away, her heels clacking on the marble floor while Bellissini tried to think up obscene and painful ways to murder her.

20

"Whee! It actually worked!" Rachel exclaimed.

Katie clutched her friend's arm, her deep brown eyes wide. "Steady on, Ray. We're here to solve a big problem."

But the problems weren't nearly as big to Rachel as her swelling excitement at having made it to *New York City!* When she started typing the "story" about her cousin Abe, she hardly dared hope that Johnny Marshall's old Remington would work as well as her original typewriter back in Warsaw and then the one the rocketship's captain had given her did at transporting people between universes.

And why did the captain's machine work? she mused. *Must have originally belonged to yet another person from our universe. I wonder who, and why they would let the machine out of their sight once they got here?*

The important thing, though, was that once again, her storytelling powers had come through. As long as she had a single faithful reader like Katie, she could go wherever she wanted and do whatever she pleased.

And it pleased her so much to be in *New York City!* America was the impossible dream of escape for her family, in that frantic final year before Nazi Germany and the Soviet Union invaded and conquered Poland, the country of her birth. Her father, a university history professor, had stood patiently in line at the U.S. Embassy in Warsaw, filled out all the forms for all three of them to apply for a visa, and even, as much as it killed him, got his hated brother-in-law Marek to agree to sponsor them.

But it had all been for nothing: the letter from the U.S. State Department, which had arrived by dreadful coincidence on the hot August day Nazi Germany and Soviet Russia announced to the world that they were now the best of friends, said he was "likely to become a public charge," which meant they thought Rachel's doctorate-holding father wanted to go to America only to go on welfare. Which also meant, if she thought about it, that some Jew-hating American bureaucrat was almost as guilty of murdering her parents as the SS guard who shoved them onto the death train.

But she didn't want to think about it. She wanted to savor being in *New York City!* The buildings were so tall it gave you nosebleed just to look up at them. The people were in such a hurry they'd knock you over if you stood around gaping. The noise of buses, trucks, and subway trains was a clangorous music. And her Aunt Debbie, Uncle Marek and Cousin Abe were just a short walk away! Life would have been just about perfect if she hadn't had to worry about all her friends who were in trouble back on Venus—Jack, and Eddie, and Helia's father, and all those N'Bialy.

And Katie didn't look happy to be here. Her face was pale. "Let's go find your cousin, Ray, and get the heck out of here."

"Don't you want to do a little sightseeing first? After all, we've got all the time we need—Helia can make it all pass in just a line or two," Rachel said slyly.

"Huh-uh." Katie shook her head. "For me, it's like being in a giant graveyard. I told you, New York was blown up by terrorists almost a hunnert years ago, back where I come from. It's how come we don't have a United States of America anymore."

Rachel shook her head. To her, New York City was the future, with its clean, soaring glass and steel skyscrapers. Maybe she could get Katie to change her mind about it, if she could get her to go there back in the other universe, the one they lived in now. But Katie was right, they did have a job to do.

"All right, we'd better go find Abe. Like I told you, he went to school with Bellissini. Da Mayor hates and fears him, so he took it out on me. Which must mean Abe knows something that can really hurt him!"

"Okay. I read in a book that the quickest way around New York was the subway, but we haven't got any money," Katie said. "Dangnabbit, we should've had Helia write some money into our pockets."

"Wouldn't that be counterfeiting, though?" Rachel mused as they walked down the street arm in arm.

Katie just rolled her eyes at that. "You writers and your imaginations. You'd be happy just standing around gawking, wouldn't you?"

"Sure I would!"

That enormous steeple over there, with the curves near its top? That had to be the Chrysler Building. Turn in another direction, and she could see the Empire State Building towering over everything.

Pity King Kong isn't here, he could pick us both up and carry us over to Abe's apartment in a jiffy!

The thought made Rachel giggle. God, she was so sick of being serious and responsible all the time. What fun it would be if she could bring Tommy here on a date! Though he'd have trouble with the gravity, more than double that of Mars.

"You know where you're goin', right, Ray?" Katie interrupted her woolgathering.

"Uh, no, not really." Rachel turned to a man in a fedora hurrying past and said, "Excuse me, sir, how can I find 341 Grand Concourse?"

"Grand Concourse? That's in the Bronx, miss," the man said, tipping his hat. Before she could ask anything more he hurried away. The next man she asked scowled at her and pushed her almost into the street.

Luckily for him he was half a block away by the time Katie clenched her fists. "Why, that rude so-and-so!"

"That's what people in New York are like. Abe told me in his letters. Anyway, what do you care? I thought this is all dead history to you, and that you're not an American at all, but a Texan."

"I *am* an American too, in a way." Katie shook her head. "It's complicated. But how do we get where we're going?"

"I wish I knew!"

"Excuse me, *maidele*, but are you lost?" a man's voice quavered.

Rachel looked up and saw a Hasid wearing a long black coat and a fur *shtreimel* hat, though it was a pleasantly cool afternoon in early spring. His beard was long and gray and all in all, he was a nearly perfect copy of her grandfather back in Poland, or of Rebbe Yitzchok in the Hasidic village on Mars.

Do these characters have to follow me everywhere?

She sighed and forced a grin. "Yes, we do need directions to the Grand Concourse."

He sucked in a breath through tobacco-stained front teeth, setting Rachel's own teeth on edge. "That's a long way uptown, *maidele*. I'd give you subway tokens if I had any."

"Do you have to call me *maidele* like I'm a little girl?"

"You want I should call you a *shikse* like your Southern belle friend here, when it's obvious you're a daughter of Israel?"

"Oh yes, ah am a very refined Southern lady!" Katie giggled, swirling an imaginary hoop skirt.

Rachel scowled at the man in black. "Don't call my friend a *shikse*, either! It's insulting!"

Katie elbowed her. "Take the chip off your shoulder, Ray, we're in a rush!"

The Hasid raised a bushy gray eyebrow. "You could stand to learn some manners and not embarrass us in front of *goyim*," he said, wagging a finger at Rachel.

How do these religious fossils always manage to wrong-foot me?

"You're both right," she mumbled, staring at the sidewalk. "I'm sorry."

"That's better," said the Hasid, and gave the girls directions. Rachel thanked him when he was done. "Don't thank me, *motik*. I can tell by your accent you come from over there," he said, his tone suddenly as soft as Aditai's scales.

Over there, across the Atlantic, where the Germans had not long ago finished turning her parents into ash that fertilized the fields of Poland. By the time she finished blinking away furious tears he was gone.

It took them the better part of an hour to make their way to the Bronx through the crowded streets of the springtime city, along avenues that all seemed to be lined with harsh white streetlights.

"How do you know for sure your family will still be where we're going, anyway?" Katie said after a while.

"Well, Aunt Debbie wrote my mother just before the war broke out that they'd saved up enough to buy the pharmacy Uncle Marek managed. So why would they have moved from the Grand Concourse?" But Rachel was crossing her fingers mentally.

The "once-upon-a-time" she'd taken herself and Katie to with her story, before turning the typewriter over to Helia, was "a few years after the end of the most terrible war Earth had ever known." She did that to make sure that Abe, who had been the same age as her, would be a grown man who could help her.

Katie had told her World War II, which Rachel would never have lived to see the end of, if not for her storytelling magic, ended in 1945. So by the late 1940's, she and Abe would both be in their early twenties.

She confirmed that it was April 1949 by glancing at the front page of the evening edition of the *New York Post* a newsboy was hawking as she rushed past. But she was wondering whether coming here, or rather coming *now*, was such a good idea after all. Wouldn't her aunt, uncle, and cousin think it was strange that she'd made it to America but waited all this time to look them up, to let the only family she had left know she was alive? She sighed. Albert Einstein, who was still alive somewhere in this time, had nothing on Rachel Zilber where twin paradoxes were concerned.

The spring night had turned chilly by the time Rachel and Katie staggered onto a grand 19th century bridge over a darkly glimmering river. But both girls were dripping with sweat. Traffic whizzed past them, and Rachel did her best to ignore the occasional wolf-whistles and honking car horns. Couldn't a girl from the past and her friend from the future go for a walk without causing such a fuss? A sign on the far bank welcomed them to the Bronx.

"We're almost there," Rachel said.

"Praise Jesus! I thought Texas was big," Katie groaned.

The sight of the Rapaport Pharmacy, which was closed for the night with a metal gate drawn down over the plate glass window, made Rachel's heart leap. She clutched at Katie's arm and exclaimed, "I was right, I was *right!* This is my uncle's pharmacy, and they live in the apartment right above it!"

Tired as they were, both girls put on a burst of speed and ran up to the building.

"There's a back staircase, beside that shipping carton!" Katie said.

Rachel looked, and her face broke out in a wide grin. "Do you see what I see, Katie?" Stenciled on the side of the carton was the word "PULPS."

Katie grinned back at her, but she couldn't have been as pleased as Rachel was, remembering the magic envelopes postmarked New York City that Abe used to send her before the war, stuffed full of *Thrilling Wonder Tales*, *Astounding Science Fiction*, *Worlds of Tomorrow*, and all the other titles that had inspired her to write Zap-Gun Jack Flash and his whole universe into existence. Would he be surprised when he learned what he had done!

The stairway was dark and dank. At the top was an unmarked door, through which they could hear voices speaking quietly in a mix of English and Yiddish. Rachel raised her hand and knocked. The voices fell silent as heavy footsteps clomped toward the door.

"Who's there?" a man's voice demanded. It sounded like Uncle Marek.

Rachel could hardly hear her own voice quaveringly saying her own name for the hammering of her heart. The door was flung wide open and there they were, her aunt and uncle in the flesh, graying and shrunken though they were *(no, not shrunken; it's just that I was a little girl, the last time I saw them)*.

"Ruchele, Ruchele baby," Aunt Debbie shrieked, pulling her inside with such fierceness she nearly lost her balance. The force of her hug was crushing, worse than hard acceleration with multiple g-forces in space.

Rachel barely noticed, she was crying so hard. Debbie looked so much like Mom … a little older, a little shorter and fatter, her eyes set a little further apart. Still, it was almost as if she had her mother back. Almost, but not quite.

Her uncle was bowing stiffly to Katie, who looked embarrassed. Then Marek turned to Rachel, and before he even opened his mouth she knew what he was going to ask.

It was inevitable and in his tactless way, he just came right out with it. "Your parents, they're here with you? They survived the war too?"

Rachel was still facing him, but she couldn't see him through floods of fresh tears. She was back in that terrible night, almost seven years ago as time had passed on this Earth but barely two years ago for her, when Sonya's father had come back to the ghetto slum apartment the two families had been forced to share, stammering that Mom and Dad had been taken away by the Germans, and Rachel had screamed that it should have been him instead *(and it WAS him, and his wife and poor little Shoshie just a few weeks later, when I was long gone, off having adventures on Mars ... and am I proud of myself, that my evil wish came true?)*

Somehow Rachel found herself sitting on a comfortable old forest-green couch beside Katie, cups of hot tea in both their hands, while Aunt Debbie fussed over them and Uncle Marek stared at her with eyes full of awkward pity.

"So you're an orphan," he said.

Rather than set her off crying again, that made Rachel pull herself together. "Never mind," she said, "a lot of people suffered in the war."

"Did you fight in the ghetto uprising? I hope you killed a few of those bastard Germans!"

"Marek, enough!" Aunt Debbie said, while Katie stared into her teacup.

"I escaped before that," Rachel said, feeling ashamed remembering what Katie had told her about the desperate Warsaw Ghetto rebellion, nine months after she sobbed herself to sleep the night of her parents' kidnapping and woke to find herself on Venus.

I should have been there fighting. But then I'd probably be dead.

Such thoughts were a black hole Rachel could orbit endlessly, as she knew from her countless lonely nights under the cold stars of the Martian sky. So she squared her shoulders and made herself focus on what she had come all this way for.

"Is Abe here? I have to talk to him," she said.

Her aunt and uncle exchanged glances, making Rachel's stomach lurch. *Oh my God, he was killed in the war. He went off to fight, and the Germans murdered him too!*

Aunt Debbie drew a deep breath and Rachel tried to steel herself for what was coming.

Did Katie and I come here for nothing? If we go back now, what will we tell the others?

She shook her head as she realized she hadn't been listening to what her aunt was saying. "I'm sorry, he went *where*?"

"He's back in New York now, but he went to Israel, to help our people fight for independence!" Uncle Marek said, his chest puffing out with pride.

Aunt Debbie shot him a murderous look. "Our people? Our place is here in America, Marek! It's sheer luck that he wasn't killed over there. If you hadn't filled his head full of all that nonsense—!"

"If our people had fought back in Europe—!"

It was like a replay of all those fights her parents had, back in the old days—only with the roles reserved. Dad had wanted to stay in Poland and Mom had wanted to go to what was then called Palestine.

It was "nobody's-going-to-make-me-run" versus "we-need-a-country-of-our-own," every single night. And when they finally agreed on America, IT WAS TOO DAMN LATE!

Rachel stood up, her face flushed with anger. "My mother, your sister, was a bigger Zionist than anybody!" she said to her aunt. "If she'd had her way we would've been settled on a kibbutz fifteen years ago! And she would still be alive, and so would my dad!"

Debbie's face crumbled and she ran from the room, sobbing into her apron and slamming the bedroom door behind her.

Rachel looked over at Katie, but she was staring at the floor, her arms folded. Tears welled up in Rachel's eyes, and when she heard a door open she turned to apologize to her aunt, but it was the stairway door that had opened, and she found herself looking at a young man only a little taller than her, with sparkling green eyes, sandy hair, and stubble the same color on his round cheeks.

He only had eyes for Marek. "Papa, what's all the yelling about? I checked down in the pharmacy, everything's all right—OH MY GOD, RUCHELE!" He leapt across the room in a single bound and swept Rachel into his arms, kissing her on both cheeks. His stubble was scratchy but she didn't mind, she was laughing and crying right along with him.

When he finally pulled away he couldn't let her go. He clamped his big hands around her upper arms and said, "Rachel, where have you been all this time? And Uncle Mordy and Aunt Rivka—?"

She shook her head, trying hard not to cry.

"Oh no, I'm so sorry."

"It was long ago now, Abie," she said quietly. *Though not as long for me as it has been for you.*

"But you, you don't look a day over seventeen. How is that possible?"

How indeed.

"I've come from far away to ask for your help with something very important," Rachel said carefully.

Abe looked at Marek and they both nodded slightly. "I fought at Latrun and Beersheba," Abe said quietly, "and I'll do whatever it takes now."

Rachel swallowed bile at the lie she was telling her cousin, but Katie came to her rescue. "I'm Rachel's friend Katie Webb. Is there somewhere we can go to talk?"

Abe nodded. "There's an all-night diner around the corner." He led the two girls down the back stairs and out onto the street, but somewhere along the Grand Concourse all three of them vanished.

21

Abe Rapaport had seen a lot in his twenty-two years. Though he had left Poland at the age of eight, he still had vivid memories of the place, of forest picnics with his mother and shopping expeditions in downtown Warsaw, but also of running home from school day after day, one step ahead of the bigger boys who called him a Christ killer and threw rocks at him and would knock him to the ground and beat him up if they caught him.

So when it finally arrived, the golden ticket to the *goldeneh medineh*, the Golden Land of America that the father he barely remembered had been saving up for years for, to send for Mom and him, he was determined from the first day he set foot in New York that things would be different, that if anyone called him a dirty Jew or a kike he was the one who would knock them to the ground and bloody their noses for them.

And more, if he caught any dirty rotten stinker picking on the smaller or fatter or weaker kids, knocking books out of the hands of a boy wearing glasses and calling him a four-eyes, or yanking on a girl's braids so hard her neck snapped back and she was left bawling in the dirt, he'd settle that no-good bully's hash. The bully, more often than not, was a pudgy, shifty-eyed kid with a greasy mop of dark hair who went by the name of Beppo Bellissini. Even the other Italian kids at the public school in the Bronx seemed to quietly approve whenever Abe got between him and one of his victims.

As the years went by and Abe grew he found his strength and co-ordination were good for more than just schoolyard fights. In sandlot games and eventually on the school baseball team, he became a reliable hitter and infielder and a fast base runner. He could have made varsity if he hadn't had to help out at his dad's drugstore, but he didn't think of complaining, because there was still a Depression on, and if it hadn't been for Dad working so hard all those years to bring him and Mom over, they'd still be stuck in Poland like his Uncle Mordy (who Dad always referred to sarcastically as "the big-shot professor"), his Aunt Rivka, and his poor cousin Ruchele. And Poland wasn't such a healthy place for a Jew to be, especially after Hitler's panzers rolled over it.

He was spoiling to get into that fight, but he was too young, always too young; cripes, he was still in basic training when America dropped the Bomb on Japan and the war ended. The only thing he could do for Rachel, before the German invasion cut off all mail delivery, was send her the pulp science fiction magazines he swiped off the racks in Dad's store when his back was turned, every number of *Thrilling Wonder Tales*, *Astounding Science Fiction*, *Worlds of Tomorrow*, and all the rest of them that she wrote back to him she loved so much.

Those neat letters in her beautiful handwriting and her too-perfect English, on the fragile crinkly paper with the half-familiar Polish stamps on the envelopes—he'd brought a cache of them to Israel with him (a fight he was finally old enough for), and told himself he was fighting in her memory, so no other little Jewish girl would ever have to live in fear because of who she was. He had wanted to stay and make his life in the new country, but it would have killed his mother, so he had reluctantly returned to America just a few weeks ago.

The prospect of undertaking an exciting new mission for the cause was too much to resist, especially with his beloved little cousin miraculously back from the dead to lead him on it.

He did not, however, expect to immediately and without warning find himself dangling upside down by a rope tied around his ankles, inside a windowless cube made of gray concrete, with Rachel on his right and Katie on his left, similarly trussed up. The room was featureless except for the metal hooks they were dangling from, a naked light bulb under their feet, and a peephole set in a heavy metal door in the direction they were facing.

"How," Abe said, coughed and swallowed, "how did we get here?" Apart from all the blood rushing to his head he felt perfectly fine—no wooziness, no telltale ache where a blackjack might have connected with his skull.

The door banged open and Bellissini strode in, grinning. "Hello, PEEPS!" a voice boomed.

"Oh, no," Rachel said, adding a torrent of Yiddish curses.

Abe was impressed. If he'd ever used those words around his parents he would have gotten the belt. But he also knew the speaker wouldn't get the full benefit of their meaning because he was—

"Beppo the creepo?" Abe said incredulously.

"Abe the ape, as I live and breathe! And so young and cute, too! Don't worry, I'll do something about your good looks before I do you in!"

Huh? Beppo always sounded like a jerk, but now he was a gray-haired jerk. How could that be?

"Beppo!" Rachel said. "Let Abe and Katie go. This is between you and me!"

"Uh-uh, sweetheart. Let's get down to brass tacks, shall we?" He strode over to Rachel and grabbed a large hank of her curly red hair with his left hand, bending her neck back so her throat was exposed. With his right hand he drew a long, gleaming knife and pressed it to her pale throat. "Now, I'm only gonna ask this once, Raggedy Ann. Where's your typewriter?"

Abe went into such a frenzy that he ended up twirling around and around on the end of his rope. Bellissini kicked him in the head, the motion jogging his knife-wielding right hand so that it drew blood from Rachel, whose lips were pressed so tightly together they were colorless.

When Abe stopped seeing stars, he gasped, "Beppo, have you actually lost the few marbles you had?"

But to his amazement, Rachel acted like the bully's demand made some kind of sick sense. "You might as well cut my throat now. I'll never tell you."

"Nah, not YOUR throat." Bellissini stepped over to Katie and pressed the knife up against her neck. A straight line of blood welled up.

"Don't you dare do it, Ray!" Katie said.

"Beppo! What would your mother say?" Abe demanded, remembering a time his own mother had gone behind his back to complain to Mrs. Bellissini about her son's behavior, and she had whipped his butt so hard he couldn't sit down for a week.

Bellissini's right eyelid twitched. "I suggest you not mention her again, unless you want me to–YAH!!!"

Katie had stretched out her dangling arms and yanked the knife out of his hands. She slashed at his arm, drawing blood, and he leapt away.

"Ooh, you're going to regret that, sweetheart," he growled, drawing a zap-gun—Jack's own Annabelle.

A beam of red light seared across Abe's field of vision, accompanied by a sizzling noise. When Abe finished blinking away tears the knife was on the floor and Katie was cradling her burnt right hand with her left hand. Bellissini stepped up to her and began thumping away at her head, neck and chest until she swung unconscious, blood dripping in spiral patterns on the floor.

"*Di erd nemt dich nit tzu*," Rachel said quietly. "The earth will spit you out when you die!"

"I'm done playing around," Bellissini said, his voice eerily calm. "I'll be back here in an hour. If you don't tell me then where the typewriter is, I'll kill you all. Delores, bring that other typewriter in here now."

"What is all this about typewriters?" Abe demanded.

"Abie, I—"

"You really don't know, do you, Abie?" Bellissini taunted as a skinny brunette hobbled into the room, her face swollen and bruised worse than Katie's.

She was carrying a folding table and chair under one arm and a typewriter trailing an orange extension cord under the other, and she set them up in front of Bellissini, cringing as he snapped his fingers in front of her glazed eyes.

"Come on, make it snappy! You see, Abie, your little cousin here dreamed this whole world up out of her imagination, and wrote it all down on her typewriter."

"You're insane."

"No, he's telling the truth, Abe," Rachel said hoarsely. "I was starting to tell you as we walked to the diner. This is what I needed your help with—stopping Bellissini from taking over the world I created. Right now, he's only in charge of one little town on Venus, but ..."

"We're on VENUS?" Abe said.

"Not on it, so much as underneath it, Abie," Bellissini said, "and you ain't never gonna see the surface, believe me. First, though, Rachel is going to tell me where she's hidden her typewriter. Just like Cherie told me where she hid mine," he chuckled to himself. "Boy, did I enjoy making her beg for mercy!"

"Trouble with your gal pal, Beppo?" Rachel sneered. "Anyway, you can disembowel me with that knife, still I won't tell."

"Oh yes, you will." He rolled a piece of paper into the machine and began typing.

"That won't work on me, Beppo. I come from the 'real' world, just like you."

"Just like me, too," Delores said, her voice cracking. "It doesn't matter." She took the paper Bellissini handed to her and read aloud, "Rachel began to sing like a canary."

Rachel opened her mouth and strange peeping noises emerged.

Bellissini growled, snatched the paper back from Delores and casually punched her in the nose. She staggered back with her hands over her face, blood seeping out between her fingers, as he amended what he had written.

"A real *man* doesn't hit women, Beppo!" Abe shouted as Da Mayor handed the page back to Delores.

"Rachel told her master where the typewriter was, and how much she lusted after him," Delores read aloud, tears streaming down her face.

"That can't possibly work," Abe said.

Rachel's face contorted hideously, her jaw muscles bulging as strange noises came out of her throat. Bellissini clamped his right hand over the bulges, forcing her mouth open.

"IT'S IN THE OUTLAW CAMP!" she shrieked. "If you were the last man alive, I'd make love to the Angel of Death instead!"

Bellissini snapped his fingers, and a short, squat man with a single eyebrow stretching across his forehead poked his head in the cell doorway. "Boss?"

"It's in the outlaw camp. Lead a squad of soldiers over there at once," Bellissini said.

"Yes, boss." The head disappeared.

"Was that really Vise-Grip Vinelli? He hated your guts in school!" Abe said.

"I know, right?" Bellissini said. "Hey Vito, you dumbass!"

The head poked back in. "Yes, boss?"

"Put that TV set in here before you go." As the little man scurried to comply, Bellissini said, "It's to keep you entertained till I have time to finish you off—you too, Delores, you can stay in here with them."

"Entertained?" Abe echoed.

"Sure! You'll get to watch me referee this planet's biggest Death-Ball match ever!"

22

Jack was on his feet at the first faint sounds from down the corridor while Lonya dozed on, slumped in his own corner of the cell. Jack nudged him awake with the toe of his boot.

"Ow! What'd you kick me so hard for?" Lonya groaned. Then he stood, flexing his hands.

"I'm sorry," Jack whispered. "Forget my own strength sometimes." *Also that my boots are steel-tipped.* "But we're about to have bigger problems. I think they're coming for us."

The commotion outside was rapidly drawing nearer.

It doesn't sound like two or three armed Bullyboys marching up to take us away. It sounds like they're bringing another prisoner, one who's trying to fight them!

The cell door banged open, slamming into the wall with a resounding metallic crash. Jack and his cellmate were expecting that, of course, and had stepped out of the way.

They had not braced themselves for the hurtling arrival of a slight but very angry black-haired woman. She bowled Jack over and bounced up, fists at the ready.

"Put down those guns and fight like men, you ridiculous pulp-magazine thugs! I'll tear off your heads!"

A giant guard laughed and kicked her in the midriff hard enough to send her crashing into the far wall. Meanwhile an equally sizable cutthroat was grabbing Lonya by the arms and hustling him out the door. Before Jack could make a move the cell door had already slammed shut and he was alone with the stranger, who got to her feet, cursing and pressing her left hand against her side.

"Who are you?" Jack said.

She glared at him. "Why, if it isn't the great hero Zap-Gun Jack Flash, come to save the damsel in distress!"

"Everybody says that about me," he sighed. "Fine, if you don't want my help, I'll leave you alone."

"So chivalrous was he, he'd never even look at a woman who wasn't the beauteous, crimson-haired Anya, Princess of Mars," the woman said sarcastically.

It sounded like she was quoting something, but for the life of him Jack couldn't figure out what that would be. He turned his back on her and folded his arms across his chest, till he heard a stream of profanity that made him frown and turn back around. The woman's knees were buckling, and she was biting her lower lip hard enough to leave tooth marks. Jack grabbed her under the arms and gently helped her sit down with her back against the wall. Her forehead had broken out in a cold sweat.

"I think that big goon broke my ribs," she said between shallow breaths.

Jack squatted down, fished around in his pocket and came up with a tiny pill bottle of aspirin. "It's all I've got," he said apologetically.

"It's more than I have. Give it here." The woman dry-swallowed three tablets, sighed and introduced herself as Cherie Morgan of Lawn Guyland, Earth.

The woman Lonya said was helping Bellissini? Guess that didn't work out so well for her.

He eyed her suspiciously but broke the news to her that she was about to play in a "Death-Ball" match.

"Yeah, that creep of a gym teacher must have gotten the idea from all those dodge-ball games he makes the poor kids play," she said, mystifying Jack. "So is it just us two who have this high honor, or—?"

Jack frowned. "No, Bellissini came down here himself to taunt me and Po Lonya—he's the Crewman who was here a second ago—that we were all going to take part. So why did those guards grab him and take him out of here? It doesn't make any sense."

"It's not so Bellissini can apologize and give him a dozen roses, you can be sure of that. How come you haven't tried breaking out of this joint yet? I thought the hero in these stupid stories always does that, and always succeeds."

She talks crazy, just like Rachel and Katie do sometimes.

"This is the cell they threw us in after we broke out of the other one. I could tunnel out of here if given enough time, but I don't think we will be."

Jack sat down beside her, wishing there was something more he could do for her than just giving her aspirin. Even if she had helped Bellissini, cold self-interest alone demanded that his Death Ball teammate be in the best fighting shape possible. That being so, he didn't like the sallow color of her face or the rapid, shallow breaths she was drawing.

"Maybe you'd better lie down."

"Maybe that's a good idea." Cherie grinned slyly as he took off his jacket, bunched it into a rough pillow, and eased her down onto it.

"Promise you won't try to take advantage of me in my weakened state, gunslinger?"

Jack jumped to his feet. "The very idea! What do you think I am, Cherie?"

She raised a hand. "Just joking, friend! I wanted to test if a fictional man such as yourself really is as pure as Sir Galahad, and sure enough you are! Only in the pulps ... I never met a guy who could stay true in real life ..."

Her face twisted in pain, then slackened, and Jack's heart began to pound. *She's obviously delirious. What if her lungs are punctured? She'll never even make it into that sicko's arena!*

But as she dozed off a little bubble of clear spit appeared at the corner of her mouth.

No blood—that's a good sign.

He watched her sleep, wondering if he'd always be fated to play the big brother to people in trouble, saving everybody else out of habit since he hadn't been able to save his own twin brother from being kidnapped right in front of his eyes. Nothing was worse than a situation like this, where he was as helpless as he'd been on that long-ago day when Martian agents grabbed Jim to press-gang him into the Martian Army.

He sighed and settled down with his back to the wall to watch Cherie sleep. She was pretty with those carved-in-ivory-features, though not remotely in Anya's league, but there had to be something wrong with her to have allied with Bellissini for any amount of time. Still, no one deserved to be murdered by him.

But how was Jack supposed to protect her during the Death-Ball match, when she was hurt so badly? He'd had enough troubles when he'd only had to worry about Lonya, who could take care of himself. But he knew he'd have felt obliged to shield this strange, cynical Earthwoman even if she hadn't been hurt. It was terrible that Bellissini had the power to stage a revival of the Roman gladiators' fights to the death, but it was infinitely worse that he'd do it to a woman.

So sue me, he sighed to himself, *I don't think women should be put in danger, even if they aren't so nice, and I think it's my duty to save them.*

It wasn't that he thought women were weaker than men, or not as smart—he'd never have gotten close to Anya if he thought like that, and he wouldn't have deserved to. It was just ... not *right* ... that brave and smart Katie Webb had been beaten so badly by King Ares's goons that she was still in a wheelchair two years later, or that beautiful and brilliant Rachel Zilber was an orphan thanks to bad men on another version of Earth ... he didn't quite understand that part ... or that this stranger didn't have a fighting chance now because Bellissini's Bullyboy Bastards had broken her bones before she even stepped into the ring. Things like that shouldn't happen in a well-ordered universe.

What kind of twisted god would dream up a world like this? was Jack's last clear thought before he too drifted off into an uneasy doze.

In another cell down the corridor, Jenny Dauphin was tending to Lonya's wounds just as Jack had tended to Cherie. He looked up in her direction, but his pupils were too big and she knew she must be nothing more than a woman-shaped blur to him.

"You're an angel," he slurred.

"Not really. I'm just a girl from Botticelli Island who wouldn't go out with Da Mayor," she said, brushing a stray lock of chestnut hair out of her face.

"Beautiful and brave," Lonya sighed. "If I was twenty years younger …"

"… you'd be a young fool rather than a middle-aged one, friend Lonya," she said with a sad chuckle as she dabbed away the last of the blood from his swollen face with a tiny square of gauze that had been hidden up the sleeves of her blouse.

"I wanted my daughter Helia to be a doctor, like you. Best profession in the world," Lonya said. "But she has other ideas. Or she did have, before Da Mayor kidnapped her."

"I'm not a doctor, Your Most Excellent Excellency. I was trying to save up for med school when Bellissini came to town and started rounding up 'the most beautiful girls on Venus.' Most of those who didn't want to go with him hid in the caves up in the mountains, but my dad was sick and I wouldn't leave him."

"Well, I'm sure your mom will look after him while—"

"She's dead. And I'm an only child." She blinked away angry tears. "What does Da Magnificent Mayor of Shining Venus care if an old Botticelli fisherman dies of zvuvit fever?"

"I'm sorry," Lonya said after a long pause.

"Don't be. You rest now, and together we'll figure out a way of surviving Death-Ball and making Bellissini the sorry one."

23

"Something's wrong," Helia said, dry mouthed as she stared at the devil-possessed typewriter.

"What are you talking about?" Sonya snapped. "Just type that Katie and Rachel appeared in the jungle outside this tunnel tree with her cousin. What are you waiting for?"

"I did type that, Sonya, and it got *erased*."

"What? Typewriters don't have erasers!"

"The more modern kinds do," Jim said, holding the guttering candle as he threw nervous glances at the entrance. "And anyhow, this is an interdestructing Corrector, not a typewriter!"

"Well, it looks like an antique typewriter, though I've never seen one quite like it," Helia said, "and Dad used to type up papers for the students at Aphrodite University when he couldn't find any other work. The point is, it just X'ed out everything I wrote! I thought if Bellissini is using his Corrector when someone tries to use this one, a vortex is created?"

"Just try again," Mark said, squeezing Helia's shoulder.

She squeezed his hand back, then realized what she was doing and slapped him away. "I have a bad feeling about this," she said, shaking her head as she wrote:

```
Rachel, Katie, and Abe disappeared from the
streets of New York and just as suddenly reap-
peared in the gray jungle of the planet Venus
more than two hundred years later.
```

Jim leaned closer with the candle, and they all watched as the typewriter carriage jerked itself hard to the left, striking out everything after the words "New York" and typing instead:

```
Abe did not expect to find himself dangling up-
side down without warning by a rope tied around
his ankles, inside a windowless cube made of
gray concrete, with Rachel on his right and Ka-
tie on his left, similarly trussed up.
```

"Bellissini!" they all exclaimed in unison.

"Where? I'll tear out his intestines and use them for a necklace!" Aditai snarled from outside.

"He'll be coming for us now!" Jim cried, grabbing Sonya under one arm and the typewriter under the other as he, Mark, and Helia bolted from the hideaway.

"*Rootz,* run for your life, Aditai!" Helia called over her shoulder as she ran.

"I will do as I like, human—" Aditai howled as a zap-gun beam hit his tail, and he took off roaring through the underbrush.

"You don't have to carry me, Jim!" Sonya yelled.

"Easier—you don't know the jungle," Jim grunted, puffing as he skirted a boggy patch.

Helia had never been off Venus herself, but she was a city girl through and through and she followed in Jim's footsteps as carefully as she had her dance teacher's when she was preparing for her debutante ball that Dad had to cancel in the end because he couldn't afford it.

Suddenly he seemed to disappear and Helia stopped, looking around in wild panic, Mark a few clumsy steps behind her. She almost screamed when a hand clamped itself around her ankle, but it was Jim's hand, dragging her down into a much smaller tunnel tree warren than the one they'd just left. All four fugitives huddled pressed up against each other as what sounded like the entire human army on Venus tramped past.

"We have to get into Aphro-Port!" Helia whispered to Jim. "They're being in held in prison there, and my dad and Jack—!"

"I know, but we can't just go up to a gate! The 'bots will flag us and we'll end up no better off than them!"

"How, then?"

"Leave it to me."

They lay there listening for a while. To Helia's relief the soldiers only seemed to be looking for the typewriter, not her or Sonya or Jim or Mark. Poor Aditai was just a convenient target for them to take a potshot at.

"Next time aim for that stupid dog's head, Sarge!" one called. "You should see the greeny-blue mush they explode into! Very satisfying!"

"Stop screwing around out here in the woods!" said a deeper voice. "B Squad needs help going through all those outlaw tents!"

"What about strip searching the outlaw girls?" called the first voice, to raucous laughter. "You never know WHAT some chick might be hiding in her panties!"

The voices were getting further away.

"Just like the Martian army!" Jim growled softly. "Same scum!" He poked his head out cautiously, looked around and spat in the mud. "That's what I think of 'warriors' who push people around. Come on everybody, follow me."

They dodged through the trees for close to an hour, getting hot and sweaty and thirsty, but neither Helia nor Sonya said a word of complaint. After all, Jim was still carrying the heavy typewriter, and Mark was shouldering most of the other supplies.

Poor Jim's going to miss his jithara, Helia thought.

At last he led them to a shallow valley shaded by giant gray palm trees, the increasingly rare Venusian tamar. The ground was covered with dense, thorny brush that Helia was afraid to wade too far into, but Jim, who seemed to know what he was looking for, simply kicked a patch of it out of the way, revealing a black, cave-like hole barely a meter across.

"Smuggling tunnels," he explained. "Pull the camouflage back into place behind you, it's good manners."

Helia did as she was told and followed Jim reluctantly—she was a bit claustrophobic, and hiding in all these tight spaces was starting to get to her, giving her sweaty palms and shallow, noisy breathing. Luckily, the crawlspace they were in stretched only a few meters before they emerged into a tunnel tall enough for Helia to stand without ducking her head. There were even light bulbs strung along every ten meters or so.

The sides of the tunnel were bare, jagged limestone, and Jim warned the others to watch their step on the numerous slippery patches and puddles.

"Who uses these tunnels?" Mark asked.

"Smugglers, like I said. When Jack and I were kids it was mostly jewelry and other luxury items people didn't want to pay taxes on, but lately it's been food and other necessities, and a rougher sort of men carrying them. We run into anybody, you let me do the talking."

He glanced at Helia and she thought she knew what was in his mind: criminals like that would take one look at her and assume she was loaded just because she was a Crewman, although in fact she'd never had much more than her black face and her useless title. Or worse, they might know exactly who she was—and that there was a price on her head.

But they got to the exit Jim was looking for without meeting anyone. Pushing through another cave-mouth, they emerged in the basement of a dusty warehouse, in a part of town Helia didn't think she'd ever been to before. The street was strangely deserted, with just a few people hurrying past under the gray light of the dome.

Jim called out to a shabbily dressed man and grabbed his sleeve when he didn't respond. "Hey, friend! I asked you where everyone's going. Don't you have any manners?"

The man was middle-aged, with a lumpy unshaven face and frightened eyes. He shook Jim off and said, "Don't you *know?* It's the Death-Ball tournament where they're going to execute Zap-Gun Jack and the other alien spies. It was supposed to be next week, but they moved it up to today." He ran off before Jim could ask him anything else.

"What do we do? Where's this horrible thing happening?" said Mark.

Jim looked at Helia, and they both nodded grimly.

"Over at Aphrodite University. Or what *used* to be the university," Helia said. "Da Mayor closed it, because he said college kids only make trouble. And he turned the biggest lecture hall into his Death-Ball stadium."

24

Jack squinted against the brightness, trying to take stock of the situation. It did not look good.

He guessed that less than ten minutes had passed since the cell door had banged open and he and Cherie were dragged out. As the Bullyboy Bastards tied his hands behind his back, just as Da Mayor had threatened, he tried to protest that the woman was injured and it wouldn't be sporting to throw her into the ring, but to no avail.

"Thanks anyway, gunslinger," she called back as they were shoved down a dank corridor at gunpoint. "But I can take care of myself."

"No you can't," said the brute holding her, shoving her through an open door and throwing Jack out after her.

By some miracle he managed not to fall flat on his face as the guards laughed maniacally behind him and a crowd he couldn't see howled. Everywhere Jack looked, he saw concrete. The floor of the basketball-court-sized space was gray concrete, the walls that rose ten meters high were off-white concrete, and down the center ran a sparkling white concrete dividing wall almost two meters high. Jack was tall enough to see someone's head over it.

He blinked in surprise and then outrage when he glimpsed the famous face of Jenny Dauphin, the most beautiful of all the beautiful women of Botticelli Island, with bruises all over her high cheekbones and her glossy chestnut hair matted with sweat.

She must have turned Da Mayor down for a date. So now she has to die.

The door opened behind her and Lonya staggered in, his mahogany face slick with sweat and badly swollen. His hands, like Jack's, were bound behind his back.

Since he's on the other side, he and I can't work together, just as Bellissini said. Guess he does keep his promises.

The crowd noise rose till it sounded like the pounding surf Jack had heard once as a child when Venus's Equatorial Typhoon swung so far north it flooded the Yarden Delta.

"HELLO, PEEPS!" Bellissini's voice boomed from high above. "WELCOME TO OUR ALL-PLANETARY DEATH BALL MATCH!" The noise was so loud it rattled the fillings in Jack's teeth.

"Bellissini, you coward!" he shouted as loud as he could. His voice echoed faintly. "Take Miss Morgan out of the match! Her ribs are broken! It isn't fair!"

"WHINING ABOUT WHAT ISN'T FAIR IS FOR LOSERS, MR. ZAP-GUN! LET'S SEE HOW GOOD YOU DO WITHOUT YOUR HANDS AND YOUR PRECIOUS ANNABELLE!"

Something huge and red cannoned down out of the glare, straight toward Jack's head.

* * * *

High up in the stands of Bellissini Stadium, Helia huddled over her typewriter, with Sonya peering over her shoulder and Jim standing guard. They weren't actually sitting on the bleachers. Instead they'd bribed a scorpion-bunny sausage vendor to take the rest of the afternoon off, politely turned down his offer of ten-to-one odds on Cherie lasting the longest in the arena, hung a "CLOSED" sign on his concession stand, and established themselves behind it.

Mark was no longer with them. As soon as they bought their tickets to the "Death-Dealing Event of the Century" and walked in the gate past a bored Bullyboy, Mark said, "Helia, you know I'm sorry for the way I treated you."

"Yes, yes, Mark, you've said so a hundred times already," she replied quietly. "Let's take care of our business first, then you can get all personal with me. Or you can give it a shot, anyhow." She gave him a dirty look. "Just don't try doing it from behind a typewriter this time, buckaroo, or I might have to get personal with *you* in a way that you won't like so much."

She more than half expected him to start blubbering, but instead he drew himself up to his full height, *barely up to my collarbones, what WAS I thinking?* and said, "I'll prove myself to you, Helia, or die trying." And he turned and started elbowing his way through the crowd before she could tell him not to be a fool.

Jim laid a gentle hand on her arm. "You'd better let him go, Helia. It's him or everybody else."

"I know, I know," she said as they climbed the stands. "It's just that he *does* care about me, in his way." She tried to push aside the thought that he might have *created* her, which was too disturbing to contemplate.

Now she hunched over the typewriter, fingers poised on the home keys, and froze. Who should she try to save first? *Who's in worse trouble?*

On the one hand, Rachel, Katie, and Abe were directly at the mercy of Bellissini. On the other hand, the crowd was roaring as the four Death-Ball contestants were pushed out onto the field, two on each side of a concrete wall, while an amplified voice bellowed their names.

Sonya poked her. "Helia! C'mon! DO something!"

"I—"

Bellissini's voice boomed out over the field.

One of the "players" shouted back—it sounded like Jack, though she couldn't make out the words—Bellissini taunted him, and a red ball zoomed down, headed straight for his head.

Helia's fingers flew over the keys:

```
Jack deflected the ball, which sailed over the
wall and exploded harmlessly on the ground.
```

Sonya read her words aloud, and sure enough, though there was a re-sounding *boom*, all four "players" were still running around down below, like ants whose hill is attacked with boiling water.

Before Bellissini could send another ball hurtling down, Helia frantically typed:

```
Rachel kicked the cell door and it flew open.
```

But Helia could do no more for Rachel, who for all she knew was already dead, or her cousin, or Katie. She was too busy trying to save Jack and Jenny and Cherie and her own father.

* * * *

Tears flowed steadily from the eyes of Bellissini's brown-haired punching bag as she worked to untie Katie. She dabbed at them with her shoulder only when they threatened to blind her.

"Why didn't I stand up to him sooner? I could have prevented all this from ever happening!"

The TV screen in the corner flickered, and everyone looked in horror at the crowd bellowing as an exploding sphere narrowly missed Jack.

"It's not your fault, Delores," Rachel said. "Nobody can stand up to the power of—"

"A typewriter wielded by a barely literate bully? Yeah, right. And my name's Denise Fink, by the way, not 'Delores Fabuloso.'"

"Oh! I'm sorry," Rachel said.

"Why are you sorry? Everybody on this crazy planet is a victim of Beppo's."

Denise caught Katie as she began to fall and eased her down to the floor. Katie moaned softly as the older woman bent over her, holding the fingers of her right hand up in a V sign. "How many fingers here, honey?"

"Wait, wait, I know thish sheen," Katie slurred, "Catch-22, right? 'I shee everything twish?'"

Denise started, then began to chuckle. "Yeah, that's right. My ex-husband was crazy about that book." She helped the Texan sit up, then eased her back against the wall. "Do you think you can walk?"

"Shorry, ansher hazhy, try the Magic Eight-Ball again," Katie said.

"Miss? Can you untie me next? I know a little field medicine," Abe said.

But there was little enough he could do for Katie with no supplies. He could, however, untie Rachel a lot faster than Denise could.

"Boy Scout training," he said with a wry grin, "my dad made me go even though we barely had enough money to put food on the table. Said it would make a 'real Yenkee.'"

"My hero," Rachel smiled, looking into his emerald eyes. *Damn, he's cute. But he's my cousin ... and Tommy's waiting for me back on Mars.* "How are you at lock-picking, Abie?"

"The Boy Scouts don't have a merit badge in burglary."

"We've got to get out of here," Rachel said, and immediately felt foolish. She kicked the door in frustration, just to hear the clang it would make ... and it swung open.

She looked at Abe, who looked back at her. "What if it's a trap?" she said.

What a relief to have someone else make the decisions for once, a voice within her whispered, but Abe only shook his head.

"Landsh shakesh, Ray," Katie slurred, staggering to her feet by leaning all her weight on Denise, who tried not to wince at the pressure on her own bruises. "Don't look a gift horsh in the mouth, ain't that the oldesht leshon in literature?"

"You told me that English expression before, and I must say I don't get it," Rachel said. "Isn't looking in the horse's mouth exactly what the Trojans *should* have done?"

"Fascinating as a debate over Greek myth would be, ladies," Abe said, and poked his head out the door, "... I think we'd best get moving while the coast is clear."

The corridor they stepped out into was as barren as the cell, with a yellow lightbulb at the far end that cast a wan glow. As they walked toward it, Katie stumbling along with one arm each around Denise and Abe, their echoing footsteps seemed to call forth a chant in Rachel's mind ... the chant of the *Kaddish*, the resonant prayer for the dead that the Malchussei had turned, obscenely, into a victory march for their leader, King Rawbaw.

"Magnified and sanctified be God's holy name ..."

But why, if this world is the creation of my own mind, should they be using that prayer? Dad's father was a Hasidic rebbe. But Dad rebelled against him, and he had no use for "religious mumbo jumbo." And yet when Grandfather died, Dad sneaked off to synagogue to say Kaddish for him. Sneaked off, like it was something shameful he was doing. All that terrible cold winter before the Germans invaded he kept it up. And now he's dead, and Mom is too, and there is no one to say Kaddish for them.

Katie's battered face turned toward her. "Ray? How come you're crying?"

"I'm not," Rachel muttered, swiping at her wet face with the back of her wrist. "A trick of the light."

They were starting up a staircase, the sound of their footsteps multiplied by the echoes.

Yisgadal vi-yiskadash shmei rawbaw ...

Was the prayer to the God she didn't believe in coming back to haunt her because she had failed to honor her parents' memory? Or—

The hallway they stepped into one level up was better lit, because it had a door opening into the concrete arena where the doomed Death-Ball players ran around like mice with a cat chasing them, while two armed guards stood in the doorway roaring with laughter, paying absolutely no attention to the corridor behind them.

"I can take these goons," Abe growled, and started forward. Just then a tremendous explosion made everybody duck.

Out in the arena, Jack's instinct was to duck as the Death-Ball came hurtling down at him, but if it exploded beside him he'd be killed anyway, so he checked his impulses, leaned back and knocked the ball away with his forehead, as if he were playing soccer. It went sailing over the concrete "net," landing midway between Lonya and Jenny, who ran in opposite directions parallel to the divider.

The ball exploded with a concussion that made Jack's ears ring and the crowd noises seem to drop to a low murmur. Glancing up and to the side, now that his eyes were adjusted to the glare from above, Jack saw rows and rows of tiny faces packed in like ants in an ant farm. A surge of rage shook him.

They're all watching to see us get killed! They get off on it!

He wished that his hands were free and that he was strong enough to lob the next ball into the stands, but he knew he'd never clear the ten-meter-high blast walls that surrounded the arena. It was diabolical.

As the ringing in his ears began to die down Jack risked a sidelong glance at Cherie to his right. She gave him a sickly smile and a thumbs up. But there was no time for words of encouragement because another Death-Ball was headed straight for him.

Again Jack used his head to bat it away, then noticed with horror that it was heading straight for Lonya. He hoped his new friend was fast enough on his feet.

Behind his back, the guards quickly recovered their composure and started yelling. "Sissies! You ain't supposed to let the ball just fall like that, without hitting anyone!"

"Yeah, bunch of yellowbellies!" the other one said. "But whaddya expect from a Crewman, an outworlder, and two *girls*."

"Maybe the next explosion will blast the chicks' clothes off," the other one said, and they both guffawed. Neither one noticed the escaped prisoners in the hallway behind them.

"You girls stay put," Abe whispered. "I'm a trained soldier. All due respect, none of you are, and Katie, you've got a concussion."

"Nuts to that! I'm a-goin' with you," said Rachel, drawing a funny look from Abe.

She was unconsciously echoing Katie, while the Texan herself swayed and leaned against Denise. The school secretary tried to drag her out of harm's way as Rachel and Abe charged ahead.

The guards were so engrossed in the show they never heard their attackers.

"Ooh! Jenny nearly got it that time!" said the one on the left, just before Abe slammed his head into the door frame. His companion lunged at Abe, but Rachel tripped him and he went sprawling as her cousin wrestled the first one's gun away.

"All right, you two, stay right where you are," Abe growled in his best streets-of-New-York accent, but Rachel started to choke as the other man grabbed her by the neck.

She clawed at his arm, red and black spots dancing before her eyes. Three or four loud bangs sounded right beside her ears. When they stopped ringing and she was able to catch her breath, both guards were lying motionless on the floor. She saw what had happened to their heads and her hand flew to her mouth.

"Rachel! Rachel come on, we've got to go!" Abe said, and dashed through the door into the arena.

He's right. I don't have time to be sick, Rachel thought, running hard on his heels.

Jack's startled face turned toward her, his mouth wide open. Behind him an oversized red rubber playground ball came sailing toward his head.

To Rachel it seemed to move as leisurely as a puffy white cloud in a clear June sky. She opened her mouth to shout, but her throat knotted up and refused to make a sound. Beside her, Abe brought his gun up and fired once.

There was a noise louder than anything Rachel had ever heard before. Something hot brushed past her neck, and she brought her hand up, feeling for a wound.

Jack staggered and sat down hard. Off to the right, Cherie folded in the middle, like a paper doll, and rolled over onto her left side. Rachel barely even glanced at her.

If she was dead, too bad, but it was her heroic creation she ran to check on …

25

Mark couldn't help it, he gagged as he walked into the giant glassed-in box at the top of the stadium where Mayor Bellissini held court over his harem. There was really no other word for the bikini-clad girls and young women who crowded the space, standing on all sides of a giant hot tub made of cedar wood imported all the way from Earth.

Look at all these hot girls hanging out with that disgusting ugly bully!

He swallowed hard, held the tray he was carrying high and put on his best smile. "Excuse me … excuse me …"

None of the girls gave him a second look, though a few stretched out slim, graceful fingers and snagged a canape as he weaved in and out among them, keeping his face turned as far away from Bellissini as possible. He wanted Da Mayor to get a good look at him for only one second, the last of his life, before he vaporized the S.O.B. with the zap-gun hidden under his apron. And when he did that and freed all these girls and the whole entire planet, Helia would see he was a hero after all and come back to him.

Getting hold of the zap-gun had been easier than he'd dared hope. All he'd had to do was make his way down from the sausage stand where the others were hiding until he spotted a lone uniformed Bullyboy, who wasn't a boy so much as a middle-aged guy with a beer belly, working security among the crowd. He tapped him on the shoulder and murmured in his ear that he wanted to place a ten-to-one bet on Cherie.

"Not here," the Bullyboy said out of the side of his mouth, "let's go into the bathroom."

"My plan exactly."

"Say, you look kind of familiar," the Bullyboy said as they made their way into the reeking space between a stall and a urinal and he pulled out a notebook and pen.

"Really?" Mark said, not looking up as he pretended to rummage in his pocket for money, then elbowed the man in the gut.

The man gagged, staggered back, and hit his head against the porcelain of the urinal. The Bullyboy couldn't free his zap-gun from its holster fast enough, and ended up wrestling Mark for it, stray beams sizzling around the restroom. The urinal shattered into a thousand pieces, pelting both of them with piss-spattered shards. Then the stall walls caved in, sweeping the Bullyboy off his feet.

Mark made a grab for the zap-gun, but its owner held it tight—too tightly, depressing the trigger once again so that a beam bounced off a mirror over a sink located directly in front of him and returned to its sender, exploding his head.

Mark, who had finished an optics unit in physics class just before departing for Venus, said faintly, "I=R: the angle of incidence equals the angle of reflection." Then he knelt down and vomited in a leaking toilet bowl.

Mark took the gun, cleaned himself up as best he could and staggered out of the bathroom, intending to make his way straight up to the skybox and take his best shot at Bellissini or die trying. But his empty stomach kept trying to turn itself inside out, slowing him down, and though he climbed higher and higher toward the skybox, the stadium was like a maze and he couldn't seem to get near it.

Space battles weren't like this in the kind of science fiction he read and wrote. In those stories, clean-cut, handsome men with strong jaws shot at each other in the vacuum of space, and when they hit they blew the other fellow clear to Kingdom Come, with no suffering or bad smells involved.

The hero never had to wipe bits of some flunky's brains off his shirt and end up discarding it to walk around in his undershirt, and for that matter the bad guy's flunkies were always scary and nasty and not some pudgy, loserish type who could have been the father of one of his classmates. And heroes didn't get LOST trying to find the bad guy! Would Helia really be so impressed if she could see him now?

"There you are!" said a voice, and Mark fumbled for the zap-gun. But it was only a man in a food-stained tuxedo and white shirt, his thinning black hair flying all over the place as he grabbed for Mark's arm—fortunately not the one he was reaching for the gun with. "Kevin and Jeff didn't show—too busy betting on the outcome, I guess, so you'll have to do. Jeez, can't you kids remember you've got to dress up when serving Da Mayor? Come on, I'll find a spare suit for you. Those appetizers need to get up there pronto."

And that was how he found himself picking his way through a skybox full of unbelievably gorgeous women, trying to swallow down the bile that kept rising in his throat at the sharp tang of champagne reacting with the evergreen aroma of the cedar wood and a pungent locker-room odor mingled with cheap cologne that rolled in waves off Hizzoner Da Mayor, whom he caught glimpses of between all the bare feminine arms and legs. The bubbly French wine was everywhere, spilling out of elegant glass flutes and mingling with the chlorine-dosed water from the hot tub that was slopping out all over the gleaming white tile floor, so that you couldn't take a step without your feet sticking to the mess.

Mark tried to slip through the crowd to get a clear line of sight to Bellissini, but the people were packed in too densely and some of them were giving him dirty looks.

Don't you know I'm here to rescue you?

A few feet away a bulky gray microphone was being passed from hand to hand toward the hot tub. It was at the end of a curly black cord that trembled with tension as it stretched tauter and tauter.

Bellissini must have grabbed the thing because he started hollering into it, in a voice that echoed around the stadium, threatening poor Jack far below. He stood up, spraying chlorine-scented champagne in all directions, and the crowd suddenly parted so Mark could see him in all his flabby glory.

His chest, covered with wiry gray hairs, hung over a pair of crimson swim trunks with a beach umbrella decal, but his arms and legs rippled with muscle as he held up his hands. There was a large gauze bandage with a wine-colored streak of dried blood stuck to his right forearm.

"Ladies! Soon you shall all be my brides!"

He had to raise his voice to be heard over the noise of explosions ricocheting around the stadium. The girls let out a cheer.

Mark wished he could see what was going on down in the arena, but he was too busy holding the tray up to shield his face as he reached for the zap-gun. As he fumbled for it he saw something behind Bellissini that froze his blood—a folding table that held a typewriter and a stack of blank paper.

"But before that happy moment," Hizzoner was saying, "let's have the results of our little sporting match!"

There were squeals of excitement. Mark's stomach flipped and he let out a tiny belch.

Well, here goes nothing!

He dropped the tray with a crash just as two more booms shook the stadium, one right after the other.

Bellissini looked at his huge gold wristwatch and clucked his tongue. "Sorry, ladies. Those of you who bet one of our gladiators would be killed within the first minute, you lose."

Several of the girls groaned. Mark tried to nudge aside a cute blond no older or taller than him, with light blue eyes and a scattering of freckles on her nose. He needed her out of the way so he could get a clear shot. But she elbowed him right back. As they struggled there was a firecracker-like pop followed by an echoing explosion.

Bellissini glanced at the glass wall and did a double take. A grin spread itself over his face like a quick-growing jungle fungus.

Dammit, move your head just a little further, Mark thought, drawing the gun from its hiding place.

"Looks like we have us some new, umm, *volunteer* gladiators," Bellissini said. "And Kayla, you win since you're the one who bet the first to fall would be—"

He broke off, his eyes narrowing as they fixed on Mark. There was silence in the skybox, although far below there were shouts, screams, gunshots, and another explosion, all to the accompaniment of the crowd ooh-ing and ah-ing.

"So," Bellissini said, staring right at Mark, "you think you can kill me just like that, do you, Mahlett?"

There were screams as everybody noticed Mark's zap-gun. Some of the women made a run for it, but the blond threw herself directly in Mark's path and tossed her magnificent mane of hair back.

"Blast me, why don't you, you little creep," she snarled. "I'll give my life for my leader!"

"What? No! I'm, I'm here to rescue you. All of you!" Mark spluttered.

Bellissini gave out with a gravelly chuckle. "Nice work, Kayla! You know the funny thing, Mahlett?"

"No, what's that?" Mark said, trying to edge around the girl, who glared at him and kept her body firmly in his way. Her chest was *directly* in his line of sight, which he found very distracting.

"She's not Corrected, not at all! Isn't that right, Kayla?"

"Less than half of your soon-to-be-brides have been Corrected, master," she chirped, "and I would know, since I'm the one doing the typing, now that that traitorous witch Cherie is down in the arena!" She smiled. "It's *such* a relief that the Bullyboys are grabbing the Martian invaders' Corrector, so that you'll be the only one with the power, master. Now you can do what you want!"

"I don't believe you. Either of you! You're lying," Mark said.

"I was surprised myself at first, at how few girls I had to Correct for this wedding," Bellissini said, sloshing the water around in his hot tub as he shifted position …

Just a little further to the left, DAMMIT!

"But then I realized it was only natural for women to be attracted to a strong, masculine leader like me. Natural as in natural selection."

"You're a filthy narcissist, Bellissini," Mark said, his voice cracking, "if you even know what a word that long means! None of these women would be with you if they weren't being forced."

"That's where you're wrong, sissy boy. Kayla, take a letter."

"Yes master," she cooed, batting blond eyelashes at him. She turned a cold blue-eyed gaze of hate on Mark for a moment as she sat down in front of the typewriter.

I should shoot her ... stop her from typing.

His finger tightened on the trigger. In an instant, those blue eyes would dissolve in their sockets, pieces of the skull with the blond hair still attached would go flying in all directions, the brain ... he couldn't do it.

"Realizing how hopeless it was to fight a man so much his better, Mark Mahlett put his zap-gun on the floor and went down on his knees before his master."

"How hopeless it was ..." Kayla murmured, her fingers flying over the keys.

I could try to shoot only her hands ... those peach-lacquered nails would turn to pulp, blood would pour out of the stumps and she might die anyway ...

The gun fell from Mark's nerveless hands and he went down on his knees.

* * * *

"I can't just stand around here anymore, Helia," Jim said. "You hold him off with that ... weapon of yours, and I'll find a way to kill the electricity." He waved a pair of wire cutters and smiled wryly. "Jim the handyman, never without his tools!"

He ran off and Helia didn't even try to stop him—she was too busy keeping the exploding balls away from the scurrying figures in the arena far below.

"Helia, this is pointless!" Sonya said, tugging at her sleeve. "You gotta get rid of Bellissini! That's the only way to stop the death-balls!"

"You're right, but I don't have time!" Helia cried as she sent a ball careening off to the top of the blast wall directly below. The explosion shook the floor below their feet, followed closely by an even louder concussion as a ball exploded in midair.

Bellissini's voice boomed from everywhere at once. It even seemed to be coming out of Helia's guts.

"EVERYBODY QUIET!" he bawled. "THIS INTRUSION WILL NOT BE TOLERATED!"

The crowd noise dropped as rapidly as if a volume control was being twisted hard to the left, and the concrete pulverized by the explosions gradually settled, clearing the air enough so one could see down into the arena.

"Go over there and tell me what's happening," Helia whispered urgently to Sonya.

Sonya ran to the nearest railing and said, "I can see Rachel! That curly red hair can't be nobody else's! She's leaning over Jack, and a lady with straight black hair is lying on her side a few meters away—and there's another guy I don't know trying to help Jack, and your daddy has just boosted a skinny lady up to the top of the wall between the two sides, and—oh, no, here come all kinds of guards!"

Just then Jim ran up holding a bullhorn and said, "I couldn't find the electrical control room, but I grabbed this from a Bullyboy. Figured it might come in handy."

"I think it just might," Helia said slowly.

"I WILL PUNISH THE MARTIAN SPIES MYSELF," Bellissini's voice boomed.

The wall of the skybox facing the arena folded out bottom first and retracted into the ceiling. With a whirr of engines, a ramp extruded itself from the skybox's floor and over the heads of the unnaturally silent crowd, all the way down to the far side of the arena.

Bellissini stepped out wearing a scarlet bathrobe, followed by a blond girl carrying a typewriter, and Mark bringing up the rear, his head hanging low. They were met at the bottom by at least two dozen guards, three or four holding each of the captives, with men to spare. As Da Mayor stepped out into the arena Bullyboys bustled around him, setting up the typewriter for his new secretary, complete with an extra-long orange extension cord, and handing Bellissini another microphone.

Sweeping it up with a flourish as if he were a Master of Ceremonies at a circus, Bellissini roared, "How do ya like your invasion now, Martian savages?"

The crowd shouted with laughter. Hizzoner chuckled at his own joke, but the grin froze on his face when he spotted Abe. He lowered the mike and rasped, "What the *hell* are you doing out of your cell, you little jewboy?"

"What are you doing here, you big bully?" Abe sneered. "But the answer is obvious: stomping people who can't fight back, as usual. Just like when we were kids in the Bronx and I used to kick your sorry ass all the time for picking on people weaker than you."

The mike dangling from Bellissini's hand caught most of what Rachel's cousin had said, and the crowd began to murmur. The dictator made a strange noise, something between a growl and a series of clucks. Then he smiled, showing all his teeth.

"But I'm in charge now," he said. "Not only of *you*, of *all of you*, but of the story. Take a letter, Kayla."

Helia looked up at Jim. "I'm going to start typing. You use that bull-horn to read what I've written as soon as Bellissini stops for breath."

Jim nodded his understanding and Helia bent low over the keyboard.

"Some people," Bellissini began, spitting the *p*, as Kayla clacked away on the typewriter, "some *parasites* on the strong, spend all their time whining that the world isn't fair." He switched to a squeaky voice. "Ooh, it's just not *fair* that weak people get beaten up! Ooh, it's just not *fair* that lazy people are poor! Ooh, it's just not *fair* to take a planet away from smelly, ugly swamp creatures! Good gosh, it's just not *fair* that LOSERS never WIN!

"That kind of thinking has almost ruined our planet. You elected me to get rid of the decadent old Crewman elites and make sure we don't turn into the Star of Love. Together, we will restore Venus to her shining glory!"

To Helia's horror, the audience roared its approval. *Well of course. He exiled everyone who thinks differently from him. So everyone still in town must be a bully like him. If they weren't, they sure wouldn't come to watch people getting blown up!*

Bellissini pointed at Rachel. "I'll tell you what kind of world this is, my dear little carrot-top. *You* imagined a world where clever inventions would make life easy for little weaklings like you, didn't you? Where everyone would be equal, the weak and the strong, the stupid and the cunning, the ugly and the beautiful, the LOSERS and the WINNERS? Well, you did, didn't you?"

He crooked his index finger and chucked her under the chin. Jack and Abe swore and struggled against their captors. Rachel herself was silent, but she kept her burning gaze fixed on him as Helia furiously typed away.

"It's not like that, little jewgirl. And there ain't no Santy Claus, nei-ther. You tried your best to make your dreams come true, didn't you, but this world didn't turn out to be the way you wanted. Not, it's like the world always is: survival of the fittest. The WINNERS live and repro-duce ..."

He grabbed Kayla's butt with his left hand, and the crowd sniggered. "Live and reproduce, I say. And do you know what happens to the LOS-ERS, Miss Zilber? What happens to cripples?"

Suddenly he spun around and looked directly at Katie. He stalked toward her, still talking.

Stop for breath, dammit! Helia willed him.

"Like you, you cow crud kicker. Weren't you a cripple when you got here? Well, there ain't no miracle cures on this planet, girlie! Once a cripple, always a cripple!"

"... always a cripple," Kayla murmured, her fingers flying over the typewriter keys.

Bellissini smirked his thanks at her. "All right, boys, let go of her a sec and she can try to walk. Let everyone see how tough this little juvenile delinquent really is!"

Katie landed on her left side on the hard concrete, but managed to get up on her hands and knees. The crowd went wild with laughter.

"Well, my little Martian hillbilly?" Bellissini said. "Everyone's waiting to see you do a karate chop on me! Or maybe you'd rather take a flying leap over the wall, there! Come on!"

Even from far above in the upper tier Sonya could see Katie straining. She rose to a squat, but no further.

"Just like that sissy boy Mahlett. Big mouth, wimpy little muscles, failure of the will," Bellissini said, casually kicking Katie in the ribs.

She sprawled face-down on the concrete as the crowd guffawed.

Then he turned his attention back to Rachel. "And you," he said, "you shouldn't be here at all, should you?"

Rachel stared defiantly at him.

"You don't belong here, in *my* world. You shouldn't even be alive! You should be dead with all the other sheep!"

"... all the other sheep," Kayla muttered, still typing furiously.

High above, Sonya blinked. Was Rachel starting to *fade*? Was that a page of *print*, where her right hand should be? Now she was looking away from Bellissini, staring at her own dissolving arms in horror, while Kayla clacked mercilessly on the typewriter just a few meters away, recording the bully's triumph for posterity.

"*NOW, JIM!*" Helia shouted, ripping the sheet from her typewriter.

Jim raised the bullhorn to his lips. "That's not the way the story goes," he said, a feedback whine cutting through his voice and making everyone look up at him. He read the words typed on the paper so everybody could hear them:

```
Beppo Bellissini was a hollow man. Everybody
knew it, and deep down inside, he knew it too.
That was why he'd tried to dominate and bully
everybody else since he was a child. But it was
never enough. No matter how much power he had,
no matter how cruelly he treated others, he knew
they despised him at heart, and so he had to
```

keep topping himself. First it was kids smaller
than him. When he got older it was girls foolish
enough to fall under his spell of phony, brag-
ging machismo, whom he repaid with broken limbs
and broken spirits. Finally a whole planet fell
under his sway, and still he wasn't satisfied.
Someone, somewhere, was still laughing at him.
Laughing at Beppo the Bold, Beppo the Brilliant.
Beppo, the Empty Braggart.

Far away on the opposite side of the stadium someone made a high-pitched noise. A cough? A bark? A strangled giggle?

Beppo pointed that way with a shaking finger. "Time was, anyone who dared laugh at Da Mayor would be lynched! Time to revive that fine old tradition!" But nobody moved a muscle.

"Not true," Jim whispered to Sonya. "That never happened on Venus!"

Snarling, Beppo delivered a clout to the side of Kayla's head. "You useless girl! Why aren't you typing the REAL story?"

She sat up, rubbing the side of her face, and typed with the rhythm of a machine-gun firing as Beppo spoke:

His enemies called him a hollow man, as if he
was someone to be pitied not feared. But Bellissini was a colossus of the ages, a man to rank
with Caesar and Napoleon. Other men followed
him and women worshipped at his feet because he
was chosen by nature to lead them into the new
dawn. You could no more stand against him than
you could argue with evolution: it was survival
of the fittest, and he was the best of the best.

"Something smells weird," Sonya said, fear creeping into her voice. "Does anybody else smell that?"

Jim shushed her because Helia was typing again.

When Bellissini paused for breath Jim raised the bullhorn and read aloud:

The more desperate he became, the louder Bellissini ranted

"What's happening to the lights?" Sonya said, her voice quavering. She pointed into the center of the arena. "It's back!" she shrieked. "The thing that almost killed us in the jungle!"

A breath of oven-hot wind swept over them, smelling faintly like broiling chalk. Helia looked up and saw a monstrous black cloud whirling dust and torn-up betting slips around at a dizzying speed as it expanded to fill the arena.

"We've got to get out of here!" Jim cried, sweeping Sonya up with his right arm and grabbing for Helia with his left.

She shook him off. "I'll be right behind you! Save yourself!" she screamed over the rising gale.

The crowd was fleeing through every available exit. People were getting trampled in the doorways. The Bullyboys in the arena down below were no exception to the panic, and stray beams from their zap-guns flew in every direction, cutting down the fleeing fans.

Mark was on his feet, grappling with Bellissini, but Kayla kicked him hard and he went flying backward and disappeared. She turned in triumph to Bellissini, her arms flung wide, but he knocked her over in his scramble for the exit and she vanished into the black hell of the other Venus.

Unnoticed amid the stampede, Cherie stopped playing dead and sat up, her mouth a perfect tiny O. Then she lunged for the Selectric, grabbed it and turned around, tripping Bellissini up in her flight. He was on his feet again in an instant but his clothes were on fire as he ran, and then he tripped over the extension cord and went flying, flames devouring his clothes as he fell.

Helia barely noticed all the commotion. She had lost track of all her friends in reality, being too busy saving them on paper:

```
The black maw began to close as Sonya wriggled
out of Jim's arms and ran ahead of him, tug-
ging on his hand to pull him out the door where
Lonya, Mark, Jack, Katie, Rachel, Jenny
```

She struck her forehead with the heel of her right hand in frustration. Who was the mysterious sandy-haired stranger at Rachel's side? Someone important, obviously, but she didn't know his name, and she was gagging as the burning stench of the other Venus closed in on her.

So she tried to pick up the typewriter and run, but it slipped out of her hands and crashed to the concrete floor, where it broke in pieces. Somehow she rescued the typed page from the platen and went barreling down the nearest stairwell as the lights went out and the concrete walls cracked beside her, letting daylight in on one side and a poisonous eternal night on the other. At the bottom she stumbled and almost fell, but recovered herself and staggered on, only to run headlong into someone with a headful of long curly red hair who was standing just outside the stadium doors, staring with glazed eyes into an infinite distance.

"Rachel? Rachel Zilber?"

Eyes green as jade turned slowly to focus on Helia. "Abe helped me escape, but the others—"

"You can save them. Take this and read it," Helia said, thrusting the paper at her. Beside them, the outer walls of the stadium trembled as if in an earthquake.

Rachel held up her arms, which ... ended, somewhere above the wrists.

Helia gasped and took an involuntary step back. No blood poured from the stumps, although flies were buzzing around them. No—Helia leaned toward Rachel—not common Venusian zvuvits with their gray heads and their twelve legs—these things were too small for that, and they made no noise. It was a cloud of *letters* swirling above her wrists.

Helia blinked once, and held up the paper. "Read this aloud. It'll fix things."

"No it won't." Rachel's voice was a lifeless buzz. "It can't. You can't. I imagined a whole new world, but that world was born dead—that's why the Malchussei chant the prayer for the dead—because I am dead, and have been for more than two hundred years. And you, you're imaginary, and imaginary people can't—"

"Rachel, I know I'm real because I can *dream*. I do dream." Helia started to reach for her, thought better of it, held the paper up before Rachel's eyes. "We have to try. Read what I wrote."

The stadium walls began to collapse inward, but only a few bits of rubble flew past their heads.

It's the hole. It's sucking everything in.

In that same hopeless voice, Rachel began to read: "The black maw began to close ..."

26

Night had finally fallen on Venus, the long darkness that lasted some four Earthly months. The human residents of Aphro-Port were greeting it with the traditional bonfires, while the Venusian natives, N'Bialy and Malchussei alike, were greeting it with their traditional four-month-long naps.

The darkness suited Rachel just fine. She was grieving for the dozens of innocent bystanders outside Bellissini Stadium who had smothered in the plume of dense, superheated carbon dioxide that had gushed from it, and even for the hundreds of people who had lost their lives in the collapse of the arena, although they had been part of a bloodthirsty mob. Several nearby buildings had corroded so badly from a cloud of sulfuric acid that also leaked from the stadium that even Aphro-Port's safety inspectors had had to leave their bribe-bought mansions long enough to condemn them.

The common theory, worked out by the well-known carefully reasoned scientific method of screaming 144-point headlines in the competing *Aphro-Port Advertiser* and *Venusian Vindicator*, was that Beppo Bellissini had used the Death-Ball match to test out poison gas for a planned attack on the Earth and Mars.

His burned corpse had been strung up and burned again—a short, muscle-bound guy with a unibrow wielded the torch—and when the ashes scattered, a piñata effigy had been strung up instead and filled with firecrackers. Rachel avoided the festivities, but Katie said he had gotten off lightly.

"Look at the bright side, Ray, at least they wrote our cover story for us," Katie said, propping herself up on one elbow in her hospital bed.

"Nobody would ever believe the truth, anyway," Helia said.

She had shooed her guard out of the private ward, shutting the door firmly in his face when he tried to insist on staying "to protect Your Radiant Excellency."

The guard had his orders from Da New Mayor, Duke Po Lonya, whom some people were already calling Po the First in expectation that he would serve only until Helia came of age and took over for him— an expectation he was doing everything to encourage. What he really wanted to do, he confided to her, was rebuild Aphrodite University and chair its history department.

"Though maybe he wouldn't be so eager to do that if he knew Venus has at least *two* histories," Helia said.

"Shh, the walls have ears," Katie said, massaging her temples. "Ooh, my aching head. At least I ain't seeing double no more. And my parents are on the way in a Royal Martian Space Navy ship to collect us.

"Hey, cheer up, Ray. We won, didn't we? We beat Beppo Bellissini and rescued my sister. My legs are working again, mostly. *And* Mayor Po got the Malchussei to give the Whispering Wood back to the N'Bialy by threatening to flood their hibernation caves."

"But so many people died," Rachel said, her eyes welling up. "Humans and Venusians both."

Katie looked out the window, but her own reflection stared back at her against the black night sky. Her face was still swollen and bandaged, her dark hair ragged and limp against her skull.

Rachel watched her watching herself and wondered what it was tough Texans did instead of crying.

"It was like a war," Katie said at last. "Jim hates that word, he hates anything military. I keep trying to comfort him by telling him at least it weren't for nothing."

You two are so good for each other, Rachel thought, glancing at the enormous vase of delicately shaded gray Venusian orchids and the stuffed teddy bears the younger Flash brother had left earlier that day, before taking Sonya on a sightseeing tour of the Yarden Delta. *But Jim hates Mars, and we live there. This could get interesting. I've heard of long-distance relationships, but that would probably set some kind of record. What happens when the GUY is from Venus and the GIRL is from Mars?*

Helia cleared her throat. "I'm sorry to do this, but I have to ask you both a few questions," she said. "I have to figure out what to tell my dad—and it's not going to be everything—but I'd like to reassure him, at least, that there aren't any more Correctors loose out there. I dropped the one I was using when I ran out of the stadium, but what about Bellissini's? Anyone see what happened to it?"

Rachel and Katie looked at each other and shook their heads.

"What about that woman who was typing for him?" Rachel asked, wringing her hands. *At least I've got hands to wring again.*

"Well, Cherie was killed in the death-ball match, and no one's seen that Kayla person since Bellissini shoved her into the vortex. Ditto for most of Bellissini's so-called fiancées." Helia smiled wryly. "Turns out it was safer for Jenny to turn him down. Though I hear she's planning to emigrate from Venus … can't say I blame her. Anyhow, I think what we choose to call reality should be safe for now, seeing as how Bellissini's 'Corrector' was right at the mouth of that monster vortex."

"You were worried enough to check on everything, though," Katie said dryly.

"Well, of course I was. But the more I think about it, the more worried I get about something else." Helia leaned over the bed, close to Katie, and beckoned Rachel to lean in too. "There must be millions of typewriters in homes and offices all around the Solar System. Billions, maybe. How come people aren't using them all the time to make their wishes come true?"

"How do you know they're not?" Rachel said.

Helia's eyes went wide, but Katie rolled hers.

"That's Ray's Polock idea of a joke," she said, swatting the redhead on the arm. "It don't work like that, near as we can tell, Helia. We used to think you had to be from the universe that Ray and I come from to change this one with a typewriter. Thanks to you we know that ain't so, but the typewriter *does* have to come from our universe … and remember, you have to have a writer *and* a reader to make it work."

Rachel frowned. "But what about the typewriter I used to rescue Sonya from Warsaw?" she asked Katie. "We got that from the captain of a rocketship in *this* universe, remember?"

"Yeah, but I picked up some of the pieces, Ray, after you done smashed it. One of them had a little metal plate on it that said, 'Made in the Lone Star Republic.' So o'course I saved it. My country started making them machines again around the time I was born, since there wasn't no computer industry left worth speaking of.

"That typewriter was born in the same world as you and me, Ray. I'd wager someone used it to write himself into *this* universe, but then he got rid of the machine 'cause he didn't want the power no more than we do. And it somehow ended up on that rocketship."

"So what you're saying is, we're safe?" Helia broke in. "The last two typewriters that could mess with people's minds, and the nature of reality, were lost in the stadium collapse?"

"That's what it looks like," Katie said. "But the secret may still be really dangerous. It helps that there's only a few of us from that other world—Mark and Denise …"

"And Abe, who's stranded here now," Rachel said. "I haven't spoken to him since the stadium collapse. I don't know how I can face him— he'll never see his parents again …"

"And you and Jim are the only 'natives' of this universe who know the whole truth," Katie said to Helia, while patting Rachel's arm absently.

"Anya and Jack, and our friends Eddie and Gun, know we ain't from around these cosmic parts, but they don't know how exactly we got here, or that we can change reality just by typin' and readin' about it."

She paused. "Or maybe they don't exactly *want* to know, if you see what I'm sayin'. So we all got to do our best not to rub nobody's nose in this tricky business that's best left to philosophers." She paused again. "Speakin' of tricky business, how are Mark and Denise gettin' on?"

"He's moved back in with her, and she's playing mommy again," Helia said. "He tried bringing me flowers yesterday and asked if I wouldn't give him another chance, but I slammed the door in his face. I don't wish him harm, but I wouldn't go out with him again for all the money in the Solar Bank. See, Denise may want *to be* his mother, but I prefer *not to be* his girlfriend.

"What is it? What's so funny, you two? Come on, let a future mayor in on the joke!"

* * * *

A few weeks later and some dozens of millions of miles away in space, a slightly larger group was holding another secret meeting. Most of them knew one another, at least by military rank, but they were going by code names and speaking in Solar rather than their native Marpolski for the benefit of their guest, whom they didn't quite trust. It made for an awkward conversation.

"Gentlemen," the guest said, looking around—they were all men, apart from her—"let's get to the point. You have vowed to free your planet from a terrible dictator—"

"Usurper," interrupted a stout man with a bristling white mustache. "Use the proper term."

"Yes, the usurper," the guest continued, swallowing her annoyance, "who has, and let's be honest here, become very popular during her reign—"

"Only with peasants and outworlders and suchlike rabble," growled the mustachioed man.

"Maybe, but together they make up what? Like, eighty percent of the planet's population?" The guest smiled a closed-lipped smile. There was unhappy muttering around the red stone table.

A man younger than the rest, with auburn hair, chiseled cheekbones and a dangerous grin, held up his hand for silence. "Stop interrupting her, Mieczyslaw—"

The mustachioed man looked daggers at him. "I'm Larry!"

"My apologies. But let the lady speak! We are all old-fashioned, chivalrous gentlemen here."

The young man ran his eyes deliberately up and down the guest's body, a gesture that she did not fail to notice and that secretly pleased her, because she'd chosen the tight black outfit carefully to set off her creamy skin and jet-black hair and help cement her control over these Martian military ninnies.

"Thank you, Andrzej," she said sweetly, relishing the way the young man jumped in his chair. "I mean, Keith! Gentlemen, you need a strong weapon if you want to overthrow a powerful, popular leader like Queen Anya. Luckily for you, I have brought such a weapon with me."

The men leaned forward as the guest lifted onto the table an attaché case so new the leather squeaked. She snapped open its shiny brass catch and they all stared in amazement for several long seconds.

"What," said the mustachioed man, "do we need an electric typewriter for?"

ABOUT THE AUTHOR

Martin Berman-Gorvine (http://www.martinbermangorvine.com/) is the author of *Monsters of Venus* and eight other science fiction and horror novels, including *Seven Against Mars* (Wildside Press, 2013), the predecessor to *Monsters of Venus*. A short story featuring Rachel and Katie, the main characters in both books, appears in the 2015 feminist science fiction anthology *Brave New Girls* under the title "Of Cats' Whiskers and Klutzes."

Martin's other science fiction novels are the Sidewise Award-winning *The Severed Wing* (Livingston Press, 2002); *36* (Livingston Press, 2012); *Save the Dragons!* (Wildside Press, 2013), which was a finalist for the Prometheus Award; *Ziona: A Novel of Alternate History* (an expansion of the short story "Palestina," published in *Interzone* magazine, May/June 2006) (Amazon/CreateSpace, 2014); and *Heroes of Earth* (Wildside Press, 2015).

The first of Martin's four-book "Days of Ascension" horror novel series, *All Souls Day*, was published in February 2016 by Silver Leaf Books, and the second book of the series, *Day of Vengeance*, is coming out in early 2017.

Martin lives in Maryland with his wife and two younger sons, four cats, and a sort of Muppet dog.

www.ingramcontent.com/pod-product-compliance
Lightning Source LLC
Chambersburg PA
CBHW020643180626
46816CB00003B/1098